Atomised

Atomised

MICHEL HOUELLEBECQ

Translated by Frank Wynne

WILLIAM HEINEMANN : LONDON

First published in the United Kingdom in 2000 by William Heinemann

1 3 5 7 9 10 8 6 4 2

Copyright © Flammarion, 1999

Translated from the French, *Les Particules élémentaires*

Translation copyright © Frank Wynne

Michel Houellebecq has asserted his right under the Copyright, Designs and Patents Act, 1988 to be identified as the author of this work

William Heinemann
The Random House Group Limited
20 Vauxhall Bridge Road, London SW1V 2SA

Random House Australia (Pty) Limited
20 Alfred Street, Milsons Point, Sydney,
New South Wales 2061, Australia

Random House New Zealand Limited
18 Poland Road, Glenfield,
Auckland 10, New Zealand

Random House (Pty) Limited
Endulini, 5a Jubilee Road,
Parktown 2193, South Africa

The Random House Group Limited Reg. No. 954009

www.randomhouse.co.uk

A CIP catalogue record for this book is available
from the British Library

Papers used by Random House are natural, recyclable products made from wood grown in sustainable forests. The manufacturing processes conform to the environmental regulations of the country of origin

Typeset by SX Composing DTP, Rayleigh, Essex
Printed and bound in Great Britain by
Biddles Ltd, Guildford and King's Lynn

ISBN 0 434 00793 5

Prologue

This book is principally the story of a man who lived out the greater part of his life in Western Europe, in the latter half of the twentieth century. Though alone for much of his life, he was nonetheless closely in touch with other men. He lived through an age that was miserable and troubled. The country into which he was born was sliding slowly, ineluctably, into the ranks of the less developed countries; often haunted by misery, the men of his generation lived out their lonely, bitter lives. Feelings such as love, tenderness and human fellowship had, for the most part, disappeared; the relationships between his contemporaries were at best indifferent and more often cruel.

At the time of his disappearance, Michel Djerzinski was unanimously considered to be a first-rate biologist and a serious candidate for the Nobel prize; his true significance, however, would not become apparent for some time.

In Djerzinski's time, philosophy was generally considered to be of no practical significance, to have been stripped of its purpose. Nevertheless, the values to which a majority subscribe at any given time determine society's economic and political structures and social mores.

Metaphysical mutations – that is to say radical, global transformations in the values to which the majority subscribe – are rare in the history of humanity. The rise of Christianity might be cited as an example.

Once a metaphysical mutation has arisen, it tends to move inexorably towards its logical conclusion. Heedlessly, it sweeps away economic and political systems, ethical considerations and social structures. No human agency can halt its progress – nothing, but another metaphysical mutation.

It is a fallacy that such metaphysical mutations gain ground only in weakened societies or those in decline. When Christianity appeared, the Roman Empire was at the height of its powers: supremely organised, it dominated the known world. Its technical and military prowess had no rival; nonetheless, it had no chance. When modern science appeared, medieval Christianity was a complete, comprehensive system which explained man and the universe; it was the basis for the government of peoples, the inspiration for knowledge and art, the arbiter of war as of peace and the power behind the production and distribution of wealth; none of these was sufficient to prevent its downfall.

Michel Djerzinski was not the primary, nor even the

principal architect of the third – and in many respects the most radical – metaphysical mutation, which opened up a new era in world history. But, in a variety of ways, his circumstances enabled his contribution to be one of the most clear-sighted and deliberate.

We live today under a new world order,
The web which weaves together all things envelops our bodies,
Bathes our limbs,
In a halo of joy.
A state to which men of old acceded only through music,
Greets us each morning as a commonplace.
What men considered a dream: perfect but remote,
We take for granted as the simplest of things.
But we are not contemptuous of these men;
We know how much we owe to their dreaming,
We know that without the web of suffering and joy which was
*   their history, we would be nothing,*
We know that they kept within them an image of us, through
*   their fear and in their pain, as they hurtled into darkness,*
As little by little, they wrote their history.
We know that they would not have survived, that they could
*   not have survived, without that hope somewhere deep*
*   within,*
They could not have survived without their dream.
Now that we who live in the light,
We who live in the presence of the light,
Which bathes our bodies,
Envelops our bodies,
In a halo of joy
Now that we have settled by the water's edge,
And here live in perpetual afternoon

Now that the light which surrounds our bodies is palpable,
Now that we have come at last to our destination

Leaving behind a world of division,
The way of thinking which divided us,
Immersed in a serene, fertile delight
Of a new Law
Now,
For the first time,
We can retrace the end of the old order.

Part One

The Lost Kingdom

1

The first of July fell on a Wednesday, so although it was a little unusual, Djerzinski organised his leaving drinks for Tuesday evening. Bottles of champagne nestled among containers of frozen embryos in the large Brandt refrigerator usually filled with chemicals.

Four bottles for fifteen people was a little miserly, but the whole party was a sham. One careless word would break it up and send his colleagues scurrying for their cars. They stood around drinking in the white-tiled basement decorated only by a poster of the Lakes of Germany. Nobody had offered to take photos. A research student who had arrived earlier that year – a young man with a beard and a vapid expression – left after a few minutes explaining that he had to pick up his car from the garage. A palpable sense of unease spread through the group. Term would be over soon. Some of them were going home to visit family, others were going on holiday. The sound of their voices snapped like twigs in the air. Shortly afterwards, the party broke up.

By seven-thirty it was all over. Djerzinski walked across the car park with one of his colleagues. She had long black hair, very white skin and large breasts. She was older than he, and would inevitably take his position as head of the department. Most of her published papers were on the DAF3 gene in the fruit fly. She was unmarried.

When they reached his Toyota he offered his hand, smiling (he had been preparing himself mentally for this for several seconds, remembering to smile). Their palms brushed and they shook hands gently. Later, he decided a handshake lacked warmth; under the circumstances, they could have kissed each other on both cheeks like visiting dignitaries or people in show business.

After they had said their goodbyes, he sat in his car for what seemed to him an unusually long five minutes. Why had she not driven off? Was she masturbating while listening to Brahms? Perhaps she was thinking about her career, her new responsibilities: if so, was she happy? At last, her Golf pulled out of the car park, leaving him alone. The weather had been magnificent all day; it was still warm now. In the early weeks of summer everything seemed fixed, motionless, radiant, though already the days were getting shorter.

He felt privileged to have worked here, he thought as he pulled out into the street. When asked 'Do you feel privileged to live in an area like Palaiseau?', 63 per cent of respondents answered 'Yes'. It was hardly surprising: the buildings were on a human scale, surrounded by lush green lawns. There were several supermarkets conveniently nearby for shopping. The phrase 'quality of life' seemed to have been coined for such a place.

The motorway back into Paris was deserted and Djerzinski felt like a character in a science-fiction film he had seen at university: the last man on earth after every other living thing had been wiped out. A post-apocalyptic wasteland.

Djerzinski had lived on the rue Frémicourt for ten years, during which he had grown accustomed to the quiet. In 1993 he felt the need for a companion, something to welcome him home in the evening. He settled on a white canary. It was a fearful animal, which sang in the mornings though it never seemed happy. Could a canary be happy? Happiness is an intense, all-consuming feeling of joyous fulfilment akin to inebriation, rapture or ecstasy. The first time he took the canary out of its cage, the frightened creature shat on the sofa before flying back to the bars, desperate to find the way back in. He tried again a month later. This time, the poor bird managed to fall from an open window. Barely remembering to flutter its wings, it landed on a balcony five floors down on the building opposite. All that Michel could do was wait for the woman who lived there to come home, and hope that she didn't have a cat. She was an editor at *Vingt Ans* and worked late. She didn't have a cat.

Michel recovered the bird after dark; it was trembling

with cold and fear, huddled against the concrete window-sill. He sometimes saw the woman again as he was taking the rubbish out. She would nod in greeting and he would nod back. Something good had come of the accident – he had met one of his neighbours.

From his window he could see a dozen buildings – some three hundred apartments. When he came home in the evening, the canary would whistle and chirp for five or ten minutes. Michel would feed the bird and change the gravel in its cage. Tonight, however, silence greeted him. He crossed the room to the cage. The canary was dead, its cold white body lying on the gravel.

He ate a Monoprix ready-meal – monkfish in parsley sauce, from their Gourmet range – washed down with a mediocre Valdepeñas. After some thought, he put the bird's body into a plastic bag and dumped it in the rubbish chute. What was he supposed to do? Say mass?

He didn't know what was at the end of the chute. The opening was narrow (though large enough to take the canary). He dreamed that the chute opened onto vast rubbish bins filled with old coffee filters, ravioli in tomato sauce and mangled genitalia. Huge worms, as big as the canary, armed with terrible beaks, would attack the body. Tear off its feet, rip out its intestines, burst its eyeballs. He woke up, trembling; it was only one o'clock. He swallowed three Xanax. So ended his first night of freedom.

2

On 14 December 1900, in a paper to the Berlin Academy entitled 'Zur Theorie des Geseztes der Energieverteilung in Normalspektrum', Max Planck introduced the idea of quantum energy. It was a concept that would play a decisive role in the evolution of physics. Between 1900 and 1920, Einstein, Bohr and their contemporaries developed a number of ingenious models which attempted to reconcile this idea with previous theories. It was not until the 1920s that it became apparent that such attempts were futile.

Niels Bohr's claim to be the founder of quantum mechanics rests less on his own discoveries than on the extraordinary atmosphere of creativity and intellectual openness he fostered around him. The Institute of Physics, which Bohr founded in Copenhagen in 1919, welcomed the cream of young European physicists. Heisenberg, Pauli and Born served their apprenticeships there.

Though some years their senior, Bohr would spend hours talking through their hypotheses in detail. He was perceptive and good humoured but extremely rigorous. However, if Bohr tolerated no laxity in his students' experiments, he did not think any new idea foolish a priori; no concept was so established that it could not be challenged. He liked to invite his students to his country house in Tisvilde, where he also welcomed politicians, artists and scientists from other fields. Their conversations ranged easily from philosophy to physics, history to art, from religion to everyday life. Nothing comparable had happened since the days of the Greek philosophers. It was in this extraordinary environment, between 1925 and 1927, that the basic premises of the Copenhagen Inter-pretation – which called into question established con-cepts of space, time and causality – were developed.

Djerzinski had singularly failed to foster such an environment around him. The atmosphere in his research facility was like an office, no better, no worse. Far from the popular image of molecular biologists as Rimbauds with microscopes, research scientists were not great thinkers, but simple technicians who read *Le Nouvel Observateur* and dreamed of going on holiday to Greenland. Molecular biology was routine. It required no creativity, no imagination and only the most basic second-rate intellect. Researchers wrote theses and studied for PhDs when a baccalauréat and a couple of years in college would have been more than enough for them to handle the equipment. 'There's no mystery to decoding the

genome,' Desplechin, the director of the biology department, liked to say, '. . . synthesising proteins, now that
takes real talent. It's hardly surprising that Gamow, the
first person to discover how to, was a physicist. But
decoding DNA, pfff . . . you decode one gene, then
another and another, feed the results into a computer and
let it work out the sub-sequences. You send a fax to
Colorado – they're working on gene B27, we're working
on C33. It's like following a recipe. From time to time
someone comes up with better equipment and they give
him the Nobel prize. It's a joke.'

The first of July was oppressively hot. In the afternoon a
storm threatened which would send the sunbathers
scattering. Desplechin's office on the Quai Anatole France
looked out onto the river. Opposite, on the Quai des
Tuileries, homosexuals, many of them wearing thongs,
walked around in the sunshine. They chatted in pairs and
groups, and shared towels. Suntan lotion glistened on
their biceps, their buttocks were glabrous and sleek.
While they talked, some massaged their genitals through
nylon briefs, or slipped a finger under their waistbands,
revealing pubic hair or the root of the penis. Desplechin
had set up a telescope beside the bay window. Rumour
had it that he was homosexual; in reality, in recent years,
he was simply a common or garden alcoholic.

On one such afternoon he had twice tried to masturbate, his eye glued to the eyepiece, staring at an adolescent
who had taken off his thong and whose cock had begun

to rise. Desplechin's penis fell, wrinkled and flaccid; he abandoned the attempt.

Djerzinski arrived punctually at four o'clock. Desplechin had asked to see him. The case was intriguing. Certainly, it was common for a researcher to take a year's sabbatical to work in Norway or Japan, or another of those sinister countries where middle-aged people commit suicide en masse. Others – especially in the Mitterrand years, when greed reached its dizziest heights – went to venture capitalists to set up companies to exploit some molecule or another commercially. Many of them had succeeded in using the knowledge they had acquired during their years of pure research to amass considerable fortunes. But for Djerzinski to take a sabbatical with no plan, no pretext nor the merest hint of an excuse, was intolerable. At forty, he was already head of department, with fifteen researchers working under him. He reported directly to Desplechin – in theory at least. His team was widely considered to be one of the best in Europe, and their results excellent. What was wrong with the man? Desplechin forced himself to be upbeat: 'So, any idea what you're going to do with yourself?' There was a minute's silence before Djerzinski answered soberly, 'Think.' This was hardly a promising start, but Desplechin kept up his cheerful façade. 'Any personal projects?' He stared into the thin face, the sad, serious eyes of the man, and suddenly he felt intensely embarrassed. What personal life? He had plucked Djerzinski from the University of Orsay fifteen years ago. It had proved to be an excellent

choice: Djerzinski was a disciplined and rigorous researcher who had built up a considerable body of work in
the intervening years. The reputation of the CNRS as a
leader in molecular biology was in no small part due to his
work. He had kept his side of the bargain.

'Well,' Desplechin concluded, 'we'll keep your log-in
to the faculty server active indefinitely, of course. You'll
have access to the results and the intranet and so forth. If
you need anything, please don't hesitate to get in touch.'

After Djerzinski left, Desplechin went back to the bay
window. He was sweating slightly. On the bank opposite,
a young, dark-haired Arab boy was taking off his shorts.
Fundamental questions remained to be answered in
biology. Biologists acted as though molecules were
separate and distinct entities defined solely by electromagnetic attraction and repulsion. Not one of them had
even heard of the EPR paradox or the Aspect experiments, nor taken the trouble to study developments in
physics since the beginning of the century. Their view of
the atom had evolved little since that of Democritus. They
accumulated reams of repetitive statistics in the hope of
finding some immediate industrial application, never
realising that the very methods they were using were
threatened. He and Djerzinski were probably the only
members of the CNRS who had studied physics and who
realised that once biologists were forced to confront the
reality of the atom, the very basis of modern biology
would be blown away.

Desplechin thought about this as night fell over the

Seine. He could not begin to imagine where Djerzinski's thinking might lead; he did not even feel able to discuss it with him. He was almost sixty years old and, intellectually, he felt that he was past it. The homosexuals had left now, and the bank opposite was deserted. Desplechin tried to remember when he had last had an erection. He waited for the storm.

3

The storm broke at about nine o'clock that evening. Djerzinski listened to the rain and sipped cheap Armagnac. He had just turned forty – perhaps he was having a mid-life crisis. Improved living standards meant that a forty-year-old nowadays was in excellent physical shape. The first signs that one had crossed a threshold – whether in physical appearance or in the slowing of the body's responses – and begun the long decline towards death, tended to appear at forty-five, perhaps fifty. In any case, the typical mid-life crisis was sexual – a sudden frantic pursuit of young girls. This was hardly the case for Djerzinski – he used his cock to piss, no more.

The following morning he got up at seven, took his copy of Werner Heisenberg's autobiography, *Physics and Beyond*, and headed for the Champs de Mars. The dawn was limpid and cool. He had had the book since he was seventeen. He sat under a chestnut tree on the Allée Victor-Cousin and re-read the chapter where Heisenberg, recounting his years as a student, tells of his first encounter with atomic theory:

It must have been in the Spring of 1920. The end of the First World War had thrown Germany's youth into a great turmoil. The reins of power had fallen from the hands of a deeply disillusioned older generation, and the younger one drew together in an attempt to blaze new paths, or at least to discover a new star by which they could guide their steps in the prevailing darkness. And so, one bright spring morning, some ten or twenty of us, most of them younger than myself, set out on a ramble which, if I remember correctly, took us through the hills above the western shore of Lake Starnberg. Through gaps in the dense emerald screen of beech we caught occasional glimpses of the lake beneath, and of the tall mountains in the far distance. It was here that I had my first conversation about the world of atoms which was to play such an important part in my subsequent life.

At around eleven the heat began to become oppressive and Michel went back to his apartment. He undressed completely and lay down. In the three weeks that followed he barely moved. It is easy to imagine that a fish, bobbing to the surface to gulp the air, sees a beautiful, insubstantial new world. Then it retreats to its world of algae where fish feed on one other. But for a moment, it has had a glimpse of a different world, a perfect world – ours.

On the evening of 15 July he phoned Bruno. His half-brother's voice on his answerphone was coolly ironic over a jazz riff. Bruno had a leather jacket and a goatee beard. To enhance his streetwise image he smoked cigars, worked out regularly and talked like a character from a second-rate cop show. Bruno was definitely in the throes of a mid-life crisis. Was Michel? A man in a mid-life crisis is asking only to live, to live a little more, a little longer. Michel, on the other hand, had had enough; he could see no reason to go on.

That evening he stumbled on a photo taken at his primary school in Charny and he cried. The child in the photograph sat at his desk holding a textbook open in front of him. The boy smiled straight at the camera happily, confidently; it seemed unthinkable to Djerzinski that he was that boy. The child did his homework, worked hard in class with an assured seriousness. He was just beginning to discover the world, and what he saw did not frighten him; he was ready to take his place in society. All of this was written on the boy's face. He was wearing a jacket with a narrow collar.

For several days Michel kept the photograph beside him on his bedside table. The mysteries of time were banal, he told himself, this was the way of the world: youthful optimism fades and happiness and confidence evaporate. He lay on his Bultex mattress, struggling to come to terms with the transience of life. There was a small round dimple on the boy's forehead – a scar he had from chickenpox; that scar had accompanied him down the years. Where was truth? The heat of midday filled the room.

4

Born to illiterate peasants in central Corsica in 1882, Martin Ceccaldi seemed destined for the undistinguished life of a farmer, which had been the lot of his ancestors for countless generations. It is a way of life long since vanished, and is fondly remembered only by a handful of radical environmentalists. A detailed description of this pastoral 'idyll' is unnecessary, but for the sake of argument, I will outline it broadly. You are at one with nature, have plenty of fresh air and a couple of fields to plough (the number and size of which are strictly fixed by hereditary principle). Now and then you kill a boar; you fuck occasionally, mostly with your wife, whose role is to give birth to children; said children grow up to take their place in the same ecosystem. Eventually, you catch something serious and you're history.

Martin Ceccaldi's singular destiny was entirely symptomatic of the role played by secularism, throughout the Third Republic, in integrating citizens into French society and promoting technological progress. His teacher quickly realised that he was an exceptional pupil, a child of considerable intelligence with a gift for abstract thought – qualities which would have little opportunity to develop in peasant society. Martin's teacher was keenly aware that there was more to his job than spoonfeeding elementary facts and figures to every untrained citizen. His task was to seek out the qualities that fitted a child to join the elite of the Third Republic. He managed to persuade Martin's parents that their son could fulfil his destiny only if he were to leave Corsica.

In 1894, funded by a bursary, the boy started school at Thiers de Marseille (an institution faithfully described in the autobiography of Marcel Pagnol; the author's well-written, realistic account of a poor-boy-made-good would remain a favourite of Martin's). In 1902 his teacher's faith was rewarded when he was admitted to the École Polytechnique.

In 1911 he accepted a position which was to change the course of his life for ever. He was to design and plan an efficient system of waterways throughout French Algeria. For more than 25 years he calculated the curve of aqueducts and the ideal diameter of pipes. In 1923 he married Geneviève July, a secretary whose family had come from the Languedoc to settle in Algeria two generations before. In 1928 their daughter, Janine, was born.

The story of a life can be as long or as short as the teller wishes. Whether the life is tragic or enlightened, the classic gravestone inscription, marking simply the dates of birth and death, has, in its brevity, much to recommend it. However, in the case of Martin Ceccaldi, it seems appropriate to set his life in a socioeconomic context; to say less about the individual than about the society of which he is symptomatic. Carried forward by the sweep of history and their determination to be a part of it, *symptomatic* individuals lead lives which are, in the main, happy and uncomplicated. A page or two are sufficient to summarise such a life. Janine Ceccaldi, on the other hand, belongs to a different and dispiriting class of individuals we can call *precursors*. Ideally adapted to their time and social status on the one hand, they are anxious that their tendency to adopt new customs, or proselytise ideas still regarded as marginal might make them appear 'above themselves'. Precursors, therefore, require a more detailed study – especially as their lives are often tortuous or confused. They are, however, merely catalysts – generally of some form of social breakdown – without the power to stamp their authority on change; which role is the preserve of *revolutionaries* and *prophets*.

From an early age, it was clear to Martin and Geneviève Ceccaldi that their daughter was extraordinarily intelligent – at least as brilliant as her father. She was an independent girl. She lost her virginity at the age of 13 – a remarkable achievement given the time and place. She spent the war years (uneventful, for the most part) in Algeria going to dances and balls in Constantine and, later, Algiers, while somehow managing to sustain flawless grades term after term. So it was that, with a first-class *baccalauréat* and considerable sexual experience, Janine left Algiers for Paris in 1945, to study medicine.

Post-war France was a difficult and troubled society: industrial production was at an all-time low and rationing would continue until 1948. Even so, a privileged few on the margins of society already showed symptoms of the compulsive, almost fetishistic desire for prepackaged pleasures that would sweep through the populace in the decades that followed. As a student in Paris, Janine had a ringside seat during the existential years. She danced to bebop at the Tabou with Jean-Paul Sartre. Though unimpressed by the philosopher's work, she was struck by his ugliness which, she maintained, amounted to a handicap; they did not meet again. She herself was a stunning Mediterranean beauty, and had many lovers before she met Serge Clément in 1952, while he was completing his surgical internship.

'You want to know what my dad was like?' Bruno liked to say, years later, 'Give a gorilla a mobile phone and you've got the general idea.' Obviously, Serge Clément could not possibly have had a mobile phone at the time, but he was, it has to be admitted, somewhat hirsute. Though certainly not handsome, he had a simple, uncomplicated virility which seduced Janine. Moreover, he had plans. While travelling in the United States, he had become convinced that plastic surgery offered excellent career prospects for an ambitious young surgeon. The use of sex in marketing and the resulting breakdown of the traditional couple, together with the economic boom he sensed was coming to post-war Europe, suggested a vast untapped market which Serge Clément was among the first in Europe – certainly the first in France – to identify. His only problem was money: he needed funds to start up in business. Martin Ceccaldi, impressed by his future son-in-law's entrepreneurial spirit, agreed to lend him money. Clément's first clinic opened in Neuilly in 1953. Promoted in a series of positive articles in women's magazines, it proved an outstanding success and Serge opened a second clinic in 1955, in the hills above Cannes.

Janine and Serge were what would later be called a 'modern' couple; her pregnancy was something of an accident. She decided, however, to have the child, believing that maternity was something every woman should experience. It was an uneventful pregnancy, and Bruno was born in March 1956. The couple quickly realised that the burden of caring for a small child was incompatible with their personal freedom and, in 1958, they agreed to send Bruno to Algeria to live with his maternal grandmother. By then, Janine was pregnant again, this time by Marc Djerzinski.

Lucien Djerzinski had left Katowice in 1919 hoping to find work in France – or, more exactly, fled the misery and famine of the small mining community into which he had been born twenty years earlier. In France, he found work on the railways as a labourer before being promoted to track maintenance. He met and married Marie le Roux, the daughter of a newspaperman from Burgundy, and fathered four children before dying in an Allied bombing raid in 1944.

Marc, their third child, was 14 when his father died. He was an intelligent boy, serious, perhaps a little sad. In 1946, with the help of a neighbour, he got a job at the Pathé studios in Joinville, where it was immediately apparent that he had a talent for film. Given the most rudimentary instructions, he could set up and light a set before the lighting cameraman had even arrived. Henri Alekan was impressed by the boy's work and when he joined the ORTF, shortly after broadcasting began in 1951, he invited Marc to be his assistant.

When he met Janine, in 1957, Marc was shooting a documentary on the 'Tropezians'. Focusing principally on Brigitte Bardot (*Et Dieu créa la Femme*, released in 1956, marked the beginning of the Bardot legend), it covered the artistic and literary scene around Saint-Tropez with particular emphasis on what would later be called '*la bande à Sagan*'. Janine was fascinated by this milieu which, despite her wealth, was closed to her. She seemed to be genuinely in love with Marc. She convinced herself that he had the makings of a great director – which was probably true. Marc made cinéma vérité documentaries. Using minimal lighting and the careful placement of objects, he could conjure scenes reminiscent of Edward Hopper: calm, prosaic but quietly desperate. Though he was surrounded by celebrities, his gaze never seemed more than indifferent. He filmed Sagan and Bardot with the same attention to detail as he might a lobster. He spoke to no one, befriended no one; he was genuinely fascinating.

Janine divorced Serge in 1958, shortly after they had packed Bruno off to her parents. It was an amicable separation, with both parties admitting fault. Serge was generous, giving Janine his share of the Cannes clinic, which guaranteed her a comfortable income. Marc proved no less a loner after he and Janine had moved into a villa in Sainte-Maxime together. She nagged him constantly, telling him he should work on his career as a director. He agreed but did nothing, simply waiting for the next documentary opportunity to come his way. If she arranged a dinner party, he would eat in the kitchen before the guests arrived and then go walking on the sea front. He would return just as the guests were leaving and explain that he was editing a film.

The birth of their son in 1958 clearly disturbed him. He would stand for minutes at a time staring at the child, who bore an uncanny resemblance to him: the same angular face, high cheekbones and piercing green eyes. Shortly after, Janine began to be unfaithful. He was probably hurt by her infidelity, but it was impossible to tell as he spoke less and less. He spent his time making small altars of pebbles, driftwood and seashells and photographing them under the blazing sky.

His documentary about Saint-Tropez was well

received in the industry, but he turned down an interview request from *Les Cahiers du Cinéma*. His reputation reached new heights in 1959 with the broadcast of a short, bilious documentary about the film *Salut les Copains* and the *yéyé* phenomenon. He had no interest in drama and twice refused an invitation to work with Jean-Luc Godard. Janine had by now taken up with a group of Americans staying on the Riviera. Something radical was happening in California. At Esalen, near Big Sur, people were living together in communes which practised sexual liberation and the use of mind-expanding drugs. Janine and Francesco di Meola became lovers. He was an Italian-American, had met Ginsberg and Aldous Huxley and was one of the founding members of the Esalen commune.

In January 1961 Marc travelled to China to shoot a documentary about the new communist society emerging in the People's Republic. He arrived back in Sainte-Maxime on the afternoon of 23 June. The house seemed deserted. A girl of about 15 sat naked and cross-legged on the floor of the living room. 'Gone to the beach', she finally said, listlessly, before sinking back into torpor. In Janine's bedroom he found a large, bearded man, naked and visibly drunk, lying snoring across the bed. Listening, Marc thought he could hear cries or screams.

Pushing open the door of one of the upstairs bedrooms, he smelled a retch-inducing stench. The sun flared violently through the huge bay window onto the black and white tiles where his son crawled around awkwardly, slipping occasionally in pools of urine or excrement. He blinked against the light and whimpered continuously. Sensing a human presence, the boy tried to escape; Marc picked him up and the child trembled in his arms.

Marc left the house and bought a child's car-seat from a nearby shop. He wrote a short note to Janine, strapped his son into his car, climbed in, and headed north. When he reached Valence, he turned into the Massif Central. It was getting dark. From time to time, between the hairpin bends, he glanced back at his sleeping son and felt overcome by a strange emotion.

Subsequently, Michel's grandmother, who had retired to live in the Yonne, brought him up. His mother moved to America shortly afterward to join di Meola's commune. He would not see her again until he was 15. He saw little of his father, either. In 1964 Marc went to Tibet to film a documentary about the Chinese occupation. He wrote to his mother to say he was well, and to tell her how much he admired Tibetan Buddhism – which the Chinese were brutally eradicating; after that, silence. The French government made approaches to the Chinese authorities, but there was no response. Though no body was ever found, he was officially presumed dead a year later.

5

It is the summer of 1968; Michel is ten years old. He has lived with his grandmother since he was two, in the village of Charny in the Yonne, near the border with the Loiret. Every morning he gets up early to make his grandmother's breakfast; he has made a list: how long the tea should brew, how many slices of bread-and-butter and so on.

He often stays in his room all morning reading Jules Verne, *Pif le Chien,* or the *Famous Five*, but he spends most of his time poring over a magazine he collects, *The Universe Explained*. There are articles about the structure of the elements, about how clouds form and bees swarm. He reads about the Taj Mahal, a palace built by an ancient king to honour his dead queen; about the death of Socrates; about Euclid's invention of geometry three thousand years ago.

In the afternoon, sitting in the garden with his back to

the cherry tree, he can feel the springiness of the grass and the heat of the sun. The lettuces soak up the sun's rays and water from the ground. He has to water them when it gets dark. He sits in the garden reading *The Universe Explained*, or one of the books in a series called *One Hundred Facts About . . .* He feeds on knowledge.

Sometimes he cycles cross-country, pedalling as hard as he can, filling his lungs with a taste of the infinite. He does not know it yet, but the infinity of childhood is a brief one. The countryside flashes past.

There is nothing in Charny but a small grocer's shop. Every Wednesday, though, the butcher's van calls round; the fishmonger's every Friday. His grandmother often makes creamed cod for lunch on Saturday. Michel does not know that this is his last summer in Charny. His grandmother suffered a heart attack some months ago, her daughters are already looking for a house in the suburbs of Paris so that she can be closer to them. She is not strong enough to cope on her own any more, nor to tend the garden all year round.

Though Michel rarely plays with boys his own age, he gets along with his peers well enough. They think of him as a bit of a loner. His schoolwork is excellent – he seems to understand everything effortlessly – and his grandmother is very proud. Yet he is not bullied by his classmates; he is happy to let them copy his work in class, always waiting for the boy next to him to finish before turning the page. Despite his excellent academic record, he always sits at the back of the class. His is a fragile kingdom.

6

One summer while he was still living in the Yonne, Michel spent an afternoon running through the fields with his cousin Brigitte. A pretty, gentle girl of 16, who some years later would marry a complete bastard. It was the summer of 1967. She grabbed his hands, swinging him round and round until they collapsed in a heap on the freshly mown grass. He pressed himself into her warm breast; she was wearing a short skirt. Next morning they were covered in spots and itched all over.

Thrombidium holosericum is plentiful in summer meadows. Two millimetres in diameter, with a fat, fleshy, bright red body, it embeds itself into the bodies of mammals causing painful itching. *Linguatulia rhinaria* is a parasite which lives in the frontal and maxilliary sinuses of dogs and, occasionally, humans. The larva is oval and has a short tail and a sharp spike near the mouth; two pairs of limbs are armed with long claws. The body of the adult is between 18 and 85 centimetres long, flat, ribbed, translucent and covered in barbed spines.

In December 1968 Michel's grandmother moved to Seine-et-Marne to be closer to her daughters. Michel's day-to-day life changed little at first. Fifty kilometres from Paris, Crécy-en-Brie was a pretty country village at the time; its old and dignified houses had been painted by Corot in his day. Tourist brochures referred to it, hopefully, as 'Venice on the Brie', a reference to the network of canals that brought water from the Grand Morin. Few villagers commuted to Paris, most working for local businesses, or in nearby Meaux.

Two months after the move, at a time when advertising had barely begun on France's then only channel, his grandmother bought a television. And so, on 21 July 1969, Michel was able to stay up and watch the first steps of man on the moon, live. Six hundred million people across the world watched with him. The broadcast, which lasted three or four hours, probably represents the culmination of the first great Western technological dream.

Though he joined the local school in Crécy in midterm, Michel adapted quickly and had no difficulty passing his end of year exams. Every Thursday he bought *Pif*, newly relaunched, with its free 'gadget' every week. Unlike most children of his age, he did not buy it for the gadget, but for the adventure stories. The dazzling sweep of history and costume of these tales did little to mask the simple moral values they exemplified. Michel slowly realised that this moral system ran through all the stories: *Ragnar the Viking; Teddy Ted and the Apache; Rahan 'Son of a Savage Age'*; and *Nasdine Hodja* in the world of viziers and caliphs. It was a realisation that would have a profound effect on him. Later, when he read Nietzsche, he was only briefly provoked, and Kant only served to confirm what he already knew: that perfect morality is unique and universal. Nothing is added to it and nothing changes in the course of time. It is not dependent on history, economics, sociology or culture; it is not dependent on anything. Not determined, it determines. Not conditioned, it conditions. It is, in other words, absolute.

Everyday morality is always a blend, variously proportioned, of perfect morality and other, more ambiguous ideas – for the most part religious. The greater the proportion of pure morality in a particular system, the happier and more enduring the society. Ultimately, a society governed by the pure principles of universal morality could last until the end of the world.

Michel liked all of the heroes in *Pif*, but his favourite was Black Wolf, the Lone Indian. He was a synthesis of the noblest qualities of the Apache, the Sioux and the Cheyenne. Black Wolf roamed the prairies ceaselessly with his horse Shinook and his wolf Toopee, instinctively coming to the aid of the weak. Black Wolf continually commented on the transcendent ethic which underpinned his actions. Often, he referred to poetic proverbs from the Dakota and the Cree; sometimes more prosaically to the 'law of the prairie'. Years later, Michel still thought of him as Kant's ideal: always acting 'as if he were by his maxims in every case a legitimating member in the universal kingdom of ends'. Some episodes, like 'The Leather Bracelet' in which the extraordinary character of the old Cheyenne chief searches for the stars, broke free of the straitjacket of the 'adventure story' for a world that was more poetic, more moral.

He was less interested in television. Every week, however, his heart in his mouth, he watched *The Animal Kingdom*. Graceful animals like gazelles and the antelopes spent their days in abject terror while lions and panthers lived out their lives in listless imbecility punctuated by explosive bursts of cruelty. They slaughtered weaker animals; dismembered and devoured the sick and the old, before falling back into brutish sleep where the only activity was that of the parasites feeding on them from within. Some of the parasites were hosts to smaller parasites, which in turn were a breeding ground for viruses. Snakes moved among the trees, their fangs bared, ready to strike at bird or mammal, only to be ripped apart by hawks. The pompous, half-witted voice of Claude Darget narrated these atrocities, his voice filled with awe and unjustifiable admiration. Michel trembled with indignation. But, as he watched, the unshakeable conviction grew that, taken as a whole, nature was not only savage, it was a repulsive cesspit. All in all, nature deserved to be wiped out in a holocaust – and man's mission on earth was probably to do just that.

In April 1970 *Pif* gave away a free gift which was to

become famous: 'Sea Monkeys'. Each copy came with a sachet of *poudre de vie* – the eggs of a tiny marine crustacean, *Artemia salina*. They had spent thousands of years in suspended animation. The process for bringing them back to life was complicated: water had to be decanted from one container into another for three days, then warmed. Only then was the powder added and the water stirred gently. In the days that followed, the bowl had to be kept near a source of light; warm water had to be added regularly to compensate for evaporation and the water stirred to keep it oxygenated. Some weeks later, the bowl was swarming with a multitude of translucent crustaceans, which were indisputably alive, if faintly revolting. Not knowing what to do with them, Michel ended up tipping them into the river Morin.

The complete adventure story in the same issue concerned the boyhood of Rahan, and told how he had come to his vocation as a lone hero in Palaeolithic Europe. When still a child, he had seen his tribe wiped out by an erupting volcano. As he knelt by his dying father, Crâo the Wise, the old man gave him a necklace of three hawk's talons. Each of the talons symbolised one of the qualities of 'those who walked upright'. The first symbolised loyalty, the second courage, and the third and most important was the talon of kindness. Rahan had worn the necklace ever since, trying always to prove himself worthy of it.

In the long narrow garden of the house in Crécy was a cherry tree only slightly smaller than the one in Michel's garden in the Yonne. There he would sit and read *The Universe Explained* and *A Hundred Facts About . . .* For his twelfth birthday, his grandmother gave him 'My First Chemistry Set'. Chemistry was mysterious and strange; it was much more exciting than physics or biology. Each substance came in a separate tube. Each had its own colour and texture, elements forever distinct from each other, but simply putting them close to each other could produce violent reactions, which, in a flash, could create some new substance.

It was as he was reading in the garden one afternoon in July that Michel realised that the elements could have been completely different. Atoms with identical valency but higher atomic weight could have taken the place of the carbon, oxygen and nitrogen which made up all living things. On another planet, where temperature and atmospheric pressure were different, the stuff of life could be silicon, sulphur and phosphorus; or germanium, selenium and arsenic; or even tin, tellurium and antimony. He had no one he could really talk to about these things. At his insistence, his grandmother bought him several books on biochemistry.

Bruno's earliest memory was one of humiliation. He was four years old, and attending the Parc Laperlier nursery school in Algiers. It was an autumn afternoon and the teacher had shown the boys how to make necklaces out of leaves. The girls, most of them in white dresses, sat on a small bank watching, their faces already betraying a hint of the dumb resignation of women. The ground was strewn with golden leaves, mostly chestnut and poplar. One after another, his friends finished their necklaces and went to place them around the necks of their little girlfriends. He could not seem to finish his. The leaves broke and crumbled in his hands. How could he tell them that he too needed love? How could he let them know without a necklace? He started to cry with rage but the teacher did not come to help. Class had finished and the children stood up and began to file out of the park. The nursery school closed shortly afterwards.

His grandparents lived in a beautiful apartment on the Boulevard Edgar-Quinet. The apartment, like many in the centre of Algiers, was designed in the bourgeois style of the great Haussmann buildings in Paris. A central hall, thirty metres long, ran the length of the apartment, ending in a drawing-room. From the balcony of the drawing-room, the whole of the 'White City' was at one's feet. Many years later, when Bruno was already an embittered middle-aged cynic, he could still remember himself, aged four, pedalling furiously down the dark hallway towards the shimmering portal of the balcony. It was at moments like this that he had come closest to true happiness.

His grandfather died in 1967. In temperate climates, the body of a bird or mammal first attracts specific species of flies (*Musca, Curtoneura*), but once decomposition has begun to set in, these are joined by others, particularly *Calliphora* and *Lucilia*. Under the combined action of bacteria and the digestive juices disgorged by the larvae, the corpse begins to liquefy and becomes a ferment of butyric and ammoniac reactions. In three short months, the flies will have completed their work. They are succeeded by hordes of coleopterans, specifically *Dermestes,* and lepidoptera like *Aglossa pinguinalis* which feed on fatty tissue. Larvae of the *Piophila petasionis* feed on the fermenting proteins with other coleopterans called *Corynetes*.

The cadaver, now decomposed, becomes a host to *Acaridae* which absorb the last traces of residual moisture. Desiccated now and mummified, the corpse still harbours parasites, the larvae of beetles, *Aglossa cuprealis* and *Tineola bisellelia* maggots, which complete the cycle.

Bruno could still see the beautiful deep black coffin with a silver cross. It was a peaceful image, a happy one: he knew his grandfather would be at peace in such a magnificent coffin. He did not learn about *Acaridae* and the host of parasites with names like Italian film stars until later. But even now the image of his grandfather's coffin was still a happy one.

He remembered his grandmother, sitting on a suitcase in the middle of the kitchen on the day they arrived in Marseilles. Cockroaches scuttled between the cracks in the tiles. It was then that she began to lose her mind. The litany of troubles in those few short weeks had over-whelmed her: the slow agony of her husband's death, the hurried departure from Algiers and the arduous search for an apartment, finding one at last on a housing estate in the north-east of Marseilles. She had never set foot in France before. Her daughter had deserted her; she had not even attended her father's funeral. Deep down, Bruno's grandmother felt certain that there had been a mistake. Someone, somewhere had made a dreadful mistake.

She picked herself up and carried on for another five years. She bought new furniture, set up a bed in the dining room for Bruno and enrolled him in a local primary school. Every afternoon she came to collect him. He was ashamed of the small, frail, shrivelled woman who took his hand to lead him home. All the other children had parents; divorce was still rare in those days.

At night she would go over and over her life trying to discover how it had come to this. She rarely managed to find sleep before dawn. The apartment had low ceilings and the rooms were stuffy and unbearably hot. During the day she pottered around in slippers, talking to herself. Sometimes she would repeat a phrase fifty times without realising. Her daughter's memory haunted her: 'Her own father's funeral and she didn't come.' She went from one room to another carrying a bucket or a saucepan whose purpose she had already forgotten. 'Her own father's funeral . . . Her own father's funeral.' Her slippers squeaked on the tiled floors. Terrified, Bruno curled himself into a ball in his bed. He knew things could only get worse. Sometimes she would get up early, still in dressing-gown and curlers, and whisper to herself 'Algeria is French . . .' and then her slippers would squeak across the floor. She walked back and forth in the tiny two-room apartment staring at some fixed, far-off point. 'France . . . France . . .' she repeated slowly, her voice dying away.

She had always been a good cook; here it became her only pleasure. She would cook lavish meals for Bruno as though she were entertaining a party of ten. Peppers marinated in olive oil, anchovies, potato salad: sometimes there would be five hors d'oeuvres before a main course of stuffed aubergine or saddle of hare with olives, sometimes couscous. The one thing she had never succeeded in mastering was baking, but every week when she collected her pension she would bring home pastries, boxes of nougat and *marrons glacés*. As time went by, Bruno became a fat, fearful child. She herself ate little or nothing.

On Sunday mornings she would sleep late and Bruno would climb into her bed and press himself against her emaciated body. Sometimes he dreamed of getting up in the night, taking a knife and stabbing her through the heart; he could see himself break down in tears beside the body; in his imagination, he always died soon after her.

Late in 1966 she received a letter from her daughter. Bruno's father – with whom she still exchanged cards at Christmas – had given her their address in Marseilles. In the letter, Janine expressed no real regret, as evidenced by her opening sentence 'I heard Daddy died and you moved to France'. She explained that she was leaving California and coming back to live in the south of France. She gave no forwarding address.

One morning in March 1967, while she was making deep-fried courgettes, the old woman knocked over the pan of boiling oil. She managed to drag herself into the hallway where her screams alerted the neighbours. When Bruno came home from school, Madame Haouzi, who lived upstairs, met him at the door. She took him to the hospital where he was allowed to see his grandmother for a few minutes. Her burns were hidden beneath the sheets. She had been given a great deal of morphine, but she recognised Bruno and took his hand in hers. Some minutes later the child was led away. Her heart gave out later that night.

For the second time, Bruno found himself face to face with death, and for a second time, he failed to grasp its significance. Years later, when he was praised for a composition or a history essay, his first thought was to tell his grandmother. He would remember, then, that she was dead, but only rarely did he face this fact; it did not interrupt the dialogue between them. When he was offered a place at university to study modern literature, he discussed the offer with her, though he was losing faith by now. He had bought a box of *marrons glacés* for the occasion. It was their last major conversation. When he had completed his studies and taken his first teaching job, he realised that something had changed; that he could not reach her any more. The image of his grandmother dissolved and disappeared.

On the morning of the funeral he witnessed something strange. His father and mother – neither of whom he had seen before – discussing what should be done with him. Bruno sat on his bed in the living room of the Marseilles apartment and listened. It was disconcerting to hear other people talk about him, especially as they seemed completely oblivious to his presence. He could almost forget that he was there; it was not an unpleasant feeling. Though the conversation was to have a profound impact on his life, at the time what they were saying simply did not seem to concern him. Later, when he thought about the conversation, as he did often, he felt nothing. As he sat listening to them that day, he could feel no link, no physical connection between himself and these two impossibly tall and youthful people. It was decided that he should be enrolled at boarding school in September. He would stay with his father in Paris at weekends. His mother would try to take him on holiday from time to time. Bruno did not object: these people did not seem to be hostile. In any case, life – his life – was the one he had shared with his grandmother.

8

The Omega Male

Bruno leans against the washbasin. He has taken off his pyjama top. The folds of his pale stomach press against the cold porcelain. He is 11 years old. He is about to brush his teeth, as he does every night; he hopes he can get out of the bathroom without anything happening. Wilmart comes up behind him and pushes him and Bruno backs away, trembling; he knows what will happen next. 'Leave me alone . . .' he says feebly.

Pelé comes up behind him now. He is short, stocky and very strong. He thumps Bruno hard and the boy starts to cry. They push him to the ground, grab his feet and drag him across the floor to the toilets. They rip off his pyjama bottoms. His penis is hairless, still that of a child. Two of them hold him by the ankles while others force his mouth open. Pelé takes a toilet brush and scrubs Bruno's face. He can taste shit. He screams.

Brasseur joins the others; he is fourteen – the oldest boy

in the *sixième*. He takes out his prick, which seems huge to Bruno. He stands over the boy and pisses on his face. The night before, he forced Bruno to suck him off and lick his arse, but he doesn't feel like it tonight. 'This'll put hair on your chest,' he jokes, 'and your balls.' He nods to the others who spread shaving cream on his genitals. Brasseur opens a cut-throat razor and brings the blade close. Terrified, Bruno shits himself.

One night in March 1968, a prefect found him curled up on the floor of the toilets in the courtyard, naked and covered in shit. He found a pair of pyjamas for the boy and took him to see Cohen, the housemaster. Bruno was terrified of being forced to squeal on Brasseur, but though he had been dragged out of bed in the middle of the night, Cohen was calm. Unlike the prefects who reported to him, he treated the boys with the same respect he did his colleagues. This was his third boarding school and was certainly not the toughest. He knew that victims almost always refused to inform on their tormentors. The only thing he could do was penalise the head prefect in charge of the *sixième* dormitory. Most of the boys were ignored by their parents, making Cohen the sole authority figure in their lives. He tried to keep a close eye on his pupils and pre-empt trouble but, with only five prefects for two hundred boys, it was impossible. After Bruno left he made himself a cup of coffee and leafed through his files. Though he could prove nothing, he knew the culprits were Pelé and Brasseur. If he could catch them, he would have them expelled. One or two cruel elements were enough to reduce the others to a state of savagery. In early adolescence, boys can be particularly savage; they gang together and are only too eager to torture and humiliate the weak. Cohen had no illusions about the depths to which the human animal could sink when not constrained by law. He had built a fearsome reputation since his arrival at the school in Meaux. He knew that he represented the ultimate sanction without which the treatment meted out to boys like Bruno would know no bounds.

Bruno was happy to repeat a year, since Pelé, Brasseur and Wilmart had graduated to the *cinquième* and would be in a different dormitory. Unfortunately, a ministerial directive taken after the riots of 1968 meant the introduction of an auto-disciplinary system in boarding schools and a reduction in staffing. The decision was very much of its time, and resulted in considerable savings in salaries. It became easier for pupils to move about at night and soon the bullies took to staging raids on the younger boys' dormitories at least once a week. They would bring one or two victims back to the *sixième* dormitory where the ceremonies would begin. Towards the end of December, Jean-Michel Kempf, a nervous, skinny boy who had arrived earlier that year, threw himself out of the window to escape his tormentors. The boy was lucky to escape with multiple fractures; the fall could easily have been fatal. His ankle was badly broken; though surgeons worked hard to reassemble the fragments of bone, he would walk with a limp for the rest of his life.

Cohen organised an inquiry, which confirmed his sus-
picions, and, despite the boy's protestations of innocence,
he suspended Pelé for three days.

Animal societies, for the most part are organised
according to a strict hierarchy where rank relates directly
to the physical strength of each member. The most
dominant male in the group is known as the *alpha male*, his
nearest rival the *beta male*, and so on down to the weakest
of the group, the *omega male*. Combat rituals generally
determine status within the group; weaker animals can try
to better their position by challenging those above them.
A dominant position confers certain privileges: the
dominant are first to feed and have the right to couple
with females in the group. The weakest animal, however,
can generally avoid combat by adopting a submissive
position (crouching, presenting the rump). Bruno, however, found himself in a less auspicious position. While
dominance and brutality are commonplace in the animal
kingdom, among higher primates, notably the chimpan-
zee (*Pan troglodytes*), weaker animals suffer acts of
gratuitous cruelty. This tendency is at its greatest in
primitive human societies and among children and
adolescents in developed societies. *Compassion*, the
capacity to identify with the suffering of others, develops
later; this *compassion* is quickly systematised into a *moral
order*. At the boarding school in Meaux, Jean Cohen
personified that moral order and he did not intend to
deviate from it. He did not believe that the Nazis had
perverted Nietzsche's philosophy. In Cohen's opinion,

the ideas manifest in Nietzsche's philosophy – the rejection of compassion, the elevation of individuals above the moral order, and the triumph of the will – led directly to Nazism. Given his qualifications and his time at the school, Cohen could have been headmaster; he remained a housemaster by choice. He wrote repeatedly to the Ministry of Education to complain about the decline of the position of housemaster in boarding schools. He received no reply.

In captivity, a male kangaroo – *Macropodides* – will often interpret the zookeeper's standing position as a threat. If the keeper hunches his shoulders, adopting the non-threatening posture of a peaceful kangaroo, the animal's aggressive impulse is defused. Jean Cohen did not intend to allow himself to become a peaceful kangaroo. The savagery of Michel Brasseur, a normal stage in the development of the ego even in lesser animals, had crippled one of his classmates; boys like Bruno would probably be psychologically scarred for life. When he summoned Brasseur to his office, he fully intended to make his contempt obvious, to let Brasseur know that he would have the boy expelled.

On Sunday evenings, when his father drove him back in the Mercedes, Bruno would start to tremble as they reached the outskirts of Nanteuil-les-Meaux. The school hall was decorated with bas-reliefs of illustrious former pupils: Courteline and Moissan. Georges Courteline was a French writer whose stories parodied the absurdities of the bourgeoisie. Henri Moissan, a chemist who was awarded the Nobel prize in 1906, had isolated silicon and fluorine, and had pioneered the use of the electric oven. Bruno's father always arrived just in time for dinner at seven o'clock. Bruno usually only managed to eat at lunchtime, when they ate with the day-pupils; at dinner, only the boarders were present. They sat in groups of eight, with a senior at the head of each table. The seniors served themselves and then spat into the bowl so that the younger boys would not touch it.

Every Sunday, Bruno tried to talk to his father, and each time he decided that it was hopeless. His father believed it was good for a boy to learn to defend himself; and it was true that other boys – some no older than Bruno – fought back. They kicked and punched until, eventually, they earned the respect of their elders.

At 42, Serge Clément was a success. While his parents ran a small grocer's shop in Petit-Clamart, Serge already owned three clinics specialising in plastic surgery – one in Neuilly, another in Vésinet and a third near Lausanne in Switzerland. When his ex-wife had left him to live in California, he had taken over the management of the clinic in Cannes, sending his wife half of the profits. He had not done any surgical work for some time but he was, as they say, 'a good manager'. He did not really know how to behave with his son. He wanted to do his best for the boy, as long as it did not take up too much of his time; and he felt a certain guilt. He would usually arrange not to see his girlfriends when Bruno came for the weekend.

He bought prepared meals from the delicatessen and they ate together, then watched television. Serge did not know how to play games. Sometimes, Bruno would get up in the middle of the night and go to the fridge. He would pour cornflakes into a bowl, add milk and cream and a thick layer of sugar. Then, he would eat. He would eat bowl after bowl of cornflakes until he felt sick. His stomach felt heavy. He felt almost happy.

9

From a moral standpoint, 1970 was marked by a substantial increase in the consumption of the erotic, despite the intervention of vigilant censors. The musical *Hair,* which was to bring the 'sexual liberation' of the 1960s to the general public, was a huge success. Bare breasts spread quickly across the beaches of the Riviera. In a few short months, the number of sex shops in Paris leapt from three to 45.

In September, Michel started the *quatrième* and took German as his second language. It was in German class that he met Annabelle.

At the time, Michel had only the most modest idea of what happiness might be. In fact, he had never thought about it. His views were his grandmother's, who had instilled them in her children. His grandmother was Catholic and voted for de Gaulle; both her daughters had married communists, but this had not changed her view of the world. She was of the generation who, as children, had suffered the hardships of war and who, at 20, celebrated the Liberation. These are the ideas they wished to bequeath to their children: a woman stays at home and does the housework (her work is made easier by a variety of electrical appliances; she has plenty of time to spend with her children). A man goes out to work but, thanks to automation, he works shorter hours, and his work is less arduous. They are happy and faithful; they live in a nice house outside the city in suburbia. In their spare time, they may enjoy gardening and crafts and appreciate the arts, or they may prefer to travel and discover other countries, other cultures, other lifestyles.

Jacob Wilkening was born in Leeuwarden, in the Netherlands. He arrived in France at the age of four, and had only a vague recollection of his Dutch childhood. In 1946 he married the sister of one of his best friends. She was 17 years old, and he was her first boyfriend. He worked for a time in a factory making microscopes before setting up his own business crafting precision lenses, principally for Angénieux and Pathé. The business flourished. There was no competition from Japan at the time, and France produced lenses that were the equal of Schneider and Zeiss. The couple had two sons, born in 1948 and 1951, and, much later, in 1958, a daughter, Annabelle.

Born into a happy family (in the 25 years they had been married, her parents had never had a serious argument),

Annabelle knew that she was destined to be happy too.
She had begun to think about such things the summer
before she met Michel, when she was going on 13.
Somewhere in the world there was a boy she had never
met, a boy who knew nothing about her, but with whom
she would spend the rest of her life. She would try to
make him happy, and he would make her happy too. But
she was disturbed that she did not have the slightest idea
of what he would look like. A girl her age had expressed
the same concern in a letter to the Disney comic *Le Journal
de Mickey*. The agony aunt tried to reassure her, and her
answer ended with these words: 'Don't worry, Coralie;
when you see him, you'll know.'

They began to spend time together doing their German
homework. Michel lived just across the street, barely 50
yards away. They spent Thursdays and Sundays together
more and more often. Michel would arrive at Annabelle's
house just after lunch; her little brother would look out of
the window and announce 'Annabelle, it's your fiancé . . .'
She would blush; but her parents did not make fun of her.
She realised that she really liked Michel.

He was an odd boy; he knew nothing about football or
pop music. He was not unpopular at school, but although
he talked to lots of people, he kept his distance. He had
never invited anyone to his house before Annabelle. He
was a solitary child, used to his own thoughts and dreams.
Little by little, he grew accustomed to her presence. They
would often set out on their bicycles up the hill at

Voulangis, then walk through the woods and fields until they came to the cliff that towered above the valley of the Grand Morin. They walked back through the meadows, slowly getting to know one another.

10

Caroline Yessayan is to blame for everything

That same year, things improved a little for Bruno when he went back to school. Now in the *quatrième*, he was one of the big boys. From the *quatrième* to the *sixième*, the boys slept in a different wing in dormitories divided into four-bed cubicles. To the bullies, he was dead meat, he had already been destroyed, humiliated; they moved on to find new victims. This was also the year that Bruno discovered girls. Sometimes — not often — there was a joint outing for the local boarding schools. On Thursday afternoons, if the weather was good, they would go to a sort of man-made beach on the banks of the Marne on the outskirts of Meaux. There was a café nearby with pinball machines and table football, though its real attraction was a python. The boys liked to torment the animal, tapping their fingers on the sides of the vivarium. The vibrations drove the snake wild and it would throw itself against the glass until it knocked itself unconscious.

One afternoon in October Bruno found himself talking to Patricia Hohweiller. She was an orphan and had to stay in school all year round, except for the holidays, when she went to stay with her uncle in Alsace. She was blonde and thin and talked nineteen to the dozen, her animated face occasionally slipping into an odd smile. He was shocked to see her the following week sitting, legs spread, on Brasseur's knee. His arm was round her waist and he was snogging her. Bruno drew no particular conclusions from this. If the thugs who had terrorised him for years were popular with the girls, it was because they were the only ones who dared to try it on. He had noticed that Pelé, Wilmart, and even Brasseur himself never bullied the younger boys if there were girls around.

Pupils in the *quatrième* were allowed to join the cinema club, which held screenings every Thursday evening in the boys' assembly hall, though girls were allowed to attend. One night in December, just before *Nosferatu the Vampire* started, Bruno took the seat next to Caroline Yessayan. Towards the end of the film – having thought about it for more than an hour – he gently placed his hand on her thigh. For a few wonderful seconds (five? seven? surely no more than ten?), nothing happened. She didn't move. Bruno felt a warm glow flood his body, he thought he might faint. Then, without saying a word, she gently brushed his hand away. Years later, when some bitch or other was sucking him off, Bruno would remember those few seconds of terrifying joy; he would also remember the moment when Caroline Yessayan moved his hand away. What the boy had felt was something pure, something gentle, something that predated sex or a need for sensual fulfilment. It was the simple desire to reach out and touch someone, to be held lovingly in someone's arms. Tenderness is a deeper instinct than seduction which is why it is so difficult to give up hope.

If Bruno had touched Caroline Yessayan's arm that evening, she would almost certainly have let him, and it would probably have been the beginning of something. While they were waiting in the queue, she had deliberately struck up a conversation and had kept a seat free to give him an opportunity to sit with her. During the film, she had put her arm on the armrest between them. She had noticed Bruno before and she fancied him; that evening, she was hoping against hope that he would hold her hand. Why did Bruno touch her thigh? Probably because Caroline Yessayan's thigh was bare, and in his innocence, he could not imagine it was bare for no reason. As he grew older, and remembered his boyhood with disgust, he came to see this as the defining moment of his life. On that December evening in 1970, Caroline Yessayan had it in her power to undo all the humiliation and the sadness of his childhood. After this first failure (for after she gently removed his hand, he never spoke to her again), everything became much more difficult. Of course, it was not Caroline Yessayan's fault. Rather the reverse; Caroline Yessayan – a little Armenian girl with doe eyes and long, curly black hair who had found herself, after endless family wranglings, among the dark and gloomy buildings of the boarding school in Meaux – Caroline Yessayan alone gave Bruno reason to believe in humanity. If it had all ended in a terrible emptiness, it was because of something so trivial that it was grotesque. Thirty years later, Bruno was convinced that, taken in context, the episode could be summed up in one sentence: Caroline Yessayan's mini-skirt was to blame for everything.

In putting his hand on Caroline Yessayan's thigh, Bruno might as well have been asking her to marry him. The beginning of his adolescence coincided with a period of social change. Aside from a handful of *precursors* – of whom his parents, of course, were a depressing example – the previous generation had made a fierce and unwavering connection between marriage, love and sex. The rise of the bourgeoisie and the rapid economic changes of the 1950s had led to a decline in *arranged marriages* – except in the rapidly dwindling aristocracy where lineage was still of real significance. The Catholic Church, which had always frowned upon sex outside marriage, welcomed this shift towards the *love-match*. It was closer to Catholic doctrine ('Male and female created He them'), and brought its objective of a world of peace, fidelity and love a step closer. The Communist party, which was the only threat to the spiritual power of the church at the time, opposed the shift for almost identical reasons. Consequently, young people in the 1950s, without exception, waited impatiently to *fall in love*. As increasing urbanisation drained the countryside and village communities vanished, the possible candidates for a future spouse became almost infinite, just as the choice itself became of the utmost importance. (At Sarcelles, in September 1955, a new political movement dedicated to the preservation of the 'extended family' was launched; proof in itself that society had now been reduced to the nuclear family.) It would be fair to say that the late 1950s and early 1960s were *the golden age of romantic love* – a time we remember today through the songs of Jean Ferrat and early Françoise Hardy.

But it was at precisely this time that Europe was flooded with prurient mass-market entertainment from America (the songs of Elvis Presley, the films of Marilyn Monroe). With the refrigerators and washing machines designed to make for a happy couple came the transistor radio and the record player, which would teach the adolescent how to *flirt*. The distinction between true love and flirtation, little remarked in the Sixties, was to dominate magazines like *Mademoiselle Âge Tendre* and *Vingt Ans* in the early Seventies. It can be summed up by the question: 'How far can you go before you get married?' The sexual, self-indulgent American option received great support from the liberal press (the first issue of *Actuel* appeared in October 1970, and *Charlie-Hebdo* in November). Although their politics were notionally left-wing, these magazines embraced the ideals of the entertainment industry: individual freedom, the supremacy of youth over age and the destruction of Judaeo-Christian values.

Torn between these conflicting pressures, teen magazines hastily cobbled together a compromise for the modern girl.

In the first stage (say, from 12 to 18), a girl would *go out with* several boys (the ambivalence of the term *go out with* reflected a very real ambiguity: what did *going out with* a boy mean? Did it mean kissing, or did it include the joys of *petting* or of *heavy petting*, or even full sexual inter-course? Should you allow a boy to touch your breasts? Should you take off your knickers? And what should you do with his *thing*?) For Patricia Hohweiller and Caroline Yessayan the problem was far from simple; their favourite magazines gave vague, often contradictory answers. In the second stage (when she had left school), the same girl could then embark on a *serious relationship* (referred to in German magazines as 'big love'). Now, the defining question was: 'Should I move in with Jeremy?' This was intended to be the final stage. The flaw in the solution offered by girls' magazines – arbitrarily recommending contradictory forms of behaviour in consecutive periods of a girl's life – only became apparent some years later with the inexorable rise in the divorce rate. Nevertheless, for many years, naïve girls, already disoriented by the speed of social change, accepted these improbable rules and tried their best to stick to them.

Things were very different for Annabelle. Last thing at night, before she went to sleep, she thought about Michel and every morning she was overjoyed to see him again. If something funny or interesting happened at school, her first thought was of the moment when she could tell Michel about it. On days when they could not see each other for some reason, she was worried and upset. During the summer holidays (her family had a house in the Gironde), she wrote to him every day. The letters were more sisterly than passionate, and her feelings more a glow than a consuming fire, but even if she were reluctant to admit it to herself, the truth slowly dawned on her: without looking, without even trying, she had found *true love*. Her first love was the real thing, she could not even imagine there could be another. It was a plausible scenario, according to *Mademoiselle Âge Tendre,* but it was best to be cautious as it almost never happened. There was irrefutable evidence, however, of rare, almost miraculous cases. It was possible, and if it happened to you it was the most wonderful thing in the whole world.

11

Michel still had a photograph taken in the garden of Annabelle's house during the Easter holidays in 1971. Her father had hidden Easter eggs in the bushes and the flowerbeds. In the photo, Annabelle was standing in the middle of a bed of forsythias, parting the tall stems, intent on her search with all the gravity of childhood. She had just begun to mature, her face was delicate and it was obvious even then that she would be exceptionally beautiful. The gentle swell of her pullover hinted at her breasts. This would be the last time there was an egg-hunt at Easter; the following year they would be too old to play games.

At about the age of 13, progesterone and oestradiol secreted by the ovaries in a girl's body produce pads of fatty tissue around the breasts and buttocks. When perfectly formed, these organs have a round, full, pleasing aspect and produce violent arousal in the male. Like her mother at that age, Annabelle had a beautiful body. Her mother's face was charming but plain, nothing could have prepared her for the painful shock of Annabelle's beauty; she was quite frightened by it. Annabelle owed her big blue eyes and the dazzling shock of blonde hair to her father's side of the family, but only the most extraordinary fluke of morphogenetics could account for the devastating purity of her face.

A girl who is plain is unhappy because she has missed her chance to be loved. People do not jeer at her, they are not cruel to her, but it is as if she were invisible – no eyes follow her as she walks. People feel uncomfortable when they are with her. They find it easier to ignore her. A girl who is exceptionally beautiful, on the other hand, who has something which surpasses the customary seductive freshness of adolescence, appears somehow unreal. Great beauty seems to portend some tragic fate.

At 15, Annabelle was one of those rare beauties who can make every man's head turn – regardless of age or physical fitness. She was one of the few who could send pulses racing in young and old and cause old men to groan with regret simply by walking down the street. She quickly noticed the silence that followed her appearance in a café or a classroom, but it would be years before she completely understood it. At the CEG in Crécy-en-Brie, it was common knowledge that she and Michel were 'together', but even if they had not been, no boy would have dared to try it on with her. The terrible predicament of a beautiful girl is that only an experienced womaniser, someone cynical and without scruple, feels that he is up to the challenge. More often than not, she will lose her virginity to some filthy lowlife in what can prove to be the first step in an irrevocable decline.

In September 1972 Michel moved to the college in Meaux, leaving Annabelle, who was in the *troisième*, in Crécy for another year. Every evening, Michel took the train home, changed at Esbly and usually arrived in Crécy on the 6.33 p.m. train where Annabelle would be waiting at the station. They would walk through the small town and along the banks of the canals. Sometimes – though not often – they would go to the café. Annabelle believed that one day Michel would want to take her in his arms and kiss her, caress her body which she could feel changing. She waited impatiently for that day, but she was not unduly worried; she knew it would happen.

Many fundamental aspects of human behaviour are innate, but experiences during the formative years of life play an important role in birds and mammals. Early physical contact with members of the same species seems to play a vital role in the development of dogs, cats, rats, guinea pigs and rhesus monkeys *(Macaca mulatta)*. Male rats deprived of maternal contact during infancy exhibit serious disturbances in sexual behaviour, especially in mating rituals. If his life had depended on it (and, in a very real sense, it did) Michel could not have kissed Annabelle. Often when he arrived at Crécy station Annabelle was so overjoyed to see him that she threw her arms around him. For a moment, they would stay in a state of happy paralysis; only afterwards would they begin to talk.

Bruno was also in the *seconde* at Meaux, though not in Michel's class. He knew that his mother had had a son by a different father, but no more than that. He saw little of his mother. Twice, he had spent his holidays in the villa in Cassis where she now lived. She regularly entertained hitchhikers and sundry young men passing through. The popular press would have characterised these young men as *hippies*. It was true that they were unemployed and Janine – who had by now changed her name to Jane – provided for them while they stayed. They lived off the profits of the plastic surgery clinic her ex-husband had set up – in other words, off the desire of well-to-do women to fight the ravages of time, or correct certain natural imperfections. They would swim naked in the creeks. Bruno always refused to take off his trunks. He felt small, pale, fat and repulsive. Sometimes his mother would take one of the boys to her bed. She was 45 years old now and her vulva was scrawny and sagged slightly, but she was still a very beautiful woman. Bruno jerked off at least three times a day. Here, he was surrounded by the vulvas of young women, sometimes less than three feet away, but Bruno realised that they were closed to him: other boys were bigger, stronger, more tanned. Much later, Bruno would come to realise that the petit-bourgeois world of accountants and middle managers was more accepting, more tolerant than the alternative scene – represented by hippies at that time. 'If I dress up as a middle manager, they'll accept me as one,' Bruno liked to say. 'All I need is a suit, a shirt and tie – eight hundred francs top whack at C&A in the sale. In fact, all I really have to do is learn to tie a Windsor knot. Not having a car is a bit of a problem – the only real problem middle managers face in life. But it can be done – take out a loan, work for a couple of years to pay it off and there you go. But there's no point in trying to pass myself off as a dropout: I'm not young enough or good-looking enough and I'm certainly not cool enough. My hair's falling out, I'm getting fat. Worse than that, the older I get, the more terrified I am of rejection. I'm just not *natural* enough, not enough of an *animal*. It's a serious handicap because no matter what I say or do, no matter what I buy, I can never overcome it, because it's a natural handicap.' From the first time he went to stay with his mother, Bruno knew he would never be accepted by the hippies: he was not and never would be a noble savage. At night, he dreamed of gaping vaginas. It was about then that he began reading Kafka. The first time, he felt a cold shudder, a treacherous feeling, as though his body were turning to ice; some hours after reading *The Trial*, he still felt numb and unsteady. He knew at once that this slow-motion world, riddled with shame, where people passed each other in an unearthly void in which no human contact seemed possible, precisely mirrored his mental world. The universe was cold and sluggish. There was, however, one source of warmth – between a woman's thighs; but there seemed no way for him to reach it.

★

It was becoming increasingly clear that something was wrong with Bruno. He had no friends, he was terrified of girls; his entire adolescence was a disaster. His father realised this with a nagging sense of guilt. He insisted that his ex-wife join them for Christmas 1972 so that they could discuss the problem. As they talked, it became clear that Bruno's half-brother was at the same school (though in a different class) and that the boys had never met. This single fact hit Bruno's father hard, for it epitomised the utter breakdown of their family, a breakdown for which they were both to blame. Asserting his authority for the first time, he insisted that Janine contact her other son and try to salvage what she could.

Janine had no illusions as to Michel's grandmother's opinion of her, but it was to prove even worse than she had expected. Just as she was parking the Porsche outside the house in Crécy-en-Brie, the old woman came out, carrying a shopping bag. 'I can't stop you from seeing him,' she said angrily, 'he's your son. Now, I'm off to do some shopping. I'll only be a couple of hours, and I don't want to find you here when I get back.' Then she turned on her heel.

Michel was in his room. Janine pushed open the door and went in. She had intended to kiss him, but when she moved towards him he stepped back quickly. He had grown to look strikingly like his father: the same fine blond hair, the same high cheekbones. She had brought him a present: a record player and some Rolling Stones albums. He took them without a word. He kept the record player, but smashed the records some days later. His room was sober, without a single poster on the wall. A maths book lay open on his desk. 'What are you working on?' she asked. 'Differential equations,' he answered diffidently. She had wanted to talk to him about his life, invite him on holiday; obviously that was out of the question. She simply told him that his brother would be coming to visit him and he nodded. She had been there almost an hour, and the silences were becoming more drawn out, when they heard Annabelle's voice from the garden. Michel ran to the window and shouted for her to come in. Janine watched the girl as she opened the gate. 'She's pretty, your girlfriend . . .' she said, her mouth twisting slightly. The word lashed Michel like a whip, his whole expression changed. Annabelle passed as Janine was climbing into the Porsche – the woman stared at her, her eyes filled with loathing.

Michel's grandmother felt no antipathy towards Bruno. In her blunt but essentially accurate opinion, he was another victim of Janine's parenting skills. Every Thursday afternoon Bruno would go to see Michel, taking the train from Crécy-la-Chapelle. If it was possible – and it almost always was – he would find a girl on her own and sit near her. Most of them wore see-through blouses or something similar and crossed their legs. He would not sit directly opposite, but at an angle, sometimes sharing the same seat a couple of feet away. He would get a hard-on the moment he saw the sweep of long blonde or dark hair. By the time he sat down, the throb in his underpants would be unbearable. He would take a handkerchief out of his pocket as he sat down and open a folder across his lap. In one or two tugs it was over. Sometimes, if the girl uncrossed her legs just as he was taking his cock out, he didn't even need to touch himself; he came the moment he saw her knickers. The handkerchief was a back-up; he did not really need it. Usually, he ejaculated across the folder, over pages of second degree equations, diagrams of insects or a graph of coal production in the USSR. The girl would carry on reading her magazine.

Years later, Bruno could never see himself in the boy. He knew that these things had happened and that they were directly connected to the fat, timid boy in the photographs of his childhood. The little boy was clearly related to the sexually obsessed adult he had become. His childhood had been difficult and his adolescence ghastly. He was 42 now; objectively, death was still a long way off. What was left? Oh, there would be other blow-jobs and he would come to accept having to pay for them. A life lived in pursuit of a goal leaves little time for reminiscence. As his erections became shorter and more infrequent, Bruno felt himself succumb to a sad decline. His only goal in life had been sexual, and he realised that it was too late to change that now. In that, Bruno was characteristic of his generation. While he was a teenager, the fierce economic pressures which France had suffered for two hundred years had abated. The prevailing opinion was that economic conditions tended towards a certain equality. The Swedish model of democratic socialism was referred to by politicians and businessmen alike. In such a society, Bruno was not motivated to distinguish himself through financial success. His sole professional objective was – quite reasonably – to fade into the 'vast, amorphous mass of the middle classes' as President Giscard d'Éstaing would later refer to it. But human beings are quick to establish hierarchies and keen to feel superior to their peers. Denmark and Sweden, which then provided the socioeconomic models for European democracies, also obliged with a model of sexual liberation. Unexpectedly, this great middle class of labourers and office workers – or, rather, their sons and daughters – were to discover a new sport in which to compete. At a language course which Bruno attended in 1972 in Traunstein, a small Bavarian village near the Austrian border, Patrick Castelli, a young French boy in his class, succeeded in fucking 37 girls in the space of three weeks. Over the same period, Bruno managed to score zero. In the end he flashed his prick at a shop assistant in a supermarket – luckily, the girl laughed it off and did not press charges. Like Bruno, Patrick Castelli was a good student from a respectable family; their career prospects were almost identical. Bruno's memories of his adolescence were all of this kind.

Later, the rise of the global economy would create much fiercer competition, which swept away all the dreams of integrating the populace into a vast middle class with ever-rising incomes. Whole social classes fell through the net and joined the ranks of the unemployed. But the savage sexual competition did not abate as a result, quite the reverse.

Bruno had known Michel for 25 years now. Over the course of this terrifyingly long period, he felt he had hardly changed at all: he firmly believed in the concept of a kernel of personal identity, some immutable core which defined him. It was true, however, that vast tracts of his intimate history had sunk without trace from his memory. There were months, years in fact which seemed as though he had never lived them. This was not true of his adolescence, which was a rich seam of memories and formative experiences. The human memory, his brother explained to him much later, resembles Griffiths' consistent histories. It was in May and they were drinking Campari in Michel's apartment. They usually talked about social and political issues, and rarely discussed the past; that evening was an exception. 'Each person has a set of memories of different points in their lives,' concluded Michel. 'The memories come in different forms; thoughts, ideas, faces. Sometimes you only remember a name – like that girl Patricia Hohweiller you were talking about earlier, you probably wouldn't be able to recognise her today. Sometimes, you remember a face without knowing why. Everything you remember about Caroline Yessayan is compacted into the precise seconds when your hand was resting on her thigh.

'Griffiths' consistent history approach was introduced in 1984 to create coherent narratives from quantum information. A Griffiths' history is constructed from a succession of more or less random quantum measurements taken at different moments. Each measurement defines a specific physical mass at a precise moment with reference to a specific set of values. As an example, in a time t_1 an electron moves at a certain speed approximately determined depending on the method of measurement. At a time t_2 it is situated at a certain point in space. At a time t_3, it has a certain spin value. From this collection of measurements it is possible to construct a *history* which is logically consistent. It cannot be said to be *true*; simply that it can be sustained without contradiction. Under a given set of experimental conditions, a finite number of all possible histories can be recreated using Griffiths' method; these are called Griffiths' Consistent Histories. In these, the world behaves as though composed of separate objects each having fixed, intrinsic properties. However, the number of consistent histories that can be created from a single set of data is generally greater than one. As a being you are self-aware, and this consciousness allows you to hypothesise that the story you've created from a given set of memories is a *consistent history*, justified by a consistent narrative voice. As a unique individual having existed for a particular period and been subjected to an ontology of objects and properties, you can assert this with absolute certainty, and so automatically assume that it is a Griffiths' history. You make this hypothesis about real life, rather than the memories of dreams.'

'I'd like to believe that the self is an illusion,' said Bruno quietly, 'but if it is, it's a pretty painful one.' Michel, who knew nothing about Buddhism, couldn't answer. It was not an easy conversation; they saw each other twice a year at most. In September 1973 they had both started in the *seconde*, and for two years they took the same maths and physics classes. Human reality, Michel was beginning to realise, was a series of disappointments, bitterness and pain. He found in mathematics a happiness both serene and intense. Moving through the half-light, he would suddenly find a way through – with an obscure formula, a factorisation – and be transported to a plane of luminous serenity. The first equation in any proof was the most poignant, because the truth fluttering in the distance was still precarious; the last was the most thrilling, the most joyful.

That same year Annabelle graduated to *seconde* in the Lycée de Meaux. The three spent their afternoons together after class, before Bruno headed back to the school, Michel and Annabelle to the train station. Then, events took a sad, strange turn. At the beginning of 1974 Michel wandered into Hilbert spaces; launched himself into the theory of measurements, discovered the integrals of Riemann, Lebesque and Stieltjes. At the same time Bruno was reading Kafka and masturbating on the commuter train. One afternoon in May he had the pleasure of letting his towel fall open and flashing his cock at a couple of 12-year-old girls at the new swimming pool at La Chapelle-sur-Crécy. The pleasure was heightened as he watched them elbow each other, clearly interested in the show. He caught the eye of one of them – a short brunette with glasses – and held it for a long time. Though he was too miserable and frustrated to be especially interested in the psychology of others, Bruno realised nonetheless that his half-brother's situation was worse than his own. They often went to the café together; Michel would wear anoraks and caps that made him look ridiculous, he was hopeless at table football and Bruno did all the talking. Michel barely moved, barely said a word; he simply stared at Annabelle, his gaze attentive but lifeless. Annabelle did not give up; for her, Michel's face was like a commentary from another world. At about that time she read *The Kreutzer Sonata* and, for a moment, she thought that she understood him. Twenty-five years later it was clear to Bruno that everything about their relationship had been lopsided, out-of-kilter, abnormal – there had never been a future in it. But the past always seems, perhaps wrongly, to be predestined.

12

A Balanced Diet

*In revolutionary times, those who accord themselves, with an
extraordinary arrogance, the facile credit for having enflamed
anarchy in their contemporaries fail to recognise that what
appears to be a sad triumph is in fact due to a spontaneous
disposition, determined by the social situation as a whole.*

(Auguste Comte – *Philosophie Positive,* Leçon 48)

France in the 1970s was marked by the controversy surrounding *Phantom of the Paradise, A Clockwork Orange* and
Les Valseuses – three very different films whose success
firmly established the commercial muscle of a 'youth
culture' based principally on sex and violence, which
would redefine the market in the decades that followed.
Those who had made their fortunes in the 1960s, now in
their thirties, found their lives mirrored in *Emmanuelle,*
released in 1974. In the context of a Judaeo-Christian
culture, Just Jaecklin's film, with its mixture of fantasy and

exotic locations, appeared as a manifesto for the leisure society.

A number of other important events in 1974 further advanced the cause of moral relativism. The first Vitatop club opened in Paris on 20 March; it was to play a pioneering role in the cult of the body beautiful. The age of majority was lowered to 18 on 5 July, and divorce by mutual consent was officially recognised on the eleventh, thus removing adultery from the penal code. Lastly, on 28 November, after a stormy debate described by commentators as 'historic', the Veil act legalising abortion was adopted, largely thanks to lobbying by the left. Christian doctrine, which had long been the dominant moral force in Western civilisation, accorded unconditional importance to every human life from conception to death. The significance was linked to the belief in the existence within the body of a *soul* – which was by definition immortal and would ultimately return to God. In the 19th and 20th centuries, advances in biology gave rise to a more determinist anthropology, radically different in its assumptions and significantly more moderate in its ethical counsel. On one hand, this change meant that the foetus, a small collection of steadily subdividing cells, was no longer recognised as a viable individual except by consensus (absence of genetic defects, parental consent). On the other hand, the new concept of *human dignity* meant that the elderly, a collection of steadily failing organs, had the right to life only as long as they continued to function. The ethical problems posed by the extremes of youth and age (abortion, and some decades later, euthanasia) would become the battleground for different and radically antagonistic worldviews.

The agnosticism at the heart of the French republic would facilitate the progressive, hypocritical and slightly sinister triumph of the determinist worldview. Though never overtly discussed, the question of the *value* of human life would nonetheless continue to preoccupy the liberal conscience. It would be true to say that in the last years of Western civilisation it contributed to a general mood of depression bordering on masochism.

In the summer of 1974 Bruno turned 18. It was a significant, possibly crucial, period in his life. Years later, it would recur in sessions with his psychiatrist. Sometimes Bruno altered or refined the details, but this is his standard version:

'It was the end of July. I was staying on the coast with my mother for a week. The house was full of people coming and going. My mother was sleeping with some Canadian guy at the time – young, built like a brick shit-house. The day I was supposed to leave, I got up early. It was already pretty hot. I went into her room. They were still asleep. I hesitated for a second or two and then I pulled the sheet off them. My mother moved and for a minute I thought she was going to open her eyes; her thighs parted slightly. I knelt down in front of her vagina. I brought my hand up close – a couple of inches away – but I didn't dare touch her. Then I went outside and jerked off. There'd always been cats round the house, mostly strays. A black cat lay sunning itself on a rock. The land around the house was stony, white and forbidding. The cat looked over at me from time to time while I was wanking, but closed its eyes just before I came.

'I bent down and picked up a rock. The cat's skull shattered and some of its brains spurted out. I covered the body with a pile of stones and went back inside. There was still nobody awake. Later that morning, driving me back to my father's house about fifty kilometres away, my mother talked to me about di Meola for the first time. Apparently, he'd left California four years earlier and had bought a big place on the hills of Ventoux near Avignon. In the summer he took in young people from all over Europe and America. She thought maybe I could go there one summer; she said it would broaden my horizons. According to her, di Meola's commune wasn't a cult, it simply passed on the teachings of the Brahman. Di Meola knew a lot about cybernetics and PNL and used deprogramming techniques he'd developed at Esalen. It was all about liberating the individual's innate potential – "Because we only use ten per cent of our brain, you know." '

'Anyway,' said Jane as they drove through the pine forests, 'there'd be kids your own age there. It would be good for you. We all thought you were pretty hung-up about sex while you were here this summer.'

The Western concept of sexuality was perverse and unnatural, she went on. In primitive societies, sexual initiation was a natural thing that took place early in adolescence under the supervision of the tribal elders. 'I am your mother,' she stressed. She did not mention that she had initiated di Meola's son David in 1963. David had been 13 at the time. The first time, she had undressed in front of him and encouraged him to masturbate. The second afternoon, she had masturbated him and sucked him off. On the third and final afternoon, he had been able to penetrate her. Jane had pleasant memories of it; the young boy's rock-hard cock never seemed to go down, even after he had come several times. It was probably this experience which converted her to young men. 'Of course,' she went on, 'the initiation should always take place outside of the immediate family itself – that's very important. It opens the world up to the adolescent.'

Bruno jumped, afraid that his mother had been awake that morning as he was staring at her vagina. In fact, his mother's remark was banal: the incest taboo is well documented in the animal kingdom, especially among mandrills and grey geese. The car sped towards Saint-Maxime.

'When I got to my father's house I realised that he wasn't well,' Bruno would go on. 'He had only taken a couple of weeks off that summer. I didn't know it at the time, but the business was doing badly and he had money problems. He told me later that it was because he had completely missed out on the market for silicone breast implants. He thought it was a passing fad that would never catch on outside the US. Which was utterly stupid. Nothing has ever caught on in America that didn't engulf Western Europe a couple of years later, nothing. One of his junior associates had left the clinic and set up on his own. He'd poached a lot of my father's clients simply by offering silicone implants as his USP.'

Bruno's father was 70 when he made this confession. He would die shortly afterwards of cirrhosis of the liver. 'History repeats itself,' he told Bruno, tinkling the ice in his glass. 'That idiot Poncet . . . (he was talking about the dynamic young surgeon who 20 years earlier had been his ruin). That idiot Poncet has just refused to diversify into penis enlargement – thinks it's too much like butchery. He doesn't think the men's market will catch on in Europe. Moron. Almost as much of a moron as I was twenty years ago. If I was thirty years old now, I'd set myself up in prick enlargement.' Having said this, he usually slipped back into a daydream at the edge of consciousness. Conversation tended to tread water at his age.

In July 1974 Bruno's father was only at the beginning of a long, slow decline. He would spend the afternoons locked in his room with a pile of cigars and a bottle of bourbon. He would come downstairs at seven and heat up something, his hands shaking. It was not that he did not want to speak to his son, he could not; he really could not bring himself to do it. After two days, the atmosphere had become oppressive. Bruno started to go out; he would spend whole afternoons at the beach.

★

The psychiatrist was less interested in the part of the story that followed, but Bruno thought it was important and had no intention of passing over it. After all, he was paying the bastard to listen to him, wasn't he?

'She was alone,' Bruno went on. 'She went to the beach every afternoon on her own. She was seventeen, a poor little rich girl – a bit like me. She was a chubby little thing, she was shy and very pale and had spots. The fourth afternoon – it was the day before I left, in fact – I put down my towel and sat beside her. She was lying on her stomach and she'd unfastened her bikini top. I remember the only thing I could think to say was "You on holiday?" She looked up. I'm sure she wasn't expecting brilliant conversation, but maybe not something quite so moronic. Anyway, we introduced ourselves: her name was Annick. I knew she would have to sit up sooner or later and I wondered would she try to fasten her bikini top behind her? Would she sit up and show me her breasts? She did something midway between the two; she turned over, holding the ends of her top together. When she'd finished, the bra was a bit lopsided and only half covered her breasts. She had big tits, which were already sagging a bit and must have got a lot worse later. I thought she was very brave. I reached over and slipped my hand under her bra, feeling her breast as I did. She didn't move, but she stiffened a little and closed her eyes. I went on stroking her tits; her nipples were hard. It was one of the most beautiful moments of my life.

'Things got complicated after that. I took her back to my house and we went up to my room. I was scared my father would see her. He had been with a lot of beautiful women in his life, but he was asleep – actually, he was completely drunk, he didn't wake up until ten o'clock that night. Strangely, she wouldn't let me take off her knickers. She told me she'd never done it before, in fact she'd never really done anything with a boy before. But she was quite happy to jerk me off, she was pretty enthusiastic; I remember she was smiling. Then I moved my cock up to her mouth; she sucked it a little bit but she didn't really like it. I didn't push it. I got on top of her, and when I slipped my cock between her tits, she moaned a bit and seemed happy. I was really turned on. I pushed down her knickers – she didn't stop me this time, she even lifted herself up to help me. She wasn't particularly pretty, but her pussy was as beautiful as any pussy in the world. Her eyes were closed. When I slipped my hands under her arse, she parted her thighs completely. I was so excited that I came right there before I could even put it in her. There was spunk in her pubic hair. I was really upset, but she said that it didn't matter, that she was happy.

'We didn't really have much time to talk. It was nearly eight o'clock and she had to get back to her parents. I remember she told me she was an only child, I don't know why. She seemed so happy, so proud to have a good reason to be late for dinner that I nearly cried. We kissed for a long time in the garden in front of the house. The next day I went back to Paris.'

When he had finished his story, Bruno paused for a moment. The psychiatrist cleared his throat and said, about nothing in particular, 'Good.' Depending on how much of the hour had elapsed, he would prompt Bruno again, or would simply say 'We'll leave it there for today?', rising a little to make it a question. As he said this, his smile was polished and effortless.

13

In that same summer of 1974, at a disco in Saint-Palais, Annabelle let a boy kiss her. She had just read an article about boy-girl relationships in *Stéphanie*. The article had propounded a miserable rationalisation on the subject of childhood friendships. It was extremely rare that a childhood friend became a boyfriend, according to the magazine. His natural role was to become a friend – a *loyal friend*; he might perhaps be a confidant and offer emotional support through the trials of first *boyfriends*.

In the seconds that followed that first kiss, despite the assertions of the article, Annabelle felt horribly sad. She felt flooded by some new, painful sensation. She left the Kathmandu and refused to let the boy come with her. She was trembling slightly as she unlocked her moped. She had worn her prettiest dress that evening. Her brother's house was only half a mile away. It was barely eleven o'clock when she arrived, and there was a light on in the living room. When she saw the light, she started to cry. It was here, on a July night in 1974, that Annabelle accepted the painful but unequivocal truth that she was an *individual*. An animal's sense of self emerges through physical pain, but individuality in human society only attains true self-consciousness by the intermediary of *mendacity*, with which it is sometimes confused. At the age of 16, Annabelle had kept no secrets from her parents, nor had she – and she now realised that this was a rare and precious thing – from Michel. In a few short hours that evening, Annabelle had come to realise that life was an unrelenting succession of lies. It was then, too, that she became aware of her beauty.

Individuality, and the sense of freedom that flows from it, is the natural basis of *democracy*. In a democratic regime, relations between individuals are commonly regulated by a social contract. A pact which exceeds the natural rights of the co-contractors, or which does not correspond to a clear retraction clause, is considered de facto null and void.

If he was willing to talk in some detail about the summer of 1974, Bruno talked little about his final year at school. In truth, all that he remembered of that year was a growing sense of unease. His memories of that time were vague and a little grey. He continued to see Michel and Annabelle regularly, and to all intents and purposes they remained close, but their *baccalauréat* was fast approaching and they would inevitably go their separate ways at the end of the year. Michel had changed: he was very intense, listened to Jimi Hendrix and rolled around on the carpet. Long after his peers, he was finally beginning to show visible signs of adolescence. He and Annabelle seemed more awkward with one another and held hands less and less frequently. In short, as Bruno summed up the situation for his psychiatrist, 'everything was going to hell in a hand-basket'.

Since his encounter with Annick, which, in hindsight, he had a tendency to embroider (he had sensibly avoided telephoning her since), Bruno felt a little more confident despite the fact that he had had no encounters since. In fact, he had been brutally rejected when he had tried to kiss Sylvie, a pretty little brunette in Annabelle's class. Still, a girl had found him attractive, and if one girl could, there might be others. He began to feel protective towards Michel. After all, he was the older brother. 'You have to do something. Everyone knows Annabelle is in love with you — she's just waiting for you to make the first move. And she's the prettiest girl in the school.' Michel would fidget in his chair and say 'Yes'. Weeks passed. He was visibly faltering on the threshold of adulthood. Kissing Annabelle was the only way for both of them to avoid crossing that threshold, though he did not realise it, lulled as he was by a sense that there would always be time. In April he vexed his teachers when he failed to fill out his matriculation papers. It was clear to everyone that, more than anyone, he stood an excellent chance of being accepted into one of the Grandes Écoles. With his *baccalauréat* barely a month away, Michel seemed to be coasting. He would sit and stare through the narrow bars of the classroom window at the clouds, the trees, the other pupils; it was as though human affairs could no longer touch him.

Bruno, on the other hand, had decided to apply to study the arts: he was bored with the developments of Taylor-Maclaurin; moreover, in arts faculties there would be girls – lots of girls. His father did not object. Like all old libertines, he had become maudlin with age and felt bitterly guilty that his selfishness had ruined his son's life – which was not entirely untrue. In May he separated from his last mistress, Julie, though she was a remarkably beautiful woman. Her name was Julie Lamour, but she had taken the stage name Julie Love. She starred in the first French porn films, long forgotten films by Burd Tranbaree and Francis Leroi. She looked a little like Janine, but was considerably more stupid. 'I'm cursed . . . cursed . . .' Bruno's father murmured over and over when, happening on a photograph of his ex-wife as a young woman, he realised the resemblance. Julie had become intolerable. Since meeting Deleuze at one of Bénazéraf's dinner parties, she had taken to giving lengthy intellectual justifications of porn. In any case, she was costing him a fortune: on set, she demanded a chauffeured Rolls-Royce, a fur coat, all of the erotic trappings which, as she grew older, seemed more pathetic. Late in 1974 he had to sell the house in Sainte-Maxime. Some months later he bought an apartment for his son – a bright, peaceful studio – near the gardens at the Observatoire. Taking Bruno to view it, he did not think of it as a gift, but rather that he was trying to make amends; in any case it was obviously a bargain. But as he looked around the apartment he became excited. 'You could have girls back,' he said inadvertently; when he saw his son's face, he regretted it at once.

Michel eventually enrolled in the university at Orsay to study maths and physics: he had been attracted by the halls of residence on campus – that was how he thought. Unsurprisingly, both boys passed their *baccalauréat*. When they went to get their results, Annabelle went with them, her face solemn; she had matured a lot over the year. A little thinner, and with an inward smile, she was more beautiful than ever. Bruno decided to take an initiative: the house in Sainte-Maxime was gone, but he could go and stay at di Meola's commune, as his mother had suggested; he suggested that they come with him. A month later, towards the end of July, they set off.

14

Summer of '75

*They will not frame their doings to turn unto their God: for the
spirit of whoredoms is in the midst of them, and they have not
known the LORD*

(Hosea, Ch. 5, v. 4)

The man who met them at the bus station at Carpentras
seemed weak and ill. The son of an Italian anarchist who
emigrated to America in the 1920s, Francesco di Meola's
life was a success story – at least in a financial sense. Like
Serge Clément, the young Italian realised that the society
emerging at the end of the Second World War would be
radically different, and that many pursuits that had been
considered marginal or elitist would become economic-
ally important. While Bruno's father was investing in
plastic surgery, di Meola was becoming involved in the
music business. He did not make as much money as many
in the industry, but he made his fair share. At 40, like

many people in California, he sensed a new movement, something deeper than simply a passing fad, calling for the sweeping away of Western civilisation in its entirety. It was this insight which brought luminaries like Allan Watts, Paul Tillich, Carlos Castaneda, Abraham Maslow and Carl Rogers to his villa at Big Sur. A little later, he had the privilege of meeting Aldous Huxley, the spiritual father of the movement. By then old and almost blind, Huxley paid him scant attention but the meeting was to leave a profound impression on di Meola.

He himself was unclear as to the reason why he left California in 1970 and bought a property in Haute-Provence. Later, close to the end, he came to think that he had wanted, for some obscure reason, to *die in Europe*; but at the time, he was only aware of the most superficial reasons. The events of May '68 had impressed him and, as the hippie movement began to ebb in California, he turned his attention to the youth of Europe. Jane encouraged him in this. Young people in France were particularly repressed, a time bomb of resentment suffocating under the legacy of Gaullist patriarchy, which, according to Jane, a single spark would be enough to detonate. For some years now, Francesco's sole pleasure had been to smoke marijuana cigarettes with very young girls attracted by the spiritual aura of the movement and then fuck them amongst the mandalas and the smell of incense. The girls who arrived at Big Sur were, for the most part, stupid little WASP bitches, at least half of whom were virgins. Towards the end of the Sixties the flow began to dwindle and he thought that perhaps it was time to go back to Europe. He found it strange that he thought of it as 'going back', since he had left Italy when he was no more than five years old. If his father had been a militant revolutionary, he was also a cultivated man, an aesthete who loved his mother tongue. This had undoubtedly left its mark on Francesco. In truth, he had always thought of Americans as idiots.

He was still a handsome man, with a tanned, chiselled face and long, thick, wavy hair, but his cells had begun to reproduce in a haphazard fashion, damaging the DNA of neighbouring cells and secreting toxins into the body. The specialists he consulted differed on most points, but on one, they were agreed: he was dying. The cancer was inoperable and he would continue inexorably to develop metastases. Overall his consultants were of the opinion that he would die peacefully and, with medication, he would probably not suffer any physical pain; and to date he had suffered only from a general tiredness. However, he refused to accept the diagnosis; he could not even imagine accepting it. In contemporary Western society, death is like *white noise* to a man in good health; it fills his mind when his dreams and plans fade. With age, the noise becomes increasingly insistent, like a dull roar with the occasional clang. In another age it was the expectant sound of the kingdom of God, now it is in anticipation of death. Such is life.

Huxley, he would always remember, had seemed

detached about the prospect of his own death, though perhaps he was simply numbed or drugged. Di Meola had read Plato, the Bhagavad-Gita and the Tao Te Ching, but none of them had brought him the slightest comfort. He was barely 60, but he was dying – the signs were there, there could be no doubt about it. He had even begun to be less interested in sex, and it was with a certain detachment that he noticed how beautiful Annabelle was. He did not notice the boys at all. He had lived around young people for a long time, and it was probably habit which made him curious to meet Jane's sons though, fundamentally, he couldn't care less. He dropped them off in the middle of the estate and told them they could pitch their tent anywhere. He wanted to go to bed, preferably without meeting anyone. Physically, he was still the epitome of a sensual man, a man of the world; his eyes twinkled with irony and perception; certain exceptionally stupid girls thought of it as a radiant and benevolent look. He did not feel in the least benevolent; moreover, he thought of himself as a mediocre actor: how could they all be so easily taken in? Decidedly, he thought sometimes, a little sadly, these young people searching for spiritual values were thick.

Moments after they climbed down from the Jeep, Bruno realised that he had made a mistake. The estate sloped gently towards the south scattered with shrubs and flowers. A waterfall tumbled into a clear green pool; nearby, a woman lay, naked, sunning herself on a flat rock while another soaped herself before diving in. Closer to them, on a rug, a bearded man was meditating or sleeping; his long blond hair looked striking against his tanned skin – he looked a little like Kris Kristofferson. Bruno felt depressed. But, then, what had he expected? Perhaps he could still leave as long as he did so immediately. He glanced across at his friends: Annabelle was calmly unfolding her tent; sitting on a tree-stump Michel toyed with the fastening of his rucksack – he seemed miles away.

Water follows the path of least resistance. Human behaviour is predetermined in principle in almost all of its actions and offers few choices, of which fewer still are taken. In 1950 Francesco di Meola had a son by an Italian starlet, a second-rate actress who would never rise above playing Egyptian slaves; eventually – in the crowning achievement of her career – she had two lines in *Quo Vadis?* They called the boy David. At 15, David dreamed of being a rock star. He was not the only one. Though richer than bankers and company presidents, rock stars still managed to retain their rebel image. Young, good-looking, famous, desired by women and envied by men, rock stars had risen to the summit of the social order. Nothing since the deification of the pharaohs could compare to the devotion European and American youth bestowed on their heroes. Physically, David had everything he needed to achieve his ends: he had an animal, almost diabolical, beauty; his eyes were a deep blue, his face, masculine but refined, his long hair, thick and black.

With the help of his father's contacts, David recorded his first single at 17; it was a complete flop. It was released, it must be said, in the same year as *Sergeant Pepper* and *Days of Future Passed,* to name only two. Jimi Hendrix, the Rolling Stones and the Doors were at the height of their powers; Neil Young had just begun recording and great things were still expected of Brian Wilson. There was little room then for a bassist who was good, but not gifted. David persisted. He played in four different groups, changed musical styles and, three years after his father, he too decided to try his luck in Europe. He got a regular gig in a club on the Riviera, that was not a problem; every night girls waited for him in his dressing room, that was not a problem either. However, no one from any of the record companies so much as listened to his demos.

When David met Annabelle he had already slept with more than five hundred women; nevertheless he could not remember ever seeing such supple perfection. For her part, Annabelle found herself attracted to him as all the others had. For days she resisted, finally giving in to him a week after they arrived. There were about thirty of them dancing outside at the rear of the house, the night was warm and starry. Annabelle was wearing a white skirt and a tee shirt with a sun drawn on it. David danced beside her, sometimes twirling her, rock-and-roll fashion. They danced tirelessly for more than an hour to the beat of a tambourine − sometimes fast, sometimes slow. Bruno leaned against a tree, alert, vigilant, his heart in his mouth.

At times Michel appeared at the edge of the bright circle, at others he disappeared into the darkness. Suddenly, there he was, barely five yards away. Bruno watched Annabelle break away from the dancers and come over to him, he distinctly heard her ask 'Are you not dancing?'; her face as she said it was terribly sad. Michel declined, his gesture immeasurably slow, like some prehistoric animal recently roused. Annabelle stood looking at him for five or ten seconds longer, then turned and went back to the dancers. David put his hand on her waist and pulled her to him. She placed her hands on his shoulders. Bruno looked at Michel again and thought he saw a smile play on his lips; he looked down, and when he looked up again, Michel had disappeared. Annabelle was in David's arms, their lips close together.

Lying in his tent, Michel waited for daybreak. In the early hours a fierce storm broke and he was surprised to discover that he was a little afraid. When at last the sky cleared, a steady rain began to fall. Raindrops fell with a dull sound on the canvas; though they were inches from his face, they could not touch him here. He had a sudden premonition that all his life he would feel as he did at this moment. Emotion would pass him by, sometimes tantalisingly close; others would experience happiness and despair, but such things would be unknown to him, they would not touch him. Several times that evening Annabelle had looked over at him while she danced. Though he had wanted to, he simply could not move; he felt as though his body were slipping into icy water. Still, everything seemed strangely calm. He felt separated from the world by a vacuum moulded to his body like a shell, a protective armour.

15

The following morning Michel's tent was empty. His things were gone, but he had left a note which read, simply, 'DON'T WORRY'. Bruno left a week later. As he boarded the train, he realised that in all the time he had been there he had not tried to flirt with anyone, or even to talk to anyone.

Late in August, Annabelle noticed that her period was late. She thought it was probably best this way. There was no problem; David's father knew a doctor in Marseilles, a fervent champion of family planning. The guy's name was Laurent, he was about 30, expansive, with a little red moustache. He insisted that she call him Laurent. He showed her the instruments and explained to her the procedure of dilation and curettage. He liked to establish a rapport with his clients; he thought of them almost as friends. He had been an advocate of women's rights from the beginning, and he believed that there was still a long way to go. The operation was scheduled for the following day; the costs would be covered by the family planning clinic.

By the time she returned to her hotel, Annabelle was distraught. She would have the abortion the following day and stay overnight at the hotel before going home; that was what she had decided. Every night for three weeks she had slept in David's tent. The first time it had been painful, but afterwards she enjoyed it. She had never thought that sexual pleasure would be so overpowering. She felt no particular affection for the guy; she knew he would quickly find someone else, he was probably with someone now.

At a dinner party that same evening, Laurent talked enthusiastically about Annabelle's case. This was precisely what they had been fighting for, he remarked, to ensure that a 17-year-old girl ('and a pretty girl, too,' he almost added) did not have her life destroyed by a holiday romance.

Annabelle was apprehensive about returning to Crécy-en-Brie, but her fears were unfounded. When she got back on 4 September her parents simply complimented her on her tan. Michel had already left, they told her, he had moved into the university hall of residence in Bures-sur-Yvette; he obviously did not suspect anything. She went to visit Michel's grandmother. The old woman seemed tired, but she greeted Annabelle warmly and managed to find her grandson's address for the girl. Yes, it was a little strange that Michel had come back from holiday before the others; and she had thought it odd that he should go to university weeks before he was due to start, but then Michel had always been a strange boy.

In the midst of nature's savagery, human beings sometimes (rarely) succeed in creating small oases warmed by love. Small, exclusive, enclosed spaces governed only by love and shared subjectivity.

Annabelle spent the fortnight that followed writing to Michel. It was hard work; several times she crossed out what she had written and started again. When finished, it ran to 40 pages; it was her first *love letter*. She posted it on 17 September, the day she went back to school; then she waited.

The University of Paris IX – Orsay – is the only one in the Paris area modelled on the American campus system. For their first year, students stay in halls of residence set in parkland. Orsay University has within its campus an exceptional physics research facility dedicated to the study of elementary particles.

Michel lived at the top of Maison 233, in a corner room on the fourth floor where he felt immediately at home. There was a small bed, a desk and some shelves for his books. His window looked out onto a lawn which ran down to the river. If he leaned out and craned his neck, he could see the grey concrete expanse of the particle accelerator on the right. With a month to go before lectures began, the halls were almost empty. There were some African students, whose problem was where to stay in August, when the halls closed completely. Michel sometimes talked to the concierge and during the day he walked by the river. He already knew that he would be here for longer than eight years.

One morning, at about eleven o'clock, he lay down on the grass beneath some indeterminate trees. He was surprised by how miserable he felt. Far removed from Christian notions of grace and redemption, and hostile to the concepts of freedom and compassion, Michel's world view had grown pitiless and mechanical. Once the parameters for interaction were defined, he thought, and allowing for initial conditions, actions took place in an empty, spiritless space; each inexorably predetermined. What happened was meant to happen; it could not be otherwise; no one was to blame. At night Michel dreamed of abstract spaces, snow covered; his body bandaged from head to foot, drifting, beneath lowering skies between steel works. During the day he would sometimes run into one of the African students, a short Malian boy with drab skin, and they would nod to one another. The university restaurant was not yet open, so Michel bought tins of tuna at the supermarket in Courcelles-sur-Yvette and went back to his rooms. Night fell. He walked the empty corridors.

In mid-October Annabelle wrote to him again – a shorter letter this time. She had phoned Bruno only to discover that he had no news either; all that he could tell her was that Michel telephoned his grandmother regularly, but would probably not be home before Christmas.

One evening in November, coming out of a lecture on analysis, Michel found a note in his pigeonhole at the halls of residence. It read: 'Phone your aunt, Marie-Thérèse. URGENT.' He had not seen much of his aunt or his cousin Brigitte for two years. He phoned back immediately. His grandmother had had another stroke and had been taken to hospital in Meaux. It was serious, very serious. Her aorta was weak; her heart might fail at any time.

As he walked through Meaux, past the lycée, Annabelle was inside reading a passage by the Greek thinker Epicurus: brilliant, liberal and, to be honest, a pain in the arse. The sky was dark and the river Marne filthy and turbulent. He found the Hôpital Saint-Antoine easily, a complex of modern glass and steel buildings which had been opened the previous year. His aunt Marie-Thérèse was waiting for him, with his cousin Brigitte, in the hall on the seventh floor; they had clearly been crying. 'I don't know if you should see her . . .' said Marie-Thérèse. He ignored the suggestion. What had to be endured, he would endure.

She was in intensive care, in a room on her own. The sheet was a cruel white against her exposed shoulders and her arms; he could barely tear his eyes away from the bare flesh, wrinkled, pale and terribly old. Her arms, perforated with tubes, were bound to the rails of the bed with straps.

Her throat had been intubated and wires ran from under the sheets to monitoring devices. They had taken away her nightdress, and had not allowed her to redo her chignon, as she had every morning for years. With her long grey hair undone, she no longer seemed like his grandmother but simply a creature of flesh and blood who seemed both very young and terribly old, given up into the hands of the medical profession. Michel took her hand; it was the one thing he still recognised. He often held her hand, even now at 17. She did not open her eyes, but perhaps she recognised his touch despite everything. He did not squeeze her hand, he simply took it in his, as he had always done; he dearly hoped that she knew it was him.

Her childhood had been grim. From the age of seven, she had laboured on the farm surrounded by semi-alcoholic brutes. Her adolescence was too short for her to have any precise memories of it. After the death of her husband, she had worked in a factory and brought up her four children; in mid-winter she drew water from the pump in the courtyard so that they could wash. At 60, having just retired from the factory, she agreed to look after her son's only child. He had wanted for nothing – clean clothes, good Sunday lunches and love. All these things she had done for him. Any analysis of human behaviour, however rudimentary, should take account of such phenomena. Historically, such human beings have existed. Human beings who have worked – worked hard – all their lives with no other motive than their love and devotion; who have literally given their lives for others, out of love and devotion. Human beings who have no sense of having made any sacrifice; who cannot imagine any other way of life than giving their lives for others – out of love and devotion. In general, such human beings are invariably women.

Michel had been in the room for about 15 minutes, holding her hand in his, when an intern came and told him that he would be in the way if he were to stay any longer. There might be something they could do; not an operation, it was past that, but something, maybe; he shouldn't give up hope.

They headed back in silence; Marie-Thérèse drove the Renault 16 mechanically. They ate without saying much, evoking a memory from time to time. Marie-Thérèse cooked and served, she needed to keep busy; now and again she would stop and cry a little and then go back to cooking.

Annabelle had been there when the ambulance came and when the Renault came back. At about one a.m , she rose and dressed – her parents were asleep – and walked to the gate of Michel's house. The lights were still on, he was probably in the living room, but it was impossible to make out anything through the heavy curtains. A light rain fell. Ten minutes passed. Annabelle knew that she could ring the doorbell and see Michel; she could also do nothing. She did not know that these ten minutes were a concrete example of *free will*; she knew only that they were terrible and that when they had elapsed, she would never be quite the same again. Many years later Michel proposed a theory of human freedom using the flow of superfluid helium as an analogy. In principle, the subtle transfer of electrons between neurons and synapses in the brain is governed by quantum uncertainty. The sheer number of neurons, however, statistically cancels out such differences, ensuring that human behaviour is as rigorously determined – in broad terms and in the smallest detail – as any other natural system. In rare cases, however – Christians refer to them as *acts of grace* – a different harmonic waveform causes changes in the brain which modify behaviour, temporarily or permanently. It is this new harmonic resonance which gives rise to what is commonly called *free will*.

Nothing of the sort happened on this occasion, and Annabelle went home. She felt much older. It would be 25 years before she would see Michel again.

At three a.m. the telephone rang; the nurse seemed truly sorry. Everything possible had been done; but there was very little that they could do. Her heart was too weak. At least they could be sure that she had not suffered. But, she had to tell them, it was over now.

Michel went back to his room, taking short steps, barely a foot long. Brigitte moved to get up but Marie-Thérèse prevented her. For a minute or two, there was silence, and then a scream, a long howl, from his room. Brigitte hurried to him. Michel was rolled into a ball at the foot of his bed. His eyes were wide open, but his expression was not one of grief, nor of any recognisable human emotion. His face was filled with abject, animal fear.

Part Two

Strange Moments

1

Bruno lost control of the car just outside Poitiers. The Peugeot 305 skidded across the motorway and hit the crash barrier on the central reservation, the car rolled onto its roof and righted itself, then stopped. 'Christ!' he muttered numbly, 'Jesus fucking Christ!' A Jaguar hurtled towards him, doing 140; the driver braked sharply and swerved, narrowly missing the crash barrier, then drove off leaning on his horn. 'Cunt!' screamed Bruno, climbing out and shaking his fist. 'Fucking cunt!' Then he got back into his car, made a U-turn and headed back.

The Lieu du Changement was founded in 1975 by a group of '68 veterans (in fact, they were more 'spirit of '68', since none of them had actually been involved in the riots). It was just south of Cholet on a vast estate scattered with pine forests that belonged to the parents of one of them. Their plan, inspired by the liberal values of the early

Seventies, was to create an authentic utopia – a place where the principles of self-government, respect for individual freedom and true democracy could be practised in the 'here and now'. The Lieu was not a commune, but had the more modest aim of providing a place where like-minded people could spend the summer months living according to the principles they espoused. It was intended that this haven of humanist and democratic feeling would create synergies, facilitate the meeting of minds and, in particular, as one of the founding members put it, provide an opportunity to 'get your rocks off'.

Just before Cholet Sud, Bruno took the slip road off the motorway and drove for 15 kilometres along country roads. The map was not very clear, and he felt hot. It was pure chance, he thought, that he finally saw the sign. In large, multicoloured letters it read 'Lieu du Changement', and, underneath: *'I am properly free when all the men and women about me are equally free'* (Mikhail Bakunin). On the right, two teenage girls were walking up a path that led to the sea. The sluts were wearing nothing under their tee shirts. Bruno watched them as they passed; his cock ached. Wet tee shirts, he thought solemnly, were a wonderful thing. The girls turned off the road; they were clearly heading to the nearby camp site.

He parked the 305 and walked over to a small wooden hut with a WELCOME sign. Inside, a woman of about 60 sat in the lotus position. Her thin, wrinkled breasts hung over her thin cotton tunic; Bruno felt sorry for her. She gave him a big, somewhat stilted smile. 'Welcome to the Lieu du Changement,' she said at last. She smiled broadly again; was she demented? 'Have you got your reservation form?' Bruno took his papers out of his leather pocket-book. 'Perfect!' muttered the hag, still smiling like an idiot.

It was forbidden to drive cars within the grounds of the camp site so he decided to work in stages: first he would find a place to pitch his tent, then he would get his things from the car. He had bought a tent from La Samaritaine before setting off ('Made in the People's Republic of China, 2/3 persons, 449FF').

The first thing Bruno noticed when he arrived in the clearing was the pyramid. It was 20 metres high and 20 metres along the base: exactly equilateral. The sides were constructed of glass panes in heavy wood frames. The dying sun glinted on some of them, while through others it was possible to see the internal framework of stairs and shutters, also constructed of dark wood. It was intended to symbolise a tree – in the centre, a large cylinder housed the central staircase. A stream of people – some alone, others in small groups; some dressed, others naked – was leaving the building. The sunset flared through the long grass, as if in a film trailer. Bruno observed the scene for two or three minutes, then took his tent under his arm and started up the first hill.

The land was hilly and wooded with clearings here and there, the ground was carpeted with pine needles and there were communal sanitary facilities at regular intervals. There were no plots marked out. Bruno started to sweat, he had heartburn; he had eaten too much at the rest stop. He was finding it difficult to think clearly, but he knew that the choice of where to pitch his tent could make all the difference to the success of his stay.

He was thinking this when he noticed a washing line strung between two trees. An evening breeze moved gently through the panties that had been hung out to dry. It might be an idea to camp here, he thought, it's easy to get to know your neighbours when camping. Not necessarily to fuck them, just to get acquainted. It was a start. He put down the tent and began to study the instructions. The French translation was abominable, the English not much better; he assumed that the other languages were just as bad. Fucking Chinks. What the hell did 'upturn the demi-poles to stable the dome' mean?

He was standing staring hopelessly at the diagrams when a sort of squaw appeared, dressed in a mini-skirt of animal pelt, her large breasts dangling in the twilight. 'Just got here?' the apparition asked. 'Need a hand setting up your tent?'

'I'll be okay . . .' he said in a strangled voice. 'I'll be okay, thanks . . . It's very good of you,' he said in a whisper. He had the impression this was a trap. Moments later, a wailing erupted from the neighbouring wigwam (where the hell had they bought this thing? Had they made it themselves?). The squaw ran off, returned with two little brats, one on each hip, and rocked them gently. They screamed louder. The squaw's brave trotted up, his cock dangling in the breeze. He was about 50, a stocky guy with long grey hair and a beard. He took one of the little monkeys in his arms and started to kiss it; it was disgusting. Bruno moved a little way off – that was close. With little monsters like that, he would not get a wink of sleep. She was obviously breastfeeding; nice tits, though.

He walked a couple of metres away from the wigwam, but he did not want to go too far from the panties. They were delicate, lacy and transparent and he could not imagine they belonged to the squaw. He finally found a spot between two Canadian girls (cousins? sisters? school friends?) and set to work.

It was almost dark by the time he had finished. In the half-light, he went back to get his suitcases. He met a number of people on the way: couples, singles; quite a few single women in their forties. At regular intervals there were signs nailed to the trees reading 'MUTUAL RESPECT'; he walked up to one of them. Underneath was a vending machine full of condoms conforming to French standards. Below, there was a white plastic pedal-bin. He put his foot on the pedal and turned on his torch; the bin was mostly full of empty beer cans, but there were also used condoms. That's reassuring, thought Bruno, it looks like this place is humming.

The trip back was difficult; he was out of breath and the suitcases cut into his hands. There were still some people circulating, the beams from their torches crossing in the darkness. There was still a lot of traffic on the road. The

Dynasty on the road to Saint-Clément had a topless night, but he didn't feel up to it. He stood motionless for half an hour. This is my life, thought Bruno, standing, watching car headlights through the trees.

When he got back to his tent he poured himself a whisky and jerked off slowly, flicking through a copy of *Swing* – 'pleasure is a right'. He had bought a copy at a service station near Angers. He had no intention of really replying to any of the small ads; he did not feel up to a *gang bang* or a *sperm fest*. The women seeking single men were generally looking for black guys, and, in any case, he did not come close to the minimum size they required. Issue after issue, he came to the conclusion that his cock was too small for the porn circuit.

In general, however, he was not unhappy with his body. The hair transplant had taken well – he had been lucky to find a good surgeon. He worked out regularly, and frankly, he thought he looked good for 42. He poured another whisky, ejaculated onto the magazine and fell asleep, almost content.

2

A Thirteen-Hour Flight

As its clientele grew older, the Lieu du Changement rapidly ran into problems. In the Eighties young people found its ideals dated. There were theatre workshops and massage therapy but, basically, it was a camp site; the accommodation and facilities were not up to the standards of package holidays. Apart from that, the anarchic spirit of the place made it difficult to control access and collect payments; its finances, which had always been precarious, became more problematic.

Their first response – a decision passed unanimously by the founder members – was to establish preferential tariffs for the young, but it was not to be enough. At the AGM in early 1984, Frédéric Le Dantec made a proposal that was to prove the salvation of the Lieu. He suggested that business was the leisure industry of the 1980s. Each of them had acquired valuable experience in humanist therapy (Gestalt, rebirth, walking on hot coals, transactional analysis, sex meditation, PNL . . .). Why not invest that experience in developing a series of residential courses aimed at businesses? After fierce debate, the proposal was adopted. Once it was accepted, work began on building the pyramid, together with 50 bungalows – basic but comfortable – where visitors could stay. At the same time, the founders organised an extensive mail-shot, targeting human resources directors in multinational companies. Some of the more left-wing of the founders found this difficult to accept. After a brief internal power struggle, the Lieu ceased to be an association under the act of 1901 and became a public limited company in which Frédéric Le Dantec was principal shareholder. After all, it was his parents' land, and Crédit Mutuel in Charente Maritime seemed willing to back the project.

Five years later, the Lieu du Changement had an excellent client list (the BNP, IBM, the Ministry of Finance, the RATP, Bouygues . . .). Inter- and intra-company courses were organised all year round and the camp site – maintained principally for reasons of nostalgia – accounted for less than five per cent of the company's annual turnover.

Bruno woke with a crippling headache and no illusions. He had heard about the place from a secretary who had been on a 'Personal Development – Positive Thinking' course at five thousand francs a day. He had asked her for the brochure. It looked good: friendly, open-minded, he got the picture. One statistic particularly attracted his attention: in July–August of the previous year, 63 per cent of visitors to the Lieu du Changement were female. That was almost two women to every man: an excellent ratio. He decided to check it out, and booked a week there in July; especially as camping would be cheaper than going on a Club Med holiday. Of course, he could guess what sort of women went there: deranged old lefties who were probably all HIV positive. But still, two women to every man, he was in with a chance – if he worked it properly, he might even pull two.

The year had started well from a sexual point of view. The influx of girls from Eastern Europe had meant prices had dropped. For 200 francs, you could get a little personal relaxation, down from 400 francs some months earlier. Unfortunately, he crashed his car in April and the repairs were expensive; worse still, it had been his fault. The bank started to squeeze him and he had to economise.

He lifted himself onto his elbow and poured himself his first whisky. The copy of *Swing* was still open at the same page. A guy wearing socks was thrusting his cock towards the camera – his name was Hervé.

Not my thing, thought Bruno, not my thing. He put on a pair of boxer shorts and walked towards the shower block. After all, he thought hopefully, the squaw from last night was more or less fuckable. In fact her big, sagging breasts were perfect for a tit wank; it had been three years since his last time. Bruno had always liked jerking off between a girl's tits, but whores did not really go for it.

Was it the fact that you came in their faces that turned them off? Did it really take more time or trouble than a blow-job? Whatever, a tit wank was not generally on offer, it wasn't on the menu, so it was difficult to get girls to do it. Girls seemed to think of it as personal. Often when he tried for a tit wank, Bruno had to make do with a hand-job or maybe a blow-job. He sometimes managed to coax one out of a girl, but as far as Bruno was concerned there were not enough tit wanks to go round.

He arrived at the showerblock, 'Body Space 8'. He had more or less resigned himself to the women being old and decrepit and was taken aback to see the teenagers. There were four of them near the showers, all between 15 and 17, opposite the wash basins. Two of them wore swim-suits and waited as the other two played under the shower like otters, chatting and laughing and splashing one another: they were completely naked. The scene was indescribably graceful and erotic. He did not deserve such a thing. His cock was hard in his boxer shorts; with one hand, he took it out and pressed himself against the wash basin as he cleaned between his teeth with a toothpick. He stabbed himself in the gum, removed the bloody tooth-pick. The head of his penis tingled unbearably, it was hot and swollen; a drop formed at the tip.

One of the girls, graceful and dark-haired stepped out of the shower, grabbed a towel and began to pat her young breasts dry contentedly. A little redhead slipped off her swimsuit and took her place under the shower – her pussy hair was golden blonde. Bruno moaned a little, he was beginning to feel dizzy. In his head, he could imagine walking over, taking his shorts off and waiting by the showers. He had every right to go and wait to take a shower. He imagined himself beside them, his cock hard, saying something like 'Is the water hot?' The showers were ten centimetres apart; if he took a shower next to the redheaded girl she might accidentally brush against his prick. At the thought, he felt increasingly dizzy and had to hold onto the porcelain washbasin. At the same instant, two boys arrived, laughing a little too loudly; they were wearing black shorts with fluorescent stripes. In an instant, Bruno's hard-on was gone; he put his penis back into his shorts and carried on picking at his teeth.

Later, still in a state of shock, he went down to the break-fast tables. He sat apart from the others and spoke to no one. As he masticated his cereal with added vitamins, he thought about the Faustian nature of sexual pursuit, its vampirism. For example, thought Bruno, people are wrong to talk about homosexuals. He had never – or very rarely – met a homosexual; on the other hand, he knew a great many *pederasts*. Some pederasts – thankfully, very few – prefer little boys; they wind up in prison for a long stretch and no one ever talks about them again. Most pederasts, however, are attracted to youths of between 15 and 25. Anyone older than that is, to them, simply an old, dried-up arsehole. Watch two old queens together, Bruno liked to say, watch them closely: they may be fond of one another; they may even be affectionate, but do they really want each other? No. As soon as some tight 15–25-year-old arse walks past, they will tear each other apart like panthers; they will rip each other to pieces just for that tight little arse; that is what Bruno thought.

In this, as in many things, so-called homosexuals had led the way for society as a whole, thought Bruno. Take him, for example – he was 42 years old. Did he want women his own age? Absolutely not. On the other hand, for young pussy wrapped in a mini-skirt he was prepared to go to the ends of the earth. Well, to Bangkok at least. Which was, after all, a 13-hour flight.

3

Sexual desire is preoccupied with youth, and the tendency to regard ever-younger girls as fair game was simply a return to the norm; a return to the true nature of desire, comparable to the return of stock prices to their true value after a run on the exchange. Nonetheless, women who turned 20 in the late Sixties found themselves in a difficult position when they hit 40. Most of them were divorced and could no longer count on the conjugal bond – whether warm or abject – whose decline they had served to hasten. As members of a generation who – more than any before – had endorsed a cult of youth over age, they could hardly claim to be surprised when they, in their turn, were dismissed by succeeding generations. As their flesh began to age, the cult of the body, which they had done so much to promote, simply filled them with disgust for their own bodies – a disgust they could see mirrored in the gaze of others.

The men of their generation found themselves in much the same position but this common destiny fostered no solidarity. At 40, they continued to pursue young women – with a measure of success, at least for those who had attained a certain position, whether intellectual, financial or social. For the women, their mature years brought only failure, masturbation and shame.

Dedicated exclusively to sexual liberation and desire, the Lieu du Changement naturally became a place of depression and bitterness. Farewell to limbs entwined in a clearing under the full moon! Farewell to the quasi-Dionysian spectacle of oiled bodies glistening under the midday sun. That, at least, is how the forty-somethings mourned as they looked at their flaccid pricks and fleshy tits.

In 1987 the first quasi-religious workshops appeared at the Lieu. Christianity was excluded, of course, but a sufficiently nebulous mysticism – for these people were spiritually impoverished – dovetailed neatly with the cult of the body beautiful which, against all sense, they continued to promote. There were still workshops on sensual massage, and the liberation of the orgone, but interest in the esoteric – astrology, Egyptian tarot, working with chakras – boomed. There were Encounters with the Angel and courses on crystal healing. Siberian shamanism made a remarkable debut when, in 1991, during the long initiation in a sweat lodge fired by sacred coals, an initiate died of heart failure. Tantric Zen, which combined vanity, mysticism and frottage, flourished. In a matter of years, the Lieu – like many centres throughout France and Western Europe – became a New Age institution, while maintaining a reputation as a hedonist's paradise, which became its unique selling point.

After breakfast Bruno retired to his tent. He considered masturbating (the image of the teenagers was still vivid), but finally decided against. The enticing girls must be the offspring of the regiments of flower children he had passed around the Lieu, so clearly some of the old hags had suc-ceeded in reproducing after all. This realisation plunged Bruno into vague, unpleasant reflections. He tore open the fly-sheet of his tent; the sky was blue, small clouds floated like spatters of sperm between the pines, the day was set to be dazzling. He glanced at the programme for the week: he had chosen option one – 'Creativity and Relaxation'. There was a choice of three workshops that morning: mime and psychodrama, painting in water-colours, and creative writing. Psychodrama, he decided, was best avoided. He had been there and done that, on a weekend course in Chantilly where he had watched 50-year-old social workers rolling around on the floor whining for Daddy to bring them their teddy bears. Painting in watercolour sounded more interesting, but would probably be outdoors: did he really want to deal with pine needles, insects and God knows what, only to turn out some crap?

The woman who led the creative writing workshop had long black hair and a full, sensual mouth outlined in carmine red (what he usually referred to as 'blow-job lips'); she wore a grey tunic and drainpipe trousers. She was beautiful; she had class. Probably just a slut, though, thought Bruno, crouching down in the ill-defined circle of disciples. To his right a fat, grey-haired woman with thick glasses and an ugly shit-coloured tan breathed noisily. She reeked of wine and it was only ten-thirty.

'To salute our selfhood,' began the leader, 'to salute the Earth and the five ways we will begin the workshop with the hatha-yoga position "salute to the sun".' She followed this with a description of an unlikely posture; the wino on Bruno's right belched. 'You look tired, Jacqueline . . .' said the yogi, 'you shouldn't do any exercise if you don't feel up to it. Lie down, the group will join you in a while.'

They all had to lie down while the teacher delivered a long, vacuous speech in the style of Contrexéville: 'You are plunging into beautiful, crystal water. You can feel it enveloping your limbs, flowing over your stomach. You give thanks to Gaia, your mother. Confidently, you press yourself to your mother, the Earth. Feel your desire. You give thanks to yourself for giving you this desire,' etc. Lying on the filthy Indian rug, Bruno ground his teeth together angrily. The dipso beside him belched regularly. Between burps, she exhaled with a great 'Haaaaaa' which was presumably intended to express her relaxation. The karma queen went on with her routine, conjuring tellurian energies to revitalise the stomach and the groin. After meandering through the four elements, and satisfied with her routine, she concluded: 'Now that you have broken the barrier of the rational and made contact with your deepest desires, open yourself to the limitless power of the creative urge.' 'Urge, schmurge,' fumed Bruno as he got to his feet with difficulty. The writing session was followed by a presentation in which each of them had to read what they had written. The only halfway-decent babe in the whole workshop was called Emma – a fit little redhead wearing jeans and a tee shirt, who had written a nauseating poem about moon-sheep. Most of the group were positively oozing with rapture at having made contact with Mother Earth, Father Sun and family. At last, it was Bruno's turn to read. Mournfully, he intoned:

> 'Taxi drivers are fucking cunts
> They never stop, the little runts'

'You feel like that . . .' said the yogi, 'you feel like that because you haven't mastered your negative energy. I can feel deep, powerful desires within you. We can help you – here and now. Let's all stand and focus the energies of the group.'

Everyone stood, joined hands and formed a circle. Reluctantly, Bruno took the hands of the old bag on his right and a revolting little bearded man who looked like Cavanna. Her whole being focused but calm, the yogi uttered a long 'Om' and they were off, everyone droning 'Om' as if they had been doing it all their lives. Bruno gamely tried to join in the resounding harmony when he suddenly felt himself pitch to the right. Hypnotised, the fat hag was toppling like a stone. He let go her hand but was unable to break his fall and found himself on his knees in front of the old bitch, now flat on her back and shaking on the mat. The yogi interrupted her meditation and said calmly: 'That's it, Jacqueline, you just lie down if you feel like it.' The two of them seemed to know each other.

The second writing session was a little better; inspired by his fugitive vision that morning, Bruno penned the following poem:

> *I'm tanning my dick*
> *(Hair on my prick)*
> *Down by the dock*
> *(Hair on my cock)*
>
> *I swear I found God*
> *In Body Space 8*
> *He has a great bod*
> *But his hair is a state*
>
> *What is our job?*
> *(Hair on my knob)*
> *To praise him in song*
> *(Hair on my dong)*

'It's humorous . . .' said the yogi, her tone somewhat disapproving. 'And mystical,' theorised the drunk, 'mystical but empty . . .' What was he going to do? Bruno wondered, how long could he put up with this? Was it really worth the effort? When the workshop ended, Bruno rushed back to his tent, not stopping to try and talk to the little redhead; he needed a whisky before lunch. Near his tent, he happened on one of the girls he had been eyeing up at the showers. With a graceful movement, which showed off her breasts, she reached up and took down the lacy panties she had hung out the night before. He felt as though he might explode, showering the camp site in a rain of fatty tissues. What had changed since his adolescence? He still had the same desires, with the knowledge that he could probably never satisfy them. A world in which the young have no respect eventually devours everyone. For lunch, he chose a Catholic. She was easy to spot: she wore a big iron cross around her neck; besides, her heavy lower lids gave her eyes the fervour common to Catholics, or mystics (though, admittedly, to alcoholics too). Long dark hair, pale complexion, slim, not bad looking. Facing her sat a girl with reddish blonde hair who was Swiss-Californian: six feet tall, perfect body, obscenely healthy. She was the leader of the workshop on Tantric Zen. In fact, her name was Brigitte Martin and she came from Créteil. She had been initiated into the mysteries of the orient in California, where she had had her breasts done and changed her name. Back in Créteil, she ran a workshop on Tantric Zen under the name of Shanti Martin; the Catholic was clearly impressed. At first, Bruno found it easy to join in their discussion, which seemed to be about macrobiotics – he had read up on wheatgerm before he came – but the conversation quickly turned to more religious themes and he found he was lost. Could Jesus be subsumed into Krishna, or perhaps into some other deity? Was Rin-Tin-Tin more loveable than Lucky Luke's

Rusty? Though Catholic, the Catholic had no time for the Pope – his medieval outlook, in her opinion, was hindering the spiritual evolution of the Western world. 'You're right,' said Bruno, 'he's an atavist.' The word earned him a new respect from the others. 'And the Dalai Lama can wiggle his ears,' he said dolefully as he finished his tofu burger.

Indefatigable, the Catholic got up before coffee was served – she did not want to be late for her personal development workshop – *The Principles of Yes-Yes*. 'Ah yes, Yes-yes is cool,' said the Swiss-Californian as she got up. 'Thanks for the chat . . .' said the Catholic, turning back with a smile. Anyway, he hadn't done too badly, thought Bruno as he headed back to his tent. 'Talking to morons like that is like pissing in a urinal full of cigarette butts, like shitting in a bog full of Tampax: everything starts to stink.' Space separates one skin from another. Words cross the space, the space between one skin and another. Unheard, unanswered, the words hang in the air and begin to decay, to stink; that's the way it is. Seen like this, words could separate, too.

At the pool, he found a sun-lounger. The girls hung around by the edge of the pool, shivering, hoping a boy might push them in. The sun was at its height; slick, naked bodies moved across the expanse of blue. Without thinking, Bruno launched into a children's book, *The Six Companions and the Gloved Man*, Paul-Jacques Bonzon's masterpiece, recently republished by the Bibliothèque Verte. In the unbearable glare of the sun, it was good to find himself back in the mists of Lyons with his stalwart companion, Kapi the dog.

The afternoon programme offered a choice between *Sensitive Gestalt-massage*, *liberating the voice* and *rebirthing* in warm water. In theory, the massage sounded sexiest. He had a brief glimpse of liberating the voice as he walked up to the massage workshop: there were about ten of them, very excited, jumping around to the directions of the Tantric woman and screeching like startled turkeys.

At the top of the hill, arranged in a circle, were treatment tables, each one covered with a large towel. The students were naked. In the centre of the circle, the instructor, a small, dark-haired man with a slight squint, gave a brief history of sensitive Gestalt-massage. Born out of Fritz Perl's Gestalt-massage, the method had evolved to integrate aspects of the sensual to become – in his opinion – the most complete form of massage. There were those at the Lieu, he realised, who did not share his point of view, but he did not wish to become polemical. Whatever the truth of it – and he would like to end on this note – there was massage and massage; in fact one might say that no two massages were alike. Having finished his pre-amble, he began the demonstration. He asked one of the women to lie on the table. 'Feel the tension in your partner . . .' he commented as he stroked her shoulders; his cock only inches from the girl's long blonde hair. 'Harmony, it's all about harmony . . .' he went on, pouring oil on her breasts. 'You must respect the wholeness of the body . . .': his hands slipped down her stomach, the girl closed her eyes and parted her thighs, visibly enjoying his work.

'There you go,' he concluded. 'Now I want you to work in pairs. Take your time; move around the space; get to know each other.' Still hypnotised by what he had just seen, Bruno was slow to react, though this was the crucial moment. You simply approached your partner of choice and quietly asked her, 'Would you like to work with me?' Everyone else seemed to know the drill and in 30 seconds, it was all over. Bruno looked around, panic-stricken, and found himself face to face with a hairy little man with dark hair and a thick penis. He had not realised that there were only five girls for seven guys.

Thankfully the other guy didn't look like a queer. Visibly furious, he lay down on the table, rested his head on his arms and waited. 'Feel the tension . . . respect the wholeness of the body . . .' Bruno poured more oil on, but couldn't get past the knees; the guy's body was stiff as a log. Even his buttocks were hairy. The oil was beginning to drip onto the towel, the guy's calves had to be saturated. Bruno looked up. Next to him were two men, lying on their backs. On his left, the man was having his pectorals massaged, the woman's breasts swayed gently; his nose was level with her pussy. The instructor's ghetto-blaster pumped out synthesiser music; the sky was a perfect blue. All around him oil-slick cocks were beginning to rise, towards the light. Everything seemed intensely real. He could not bear it any longer. On the far side of the circle, the instructor was advising a couple on technique. Bruno grabbed his rucksack and hurried off towards the pool where it was clearly rush hour. On the nearby lawn, naked women lay chatting, reading, or simply taking the sun. Where should he sit? Towel in hand, he wandered erratically across the lawn, tottering between the vaginas – as it were. He decided it was time to get off the fence when he spotted the Catholic talking to a dark-skinned rugged little guy with bright eyes and dark curly hair. He waved to her – she did not notice – and sat nearby. 'Hey, Karim!' someone called to the dark-skinned man as he walked past. Karim waved and went on talking to the Catholic, who lay quietly on the lawn listening. She had a pretty muff of curly black hair between her thighs. As they chatted, Karim gently kneaded his balls. Bruno rested his head on the grass and concentrated on the gentle world barely two feet away within the Catholic's pubic hair. He quickly fell asleep.

On 14 December 1967 the Government passed the Neuwirth Act on contraception at its first reading. Although not paid for by Social Security, the pill would now be freely available in pharmacies. It was this which offered a whole section of society access to the sexual revolution, which, until then, had been reserved for professionals, artists and senior management – and some small businessmen. It is interesting to note that the 'sexual revolution' is usually portrayed as a communist utopia, whereas in fact it was simply another stage in the rise of the individual. As the lovely phrase 'hearth and home' suggests, the couple and the family were to be the last bastion of primitive communism in a liberal society. The sexual revolution was to destroy the last unit separating the individual from the market. The destruction continues to this day.

The steering committee of the Lieu du Changement regularly organised dinner dances. For a place open to new spiritual ideas, this might seem surprising, but it only confirmed the dinner dance as the ideal means of sexual selection in non-communist societies. As Frédéric le Dantec pointed out, primitive societies were brought together by feasting, dancing and the pursuit of collective trance.

A bar and a sound system were installed on the lawn and people danced in the moonlight into the small hours. For Bruno, this was a second chance. Actually, the teenagers at the camp rarely attended these occasions, preferring to go to local clubs (Bilbo-quet, Dynasty, 2001 and later Pirates) which hosted theme nights with foam parties, male strip shows and porn stars. A handful of needle-dick dreamers stayed behind, happy to spend their evenings in a tent gently strumming an out-of-tune guitar while their peers despised them. Bruno felt a keen sympathy for these young men. In the absence of girls he could never hope to pull, he would happily – to quote a reader of *Newlook* he had met in a café in Angers – 'stick his knob in any available hole'. It was in hope that he left his tent at 11, wearing white trousers and a blue polo neck, and headed down to the source of the uproar.

Glancing around the mass of dancers, he spotted Karim, who had abandoned the Catholic in favour of a ravishing Rosicrucian. She and her husband, tall, staid and slim, had arrived that afternoon; they seemed to be from Alsace. The husband had taken four hours to work out the arrangement of the numerous fly-sheets and guy-ropes of their convoluted tent. Earlier, he had taken Bruno aside and initiated him into the hidden mysteries of the Rosy Cross. Eyes glittering behind his small, round glasses, he looked every inch a zealot; Bruno listened without hearing. According to him, inspired by the work of the alchemists, the fellowship of the Rosy Cross had been founded in Germany, but was intricately linked to Rhenan mysticism. It was obviously a cabal of queers and Nazis. 'You can stick your cross up your arse . . .' Bruno thought flippantly, watching the man's beautiful wife out of the corner of his eye as she crouched by the gas stove. 'Not to mention the rose . . .' he added, as she stood up, flashing her breasts, and called to her husband to come and change the baby.

In any case, now she was dancing with Karim. They made a strange couple: the stocky, cunning little man, a good six inches shorter than this skinny Germanic beanpole. He chatted and smiled as they danced, as though he had forgotten why he had picked her up in the first place; she smiled too and stared at him, clearly fascinated; once, she even laughed out loud. On the far side of the lawn her husband was explaining the origins of the Rosicrucian fellowship in Lower Saxony in 1530 to another potential convert. At regular intervals his three-year-old son, a blond-haired, snot-nosed brat, screamed that he wanted to be put to bed. Once again Bruno was faced with a slice of *real life*. He overheard two skinny, priestly individuals commenting on the rake's progress. 'He's very expressive, very emotional, you see . . .' said one. 'On paper, he's out of his league: he's not good-looking, he's got a beer belly and he's a lot shorter than she is. But he's a charming bastard, and that makes all the difference.' The other nodded, seeming to toy mournfully with an imaginary rosary. As he finished his vodka and orange, Bruno noticed that Karim had managed to inveigle the Rosicrucian onto a grass bank. He slipped his arm round her shoulders, talking as he did so, and slipped his other hand up her dress. 'She's opened her legs for him, the Nazi slut,' Bruno thought as he walked away from the dancers. Just as he stepped out of the light, he had a vision of the Catholic girl having her arse felt up by someone who looked like a ski instructor. He still had some tins of ravioli in his tent.

Before heading back, in an act of desperation, he phoned to check his answering machine. There was one message: 'You're probably on holiday . . .' said Michel's voice calmly. 'Call me when you get back. I'm on holiday, too – indefinitely.'

4

He walks, reaches the border. A flock of vultures circle around something – probably a corpse. The muscles in his thighs respond to the irregularities of the path. The hills are shrouded in dry grass, stretching out to the east as far as the horizon. He has not eaten since the night before; he is no longer afraid.

He wakes, fully dressed, lying across his bed. A truck is unloading a consignment outside the delivery entrance of Monoprix. It is a little after seven o'clock.

For years, Michel had lived a purely intellectual existence. The world of human emotions was not his field; he knows little of it. Nowadays life can be organised with minute precision; supermarket cashiers respond to an imperceptible nod. There has been much coming and going in the ten years he has lived here; from time to time, a couple formed and he watched as the new lover moved in.

Friends carrying boxes and lamps up the stairs. They were young and sometimes he heard them laugh. Often (but not always), when they split up, the ex-lovers moved out at the same time and there was an empty apartment. What conclusions could he draw for such things? How should he interpret these comings and goings? It was puzzling.

He himself wanted nothing more than to love someone, he asked for nothing. Nothing in particular, anyway. Life should be simple, thought Michel, something that could be lived as a collection of small, endlessly repeated rituals. In time, such a life might become tedious, but the rituals give you something to believe in. A life without risk, without drama. But life was not like that. Sometimes he went out and watched the teenagers and the houses. One thing seemed clear to him: no one knew how to live any more. Perhaps that was an exaggeration: some people seemed motivated, passionate about some cause, and their lives seemed easier. Hence ACT-UP activists thought it was important to run ads which others thought pornographic, depicting homosexual practices in close-up. Their lives seemed busier and more fulfilled, full of exciting incident. They had multiple partners, fucked each other in back rooms; sometimes the condom split or slipped off and they died of AIDS. Even then, their deaths seemed radical, dignified. Television gave lessons in dignity, especially TF1. As a teenager, Michel believed that suffering conferred dignity on a person. Now he had to admit that he had been wrong. What conferred dignity on people was television.

*

Despite the constant small pleasures television offered him, he thought it best to get out sometimes. In any case, he had to do his shopping. The only conclusion he could draw was that, without points of reference, a man melts away.

On the morning of 9 July (the feast of Saint Amandine) he noticed that ring-binders, exercise books and pencil cases were already on display in his local Monoprix. He found the advertising slogan – 'Back to school – no headaches!' – less than persuasive. What was education after all, if not one long headache?

The following morning he found the autumn/winter catalogue from 3 Suisses in his mailbox. The massive hard cover was not addressed – had it been hand delivered? As a long-standing subscriber to trade publications, he was used to the little extras that came with being a loyal customer. Time rolled on. Despite the glorious summer weather, marketing campaigns were already looking to the autumn, though July had barely begun.

As a young man, Michel had read some absurdist literature, existentialist novels about the meaningless march of time; he found such extremes of opinion only half-convincing. At the time he was seeing a lot of Bruno, who dreamed about becoming a writer; he covered pages and pages in ink and masturbated continually; he introduced Michel to Samuel Beckett. Beckett was presumably what they called a *great writer*, though Michel had never managed to finish a single one of his books. That was late in 1970; he and Bruno were 20 and already they felt old. As time went on, they felt older still, and they felt shamed by the fact. Their generation was about to make a dramatic shift – substituting for the tragedy of death with the more general humiliation of old age. Twenty years on, Bruno had never seriously thought about death and he was beginning to wonder whether he ever would. He wanted to live to the end, to be a part of life, to fight against physical infirmity and the petty misfortunes of the everyday. With his last breath, he would still plead for a postponement, plead to live a little longer. In particular, he would continue his quest for the ultimate pleasure to the end; one last indulgence. However transitory, a good blow job was a real pleasure and that, thought Michel, as he flicked through the lingerie section *(Sensual Suspenders!)* of his catalogue, was something that could not be denied.

He himself masturbated rarely; his fantasies as a young research student, whether inspired by the Minitel, or by actual women (usually reps from large pharmaceutical companies), had gradually faded. Now he calmly observed the slow decline of his virility, relieved only by an occasional wank for which his 3 Suisses catalogue, supplemented now and then by a risqué CD-ROM (79FF), proved more than sufficient. Michel knew that Bruno, by contrast, was frittering away his prime chasing neurotic Lolitas with firm breasts, round buttocks and eager mouths; thank God he was a civil servant. It was not absurd: it was a melodrama where the characters were babes and dogs, hot guys and bitches; that was Bruno's world. Michel, on the other hand, lived in a world where everything was precisely regulated, a world without history where the seasons were all commercial ones: Roland Garros, Christmas, New Year's Eve, the biannual arrival of the 3 Suisses catalogue. If he were homosexual, he would be able to take part in the AIDS marathon or Gay Pride. If he were a libertine, he could look forward to the *Salon de l'Érotisme*. If he were a sportsman, he would be in the Pyrenees, right now, watching a *stage* in the Tour de France. Though an undiscriminating shopper, he was delighted when his local Monoprix had an 'Italian Fortnight'. This life so well organised, on such a human scale; happiness could be found in this; had he wanted for more, he wouldn't know where to find it.

On the morning of 15 July he took a Christian tract out of the litter bin in the hall. It included several life stories, each converging towards a happy ending: an encounter with the risen Christ. For several issues, he had been following the story of a young woman ('Isabelle was in a state of shock – her university career was on the line'), though he had to admit that Pavel's experience was closer to his own ('As an officer in the Czech army, commanding an anti-aircraft station was the pinnacle of Pavel's military career'). He had no difficulty identifying with Pavel in the next paragraph: 'As a technical expert, who had studied at a distinguished academy, Pavel should have been in love with life. Instead, he was depressed, constantly searching for a reason to live.'

The 3 Suisses catalogue, on the other hand, offered a more thoughtful, historically informed insight into Europe's current malaise. The impression of a society in flux implicit in its opening pages is finally given precise formulation on page 17. Many times, Michel had been struck by the lines that summed up the philosophy of the collection: 'Optimism, generosity, complicity and harmony make the world go round. THE FUTURE IS FEMALE.'

On the eight o'clock news, Bruno Masure announced that an American study had detected signs of fossil life on Mars. The fossils were of bacterial organisms, probably methane-based archaea. It seemed that biological macromolecules had succeeded in forming on earth's closest neighbour, giving rise to nebulous self-replicating life forms comprising a nucleus and an ill-defined membrane. It had all ended there, however, presumably the result of climatic changes that made reproduction increasingly difficult to sustain, until eventually it ceased entirely. The story of life on Mars was a modest one. However (and Bruno Masure did not seem to understand this), this brief, feeble misfire brutally refuted all the mythological and religious constructs which had privileged the human race. There had been no unique, wondrous act of creation; no chosen people; no chosen species or planet, simply an endless series of tentative essays, flawed for the most part, scattered across the universe. It was all so distressingly banal. The DNA of the Martian bacteria seemed to be similar to that of terrestrial bacteria. It was this more than anything that saddened him, in itself a sign of depression. In normal circumstances a scientist, any scientist, would be excited by the similarities, and would see in them the promise of a unifying synthesis.

When he first met Desplechin in 1982, Djerzinski was in his third year at the University of Orsay. As part of his studies, he took part in Alain Aspect's groundbreaking experiments showing that the behaviours of successive photons emitted from a single calcium atom were inseparable. Michel was the youngest researcher on the team.

Aspect's experiments – precise, rigorous and perfectly documented – were to have profound repercussions in the scientific community. The results, it was acknowledged, were the first clear-cut refutation of Einstein, Podolsky and Rosen's 1935 objections when they claimed that 'quantum theory is incomplete'. Here was a clear violation of Bell's inequalities – derived in part from Einstein's hypotheses – since the results tallied perfectly with quantum predictions. This meant that there were only two possible hypotheses. Either the hidden properties which governed the behaviour of sub-atomic particles were non-local – meaning that they could influence one another at an arbitrary distance – or the very notion of particles having intrinsic properties in the absence of observation had to be abandoned. The latter opened up a deep ontological void – unless one adopted a radical positivism and contented oneself with developing a mathematical formalism which predicted the observable and gave up on discovering the underlying reality. Naturally, it was this last option which rallied the majority of researchers.

The first paper on Aspect's experiments – 'Experimental Realisation of Einstein–Podolsky–Rosen *Gedankexperiment*: a new violation of Bell's inequalities' – was published in issue 48 of the *Physical Review*. Djerzinski was credited as a co-writer of the article. A few days later he had a visit from Desplechin. At 43, he was director of the Institute of Molecular Biology at Gif-sur-Yvette. He was increasingly aware that there was something fundamental missing in their analysis of gene mutations; and that this was probably related to phenomena at the atomic or sub-atomic level.

Their first interview took place in Michel's university rooms. Desplechin was unsurprised by the dreary austerity of the surroundings: they were more or less what he had expected. Their conversation continued late into the night. Desplechin pointed out that it was the existence of a finite list of chemical elements which had prompted Niels Bohr's first thoughts on the subject. A planetary theory of the atom based on gravitational and electromagnetic fields should, in principle, provide an infinite number of solutions, and an infinite number of possible chemical elements. The universe, however, was made up of about a hundred elements; a list which was fixed and stable. It was this anomalous situation, which contradicted

Maxwell's equations and the classical laws of electro-magnetics, that led to the development of quantum mechanics. In Desplechin's opinion, contemporary biology was in a similar position. The existence of immutable macromolecules and cellular ultrastructures, which had remained consistent throughout evolutionary history, could not be explained by the classical laws of chemistry. In some way as yet impossible to determine, quantum theory must directly impact on biological events. This would create an entirely new field of research.

That first evening, Desplechin was struck by his young interlocutor's calm and his open-mindedness. He invited Djerzinski to dinner at his home on the rue de l'École-polytechnique the following Saturday, where one of his colleagues – a biochemist who had published extensively on RNA transcriptases – would join them.

When he arrived at Desplechin's apartment, Michel felt as though he had walked onto a film set. Before this he had scarcely imagined such surroundings, leisurely, culti-vated and refined, with a confident sense of taste. Mahogany furniture, kilims, afghan rugs, reproductions of Matisse . . . Now he could imagine the rest – the house in Brittany, maybe a small farm in the Lubéron. 'And a boxed set of Bartok quintets, I bet . . .' he thought fleet-ingly as he began to eat. They had champagne with dinner; dessert was a charlotte of soft fruits accompanied by an exceptional semi-sweet rosé. It was at this point that Desplechin outlined his project. He could arrange for a post to be created in his department at Gif on a contractual basis. Michel would need to acquire the basic concepts of biochemistry to complement his studies, but that was easily done. Meanwhile, Desplechin would supervise his final thesis personally. Once that was completed, Michel could apply for a permanent post.

Michel glanced at the small Khmer statue on the mantelpiece; the clean lines of the figure of the Buddha touching the ground to ask Nature to witness his resolve to reach enlightenment. Michel cleared his throat and accepted.

In the decade that followed, remarkable technical advances and the use of radioactive markers made it possible to amass a substantial number of results. Though as far as the theoretical questions Desplechin had raised at their first meeting were concerned, thought Djerzinski, there had been zero progress.

In the early hours of the morning, he found himself preoccupied with the Martian bacteria. He found a dozen messages on an Internet newsgroup, mostly from American universities. Proportions of adenine, guanine, thiamine and cytosine had been found to be typical. Randomly, he clicked on the Ann Arbor site where he found a message about ageing. Alicia Marcia-Coelho had found evidence to suggest that DNA sequences were lost through the repeated subdivision of fibroblasts from non-striated muscles; this was hardly a surprise. Michel knew Alicia – in fact it was she who had relieved him of his virginity ten years before, after a particularly drunken dinner at a genetics seminar in Baltimore. She had been so drunk that she couldn't help him take off her bra. It had been a difficult moment, painful even. She had just split up with her husband, she confided as Michel struggled with the clasps. After that, everything went normally; he was surprised to discover that he could get a hard-on and even ejaculate inside this woman's vagina without feeling the slightest pleasure.

5

Many of the people who went to the Lieu du Changement were, like Bruno, over 40 and, also like him, many worked in the public sector or in education and were safeguarded from poverty by their status as civil servants. Most of them would have put themselves on the political left; most of them lived alone, usually as the result of divorce. He was, therefore, a pretty typical visitor. After a few days he noticed that he felt somewhat better than usual. The women were intolerable at breakfast, but by early evening the mystical morons were hopelessly vying with their daughters' generation once again. Death is a great leveller. On Wednesday afternoon he met Catherine, a 50-year-old who had been a feminist of the old school. She was tanned, with dark, curly hair; she must have been pretty when she was 20. Her breasts were still in good nick, he thought, when he saw her by the pool, but she had a fat arse. She had reinvented herself through Egyptian symbolism, tarot and the like. She was talking about the god Anubis as Bruno stepped out of his boxer shorts; he decided that she would probably not be offended by his erection and they might become friends. She had a medicine ball gripped tightly between her thighs. They parted on less than friendly terms.

That evening, just before dinner, a guy called Pierre-Louis introduced himself. He was a maths teacher, and he looked the part. Bruno had noticed him a couple of days earlier at the theatrical evening; he had done a stand-up routine about a mathematical proof that went round in circles – some kind of surreal humour, presumably – it wasn't the slightest bit funny. He scribbled furiously on a white board. From time to time he would stop abruptly, marker raised, motionless, bald head furrowed in thought, eyebrows raised in an expression that was supposed to be funny, before scribbling furiously and babbling faster than ever. When the sketch was over, five or six people applauded out of pity. He blushed wildly; it was over.

In the days that followed, Bruno had managed to avoid him on several occasions. He was at least six feet six and skinny, but he had a bit of a paunch, and he made a curious sight, walking along the diving board with his fat little belly. He was probably about 45.

That evening Bruno again made a quick getaway while the beanpole joined the others in an improvised African dance. He walked up the hill towards the communal restaurant. There was a seat free beside the ex-feminist, who was sitting opposite a sister symbolist. He had barely started his tofu ragout when Pierre-Louis appeared at the far end of the table; he beamed when he noticed a vacant seat opposite Bruno. He had been talking for some time before Bruno noticed, partly because he had a rather bad stammer, and partly because of the shrill wittering of the imbeciles next to them. What about the reincarnation of Osiris? What do you think of Egyptian marionettes? They were paying not the slightest attention to the men. At some point Bruno realised that the poor fool was asking him about his job. 'Oh, nothing much . . .' he replied vaguely; he was happy to talk about anything except the national curriculum. The meal was beginning to get on his nerves; he got up and went off for a cigarette. Unfortunately, it was at precisely that moment that the symbolists left, swinging their hips, without so much as a glance in their direction. It was probably this which triggered the incident.

Bruno was about ten metres from the table when he heard a loud whistle, or rather a strangled cry, high-pitched, almost inhuman. He turned around: Pierre-Louis was red-faced, his fists balled; from a standing start, he leapt onto the table. He took a deep breath and the wheezing from his chest stopped. He started to pace up and down the table, thumping himself on the head as the glasses and plates danced around him. He kicked out at everything within reach, screaming 'You can't do this! You can't treat me like this . . .' For once, he didn't stutter. It took five minutes to calm him down. He was admitted to the psychiatric ward of the hospital in Angoulême that evening.

At three a.m. Bruno woke with a start and scrabbled his way out of the tent, soaked in sweat. The Lieu was quiet, the moon was full and the monotonous croak of tree frogs filled the air. He sat by the pond and waited for daybreak. Just before dawn, he felt a little cold. The morning sessions would start at ten o'clock. At a quarter past ten he walked down to the pyramid. He hesitated outside the creative writing workshop, then went down to the next floor, where he studied the programme for the water-colour class for about 20 seconds before walking up the steps. The stairway was made up of straight flights each with a curved section in the middle. The steps grew wider towards the middle and narrowed again as one approached the landing. In the curve was a step which was wider than all the others. It was here that Bruno sat, leaning against the wall. He began to feel happy.

As a schoolboy, he would often sit on a step between floors just after class began; these were his rare moments of happiness. Midway between landings, he would lean back against the wall, eyes half-closed, sometimes wide open, and wait. Of course, someone might come, in which case he would have to get up, pick up his schoolbag and walk quickly to his classroom where class had already started. But often no one came, and here on the grey tiled steps (he wasn't in History class any more, he wasn't in Physics class yet) everything was so peaceful; then gently, almost furtively, his heart soared in short bursts towards joy.

The circumstances were very different now: he had chosen to come to the Lieu; chosen to take part in its activities. Upstairs, there was a creative writing class; just below, a workshop on watercolour; further down there would be classes on massage or holotropic breathing; further still, the African dance classes had clearly started up again. All around human beings were living, breathing, striving for pleasure or trying to develop their personal potential. On every floor, human beings were improving, or trying to improve, their social, sexual or professional skills or find their place within the cosmos. They were 'bettering themselves', in the expression commonly used in the Lieu. Bruno was being to feel a little tired. He had stopped wishing, he had stopped wanting, he was nowhere. Slowly, by degrees his spirit soared to a state of nothingness, the sheer joy that comes of not being part of the world. For the first time since he was 13, Bruno was happy.

Would you mind telling me where I might find the nearest sweet shop?

He went back to his tent and slept for three hours. When he awoke he was still happy, and he had a hard-on. Sexual frustration in the human male manifests itself as a dull ache in the lower abdomen as though the sperm flows up, and shooting pangs towards the chest. The penis itself is painful, constantly hot and slightly sweaty; Bruno had not

masturbated since Sunday, which had probably been a
mistake. The remaining myth of Western civilisation was
that sex was something to do; something expedient, a
diversion. He put on a pair of swimming trunks and
slipped some condoms into his bag – snorting with
laughter as he did so. He had been carrying condoms
around for years and he had never used one of them – after
all, whores always had their own.

The beach at Meschers was crawling with wankers in
shorts and bimbos in thongs; it was reassuring. He bought
a portion of chips and circulated among the holidaymakers before settling on a girl of about 20 with beautiful
breasts – round, firm and pert, with caramel-coloured
nipples. 'Hello . . .' he said. He waited a beat; the girl
frowned nervously. 'Hello,' he said again. 'Would you
mind telling me where I might find the nearest sweet
shop?'

'Hmm?' she said, raising herself up onto one elbow. It
was then that he noticed she was wearing a Walkman; he
backed off, waving his arm like Peter Falk in *Columbo*.
There was no point in pushing it, it was just too
complicated, too late-twentieth-century.

As he walked through the crowd towards the surf he
tried to keep an image of the girl's breasts in his mind.
Suddenly, directly in front of him, three teenage girls
stepped out of the waves. They couldn't be more than 14,
he decided. He noticed their towels and spread his own
on the sand a couple of feet away. They hadn't even
noticed him. He quickly took off his tee shirt and draped

it across his lap, rolled onto his side and took out his penis. With the precision of synchronised swimmers, the girls rolled down the tops of their swimsuits to get the sun on their breasts. Before he had time to touch himself, Bruno came violently on to his tee shirt. He let out a moan and rolled over on the sand. It was done.

The primitive rituals of 'Happy Hour'

The high point of social life at the Lieu du Changement was over apéritifs, which usually featured live music. That evening there were three guys playing tom-toms to 50 or so guests who waved their arms and danced on the spot. These were harvest dances, apparently, which some of them had been practising in the African dance workshop; customarily, after a number of hours, some of them would go into a trance – or pretend to go into a trance. The archaic or literal sense of the word *trance* is fear, to be numb with fear at the idea of imminent danger. 'I would rather leave my home than go on living through such a trance' (Émile Zola). Bruno offered the Catholic girl a glass of Pineau des Charentes. 'What's your name?' he asked.

'Sophie,' she replied.

'Not dancing?'

'No, I don't really like African dance, it's too . . .'

Too what? He understood her dilemma. Too primitive? Certainly not. Too rhythmic? Even that bordered on racism. There was nothing you could say about African fucking dance. Poor Sophie was trying her best. Her face was pretty: pale skinned with blue eyes framed by her dark hair. She had small breasts, but they were probably very sensitive. She had to be Breton.

'Are you from Brittany?' he asked.

'Yes – from Saint-Brieuc!' she replied happily. 'But I really like Brazilian dance . . .' she added, obviously trying to absolve herself for her dislike of African dance. Much more of this and Bruno would get really irritated. He was starting to get pissed off with the world's stupid obsession with Brazil. What was so great about Brazil? As far as he knew, Brazil was a shitheap full of morons obsessed with football and Formula One. It was the *ne plus ultra* of violence, corruption and misery. If ever a country were loathsome that country, specifically, was Brazil.

'Sophie,' announced Bruno, 'I could go on holiday to Brazil tomorrow. I'd look around a *favela*. The windows of the minibus would be bulletproof. In the morning, I'd go sightseeing. Check out eight-year-old murderers who dream of growing up to be gangsters; thirteen-year-old prostitutes dying of AIDS. I'd spend the afternoon at the beach surrounded by filthy rich drug barons and pimps. I'm sure that in such a passionate, not to mention liberal, society I could shake off the malaise of Western civilisation. You're right, Sophie: I'll go straight to a travel agent as soon as I get home.'

Sophie considered him for a moment, her expression thoughtful, her brow lined with concern. Eventually she said sadly, 'You must have really suffered . . .'

'D'you know what Nietzsche said about Shakespeare,

Sophie?' said Bruno. ' "The man must have suffered greatly to have such passion for playing the fool!" Personally, I've always thought that Shakespeare was overrated, but now that I think about it, he is a fool.' He stopped and realised to his surprise that he was beginning to suffer. Sometimes women were so compassionate; they met aggression with empathy, cynicism with tenderness. No man would do such a thing. 'Sophie,' he said with heartfelt emotion, 'I'd like to lick your pussy . . .' but she didn't hear him. She had turned away and struck up a conversation with the ski instructor who had groped her arse three days earlier. Bruno stood, speechless for a moment or two before crossing the lawn to the car park. The Leclerc supermarket at Royan was open until ten o'clock. As he wandered through the aisles he thought about Aristotle's claim that small women were of a different species. 'A small man still seems to me to be a man,' he wrote, 'whereas a small woman appears to me to belong to a new type of animal.' How could you square such a strange assertion with the habitual good sense of the Stagirite? He bought a bottle of whisky and a packet of ginger biscuits. By the time he got back to the Lieu it was dark. As he passed the jacuzzi, he heard whispering and a muffled laugh. He stopped and peeked through the branches, plastic bag in hand. There were two or three couples; they were quiet now, there was only the rippling sound of the water. The moon came from behind the clouds. At that moment another couple arrived and began to undress. The whispering began again. Bruno put down the plastic bag, took out his penis and started to masturbate. He ejaculated quickly, just as the woman was slipping into the warm water. It was Friday night, he was going to have to extend his stay by a week. He had to sort himself out, find a woman, talk to people.

6

On Friday night Bruno barely slept. He had a bad dream. He was a piglet, his little body fat and glabrous. With the other little piglets, he was sucked by a vortex into a vast, dark tunnel, its walls rusted. He was carried by the slow drift of the current. At times, his feet touched the bottom, but then a powerful swell would carry him on. Sometimes he could make out the whitish flesh of his companions as they were brutally sucked down. He struggled through the darkness and a silence broken only by the scraping of their trotters on the metal walls. As they plunged deeper, he could hear the dull sound of machines in the distance. He began to realise that the vortex was pulling them towards turbines with huge, razor-sharp blades.

Later, he saw his severed head lying in a meadow below the drainage pipe. His skull had been split from top to bottom, though what remained, lying on the grass, was still conscious. He knew that ants would slowly work their way into the exposed brain tissue to eat away at the neurons and finally he would slip into unconsciousness. As he waited, he looked at the horizon through his one remaining eye. The grass seemed to stretch out forever. Huge cogwheels turned under a metallic sky. Perhaps this was the end of time; at least the world that he had known had ceased to exist.

Over breakfast he met the leader of the watercolour workshop – a veteran of '68 who lived in Brittany. His name was Paul Le Dantec, one of the founding members of the Lieu; his brother was the current manager. He was the archetypal old hippie: long grey beard, Indian waistcoat and an ankh on a chain round his neck. At 55 this oldster lived a peaceful life. He would get up at dawn to go bird-watching in the hills, then sit down to a bowl of coffee and Calvados, and roll a cigarette amid the human traffic. The watercolour class didn't start until ten o'clock; he had all the time in the world to chat.

'As a veteran of the Lieu,' said Bruno, laughing to establish a sense of complicity, however false, 'you must have a lot of stories about this place when it first opened – the Seventies, sexual liberation . . .'

'Liberation my arse,' groaned the old hippie. 'There were always women who could knit in the middle of an orgy and there were always blokes who just stood there waving their dicks. Take it from me, nothing much has changed.'

'But I thought AIDS changed everything,' said Bruno.

'I suppose it's true that it used to be easier for men,'

admitted the watercolourist. 'You'd find a mouth or a pussy wide open and you could dive right in – no standing on ceremony. But for that, it had to be a proper orgy, invitation only, usually only couples. I tell you, I saw women with their legs wide open, wet and up for it, spending the whole evening masturbating because no one would fuck them. They couldn't even find someone to get them off – you had to be able to get it up first.'

'So, what you're saying,' said Bruno thoughtfully, 'is that there never was real sexual liberation – just another form of seduction.'

'Oh, yeah . . .' agreed the hippie, 'there's always been a lot of seduction.'

This didn't exactly sound promising. Still, it was Saturday, so there would probably be a crop of new-comers. Bruno decided to chill out, take things as they came, go with the flow. He would try to get through the day without bother, and, ideally, without incident. At about eleven o'clock that evening he went down to the jacuzzi. A delicate haze rose above the gentle roar of the water, lit by the full moon. He approached soundlessly. A couple were entwined on the far side of the pool; it looked as if she had mounted him like a horse. 'I have as much right as they have . . .' thought Bruno furiously. He undressed quickly and slipped into the jacuzzi. The night air was cool, the water, by contrast, was deliciously warm. Between the twisted branches of the pine trees he could see the stars, he could feel himself relax a little. The couple paid no attention to him; the girl continued to pump up and down on the guy, she started to whimper. It was impossible to see her face. The man began to breathe heavily too. The woman's rhythm began to pick up tempo; she threw her head back and, for a moment, the moon lit up her breasts, her face still hidden behind a dark mass of hair. Then she crushed herself against her partner and wrapped herself around him; his breathing was heavier now, then he let out a long moan and was silent.

They stayed there for a minute, wrapped around one another, then the man stood up and got out of the pool. He unrolled the condom on his penis before dressing. Bruno was surprised to see that the woman was not leaving with him. The man's footsteps died away and there was silence once more. She stretched out her legs in the water. Bruno did likewise. He felt her foot on his thigh, brushing against his penis. With a soft splash she pushed herself from the edge and came to him. Clouds shadowed the moon; the woman was barely a foot away but still he could not make out her face. He felt an arm against his thigh and another wrap around his shoulder. Bruno pressed his body to hers, his face against her small, firm breasts. He let go of the edge and gave himself up to the moment. He could feel her drawing him towards the centre of the pool, then slowly she began to turn. He felt the muscles in his neck give, his head felt suddenly heavy. Below the surface, the gentle murmur of the water became a thunderous roar. He saw the stars as they wheeled slowly overhead. He relaxed into her arms, his erect penis broke the surface of the water. She moved her hands gently, barely a caress. He was completely weightless. Her long hair brushed his stomach and then her tongue touched the tip of his glans. His whole body shuddered with pleasure. She closed her lips and slowly, so slowly, took him in her mouth. He closed his eyes, his body shuddering in ecstasy. The thunderous underwater roar was regular and reassuring. When he felt her lips at the base of his penis, he could feel the movement of her throat. He felt himself flooded with intense waves of pleasure and buoyed up by the thunderous whirlpool. All at once he felt very hot. She gently allowed her throat to contract around him; all the energy in his being rushed suddenly to his penis. He howled as he came; he had never felt such fulfilment in his life.

7

Conversation in a Caravan

Christiane's caravan was about 50 yards from his tent. She turned the lights on, took out a bottle of Bushmills and poured two glasses. Slim, shorter than Bruno, she had probably been quite pretty once, but her delicate features had faded a little and her skin was blotchy. Only her silky, black hair remained perfect. Her eyes were blue and a little sad. She was probably about 40.

'I just get that way sometimes, I just get it on with everyone,' she said. 'The only rule is that if they want to fuck, they wear a condom.'

She moistened her lips and sipped the whiskey. Bruno watched her. She had thrown on a grey sweatshirt but nothing else. The curve of her mons was beautiful even if her labia sagged a little.

'I'd like to make you come, too,' he said.

'There's no rush,' she said. 'Finish your drink. You can

sleep here if you like, there's plenty of room,' she nodded to the double bed.

They talked about caravan rentals. Christiane couldn't sleep in a tent, she had back problems. 'It's pretty bad,' she said. 'Most guys prefer a blow job,' she said, 'they're not really into fucking, they find it difficult to keep it up. But take some guy's cock in your mouth and he's like a little kid again. I think feminism has hit them harder than they like to admit.'

'There are worse things than feminism,' Bruno said soberly. He knocked back half of the whiskey before deciding to continue: 'Have you known the Lieu long?'

'Pretty much since the beginning,' she explained. 'I stopped coming while I was married. Now I come two or three times a year. When it started up, it was very alternative, very New Left; now it's more New Age. It hasn't really changed much. They were into oriental mysticism here in the Seventies; now it's more about jacuzzis and massage. It's a nice place – but it's a bit sad. There's a lot less violence here than in the outside world. The whole spiritual thing makes the pick-up lines seem less brutal. A lot of women suffer here, though. Men who grow old alone have it easier than older women. They drink cheap booze and fall asleep, their breath stinks, then they wake up and start all over again; they tend to die young. Women take tranquillisers, go to yoga classes, see a shrink; they live a lot longer and suffer a lot more. They try to trade on their looks, even when they know their bodies are sad and ugly. They get hurt, but they do it anyway, because they can't give up the need to be loved. That's one delusion they'll keep to the bitter end. Once she's past a certain age, a woman might get to rub up against some guy's cock, but she has no chance of being loved. That's men for you.'

'Christiane,' Bruno said gently, 'I think you're being a bit harsh . . . I mean, I'm here and I want to make you happy.'

'I believe you. I have a feeling you're a nice man. Selfish, but nice.'

She took off her sweatshirt and lay across the bed. She placed it under her buttocks and spread her legs. Bruno started by licking around her cunt for a while before tonguing her clitoris in short, quick strokes. Christiane exhaled with a deep moan. 'Put your finger in . . .' she said. Bruno did as she asked, turning himself so he could caress her breasts as his tongue continued to flicker over her pussy. He could feel her nipples harden; he looked up. 'Don't stop, please . . .' she said. He laid his head on her thigh and stroked her clitoris with his index finger. Her labia minor began to swell. A sudden burst of joy overwhelmed him and he began to lick her tenderly. Christiane let out a little whimper. For an instant, he saw his mother's thin, crumpled vagina again and then the image dissolved. He fingered her clitoris faster as his tongue lapped her labia eagerly. Her belly began to redden and her breath came in short gasps. She was wet now and deliciously salty. Bruno paused for a moment and then slipped a finger into her anus and another into her vagina as the tip of his tongue fluttered quickly over her clitoris. Her body shuddered and jolted as she came. He stayed there, face pressed against her moist vulva, he reached his hand towards her and felt her fingers interlace with his. 'Thanks,' she said. Then she got up, put on her sweatshirt and filled their glasses again.

'It was really good – in the jacuzzi just now . . .' said Bruno. 'We didn't say a word and when I felt your lips on my cock, I still hadn't really seen your face. There was something pure about it – no seduction.'

'It all depends on Krause's corpuscles,' Christiane said, smiling. 'Sorry – I'm a professor of natural science.' She took a gulp of Bushmills . . . 'The shaft of the clitoris and the glans of the penis are covered in Krause's corpuscles, rich in nerve endings. When touched, they cause a powerful flow of endorphins in the brain. The penis and the clitoris have about the same number of Krause's corpuscles – sexual equality goes that far, but there's more to it than that – as you know. I was very much in love with my husband. When I stroked his penis or licked it, I worshipped it; I loved to feel him inside me. I was proud that I could make him hard. I kept a photograph of his erect cock in my wallet, it was like a sacred image to me. My greatest pleasure was to give him pleasure. Then he left me for someone younger. Just now, I could tell you didn't really like my pussy – it already looks a bit like an old woman's cunt. Increased collagen bonding and the breakdown of elastin during mitosis in older people means that human tissue gradually loses its suppleness and firmness. When I was twenty, I had a beautiful pussy, now I know that my labia are sagging a little.'

Bruno drained his glass; he couldn't think of anything to say to her. Shortly afterwards, they lay down. He put his arm around Christiane's waist and they fell asleep.

8

Bruno was the first to wake. High up in the trees a bird sang. The covers had slipped off Christiane during the night. Her buttocks were still beautiful, round and very inviting. He remembered a line from *The Little Mermaid*. He had it at home, on a scratched 45 with the Frères Jacques singing the '*La chanson des Matelots*' on vinyl. She had endured many trials, given up her voice, her home, her beautiful mermaid's tail; all in the hope that she might become a woman and win the love of a prince. In the dead of night, a storm cast her onto a beach and here she drank the magic elixir. A pain ripped through her, so terrible that she felt as though she had been cut in two. She slipped into unconsciousness. At this point, a sequence of different chord changes seemed to open up a different world. A woman's voice, the storyteller, said the words which had so marked Bruno as a child: *'When she awoke, the sun was shining and the prince stood before her.'*

Then he thought about the conversation he had had with Christiane the night before; he thought he might grow to love her sagging, but soft labia. He had a hard-on, as he did every morning, as did every man. In the half-light of dawn, Christiane's face seemed pale surrounded by the thick mass of her black hair. Her eyes opened slightly as he entered her. She seemed a little surprised, but she parted her legs. He began to move in her, but he could feel himself soften as he did. He felt terribly sad about this, but worried and ashamed too. 'Do you want me to use a condom?' he asked. 'Yeah, please,' she said, 'they're in the washbag on the side.' He tore open the packet – they were Durex Technica. Of course, by the time he got the rubber on, he had completely lost his hard-on. 'I'm really sorry,' he said. 'Don't worry about it,' she said gently, 'come back to bed.' Clearly AIDS had been a blessing for men of his generation. Sometimes by the time the condom was out of the packet, they were completely flaccid. 'I never really got used to them . . .' This little ritual over, and their manhood safe, in principle, they could go back to bed, snuggle up against the woman and fall asleep in peace.

After breakfast they walked down past the pyramid. The pond was deserted. They lay down in the sunny meadow. Christiane slipped off his shorts and began to masturbate him. She wanked him gently, delicately. Later when, at her instigation, they joined the wife-swapping set, Bruno came to realise that this was a rare quality. Most of the women in the group jerked men off crudely; they had no technique. They gripped the cock too tightly and shook it frantically, probably trying to imitate something they had seen in a porn film. It might have been spectacular on screen, but on the receiving end, it was mediocre, sometimes painful. Christiane, on the other hand, worked delicately, wet her fingers regularly, flickered over the most sensitive areas. A woman wearing an Indian tunic passed them and sat at the edge of the water. Bruno inhaled deeply and held back, not wanting to come yet. Christiane smiled at him; the sun was beginning to get warm. He realised that his second week at the Lieu would be very gentle. Perhaps they would see each other afterwards, they might grow old together. From time to time she would offer him a little physical pleasure, together they would live out their declining libidos. They would go on like that for years and then it would be over; they would be old, for them the comedy of sexual manners would be over.

While Christiane was taking a shower, Bruno studied the beauty care 'daily protection for young-looking skin, now in micro-capsules' she had bought at Leclerc the day before. The packaging made much of the 'new' concept of 'micro-capsules', but the directions, which were more comprehensive, outlined three principal actions: protection against the sun's harmful rays, all-day moisturising action and the elimination of free radicals. His reading was interrupted by the arrival of Catherine, the reinvented feminist turned Egyptian tarot reader. She had just come from a workshop on personal development and was itching to talk about it. *A successful career through dance* was about finding your vocation through a succession of symbolic games intended to liberate the 'hero within' each student. By the end of the first day, it was apparent that Catherine's personality had aspects of the witch, but also aspects of the lioness, which usually pointed to a career in sales management.

'Hmm . . .' said Bruno.

Just then, Christiane arrived back, a towel around her waist. Catherine trailed off, visibly irritated. She beat a rapid retreat on the pretext that she had a workshop on *Zen and the Art of the Tango*.

'I thought you were doing *Tantric Accounting* . . .' shouted Christiane as she disappeared round the corner.

'Do you know her?'

'Oh, yeah – I've known the bitch for twenty years, pretty much since this place opened.'

She shook her hair and wrapped the towel into a turban. They walked back up together. Bruno had the sudden desire to take her hand. He did.

'Never could abide feminists . . .' continued Christiane when they were halfway up the hill. 'Stupid bitches always going on about the washing up and the division of labour; they could never shut up about the washing up. Oh, sometimes they'd talk about cooking or vacuuming, but their favourite topic was the washing up. In a few short years, they managed to turn every man they knew into an impotent, whinging neurotic. Once they'd done that, it was always the same story – they started going on about how there were no real men any more. They usually ended up ditching their boyfriends for a quick fuck with some macho idiot. I've always been struck by the way intelligent women go for bastards, brutes and ass-holes. Anyway, they fuck their way through a couple of bastards, maybe more if they're really pretty, and wind up with a kid. Then they're off making jam and collecting recipe cards from *Marie Claire*. It's always the same story, I've seen it happen a dozen times.'

'That's all in the past now,' said Bruno in a conciliatory tone.

They spent the afternoon by the pool. On the opposite side, the teenage girls were jumping up and down listen-ing to a Walkman. 'Cute, aren't they?' said Christiane. 'The blonde one, the one with the small breasts, is really pretty . . .' Then she lay down on the bath towel. 'Pass me the suntan lotion.'

Christiane didn't attend any of the workshops. In fact, she was rather condescending about what she referred to as 'that crazy shit'. 'Maybe I'm being a bit hard,' she added, 'but I know what the veterans of 'sixty-eight are like when they hit forty, I'm practically one myself. They have cobwebs in their cunts and they grow old alone. Talk to them for five minutes and you'll see that they don't believe any of this bullshit about chakras and crystal healing and light vibrations. They force themselves to believe it and sometimes they do for an hour or two. They feel the presence of the Angel or the flower blossoming within but then the workshop's over and they're still ugly, still ageing, still alone. So they cry for a bit – have you noticed? They do a lot of crying here – especially after the Zen workshops. They don't have much choice really – most of them have money problems too. A lot of them have been in therapy and they're completely broke. Mantras and tarot may be stupid, but they're a lot cheaper than therapy.'

'Or the dentist . . .' said Bruno obscurely. He laid his head on her thighs and knew that he would fall asleep there.

When it got dark they went back to the jacuzzi; he asked her not to let him come. Back in the caravan, they made love. 'Don't bother . . .' said Christiane when he reached for the condoms. When he entered her, he could tell she was happy. One of the most surprising things about physical love is the sense of intimacy it creates the moment there is any trace of mutual affection. Suddenly – even if you met the night before – you can confide things to your lover that you would not tell another living soul. And so, that night, Bruno told Christiane things that he had never told anyone – not even Michel – much less his therapist. He talked to her about his childhood, his grandmother's death, how he was bullied at boarding school. He told her about his adolescence, about masturbating in the train with a girl only a few feet away; he told her about the summers he spent at his father's house. Christiane stroked his hair and listened.

They spent the week together, and the evening before Bruno left they had dinner at a seafood restaurant in Saint-Georges-de-Didonne. The air was warm and still, the candlelight on the tablecloth barely flickered. The restaurant overlooked the estuary of the Gironde. In the distance they could just make out the headland at Grave. 'When I look at the moonlight on the water,' said Bruno, 'it's clear to me we have nothing – absolutely nothing to do with this world.'

'Do you really have to leave?'

'Yeah. I have to spend a couple of weeks with my son. I should really have left last week, but this time I really have to go. His mother's already booked her holiday – she's flying the day after tomorrow.'

'How old is your son?'

'Twelve.'

Christiane sipped her Muscadet and thought. She was wearing a long dress and had put on make-up. She looked like a girl. Her breasts were just discernible through the lace blouse of the dress; the reflected candles blazed small flames in her eyes. 'I think I might be a little bit in love . . .' she said. Bruno waited, hardly daring to breathe, perfectly motionless. 'I live with my son in Noyon,' she went on. 'Things were okay until he was thirteen. I suppose he missed his father, I don't know . . . Do kids really need a father? One thing I do know, his father didn't need him. Oh, he took him to the cinema or to McDonald's a couple of times in the beginning, though he always brought him back early. After a while he came round less and less often. Then he moved down south to be with his girlfriend, and he stopped visiting altogether. After that, I brought him up on my own. Maybe I let him get away with too much. About two years ago he started going out a lot, hanging around with a bad crowd. Noyon can be pretty violent – you'd be surprised. There're a lot of blacks and Arabs, the *Front National* got forty per cent of the vote in the last election. I live on a housing estate in the suburbs. I've had my letter box broken into, I can't leave anything in the cellar. I'm scared sometimes. Sometimes I hear gunshots. When I get back from school I basically barricade myself in the apartment and I never go out at night. Sometimes I go on the Minitel and hang out in the chat rooms, that's about it. My son gets in late – sometimes he doesn't come home at all. I don't say anything. I'm terrified of him.'

'Are you far from Paris?'

She smiled. 'No. Noyon is out in the Oise – it's about seventy kilometres . . .' She stopped and smiled again, her face for a moment filled with gentleness and hope. 'I used to love life,' she went on, 'I loved life. I'm very tactile, very demonstrative, and I always loved making love. Something went wrong. I'm not really sure what, but something went wrong with my life.'

Bruno had already folded up his tent and packed his things into the car; he spent the last night in the caravan. In the morning, he tried to make love to Christiane but he couldn't – he was too nervous, too agitated. 'Come all over me,' she said. She smeared his come over her face, her breasts. 'Stop by and see me,' she said again as he closed the door. He promised he would. It was Saturday, the first of August.

9

Unusually, Bruno drove back along minor roads. He stopped just before Parthenay. He knew he needed to think, but what exactly did he need to think about? He was parked on a peaceful, boring stretch of countryside by a canal where the water was so still it seemed motionless. Water plants sprouted or rotted, it was difficult to say which. The silence was broken by a faint trilling sound – insects, probably. As he stretched out on the grassy bank, he noticed a gentle current, the canal was flowing slowly to the south. He could not see a single frog.

Just before he started university in October 1975, Bruno moved into the studio his father had bought for him. He felt a whole new life beckoning him. He was quickly disappointed. There were girls, of course, in fact rather a lot of girls enrolled in the arts faculty at Censier, but they all seemed to be taken, or if they weren't, they weren't prepared to be taken by him. In an attempt to make friends he went to every lecture, every tutorial, and quickly became an exceptional student. He watched the girls in the cafeteria, listened to them chatting about going out, meeting friends, inviting each other to parties. He started to eat. His diet quickly settled into a nutritious trip down the Boulevard Saint-Michel. He would start with a hot dog from the takeaway on the corner of the rue Gay-Lussac; further down, he would have a slice of pizza or a kebab. At McDonald's on the Boulevard Saint-Germain, he'd stuff himself with cheeseburgers washed down with coke or a banana milkshake before staggering down the rue de la Harpe to finish off with some Arab pastries. On his way home he would stop in front of the Cinéma Latin which had a porno double-feature. Sometimes he would stand for half an hour pretending to look at the bus time-table in the always vain hope of seeing a woman or a couple go inside. More often than not, he would end up buying a ticket. He always felt better once he was inside; the usherette was the soul of discretion. The men sat far apart – always leaving several seats between them. They would quietly wank watching *Naughty Nurses, The Hitchhiker Always Comes Twice, Teacher Spreads Her Legs, The Wild Bunch,* whatever was on. He had to be careful as he left: the cinema was on the Boulevard Saint-Michel, he could easily bump into a girl from college. Usually, he waited for someone else to leave and walked just behind him – it seemed less humiliating that he might have gone to a porn movie with a friend. He usually got back just before midnight and read for a while: Chateaubriand or

Rousseau. He decided to change his life once or twice a week, to take some radical new direction. This is how it went: first, he would take off his clothes and look at himself in the mirror. He had to confront his shame head on, to face up to the humiliating sight of his fat belly, his flabby cheeks and his sagging buttocks. Then, he would turn out the lights and, feet together, arms folded across his chest, he would drop his head forward the better to go into himself. Then he would breathe slowly, deeply, expanding his chest and his revolting belly, then exhaling slowly, pronouncing a number as he did so. It was essential not to let his concentration waver – every number was important, but the most significant were four, eight and, the final number, sixteen. He would exhale completely as he reached sixteen; when he raised his head he would be a new man, finally ready to face life, to swim with the flow. He would no longer feel guilty or ashamed; he would eat properly and would behave normally around girls. 'Today is the first day of the rest of your life.'

This little ritual had no effect whatever on his self-esteem, but was sometimes effective in controlling his overeating; sometimes he would manage to get through two days before backsliding. He put the failure down to lack of concentration, but soon afterward he would begin to believe again. He was still young.

One evening he ran into Annick as he came out of the Tunisian bakery. He had not seen her since their brief meeting in the summer of '74. She was uglier now, practically obese. She wore thick, square glasses with heavy black frames that made her brown eyes seem smaller and accentuated the sickly pallor of her skin. They had coffee together, both of them distinctly uneasy. She was studying literature too, at the Sorbonne; she had a bedsit nearby, with a view onto the Boulevard Saint-Michel. She gave him her telephone number when they parted. In the weeks that followed he went to see her several times. She was too ashamed of her body to get undressed, but she offered to give him a blow job. She didn't say it had anything to do with her body, she said it was because she wasn't on the pill. 'Really, I prefer it . . .' She stayed in every night, never went out. She took slimming pills, tried dieting, but nothing seemed to work. Once or twice Bruno tried to take off her trousers, but she just curled up and pushed him away fiercely. He gave up and took out his penis. She would suck him off quickly, a little brutally, and he would come in her mouth. Sometimes they talked about their studies, but not often; he would usually leave quickly. True, she wasn't very pretty and he would have been embarrassed to be seen with her in the street, in a restaurant or in a cinema queue. He'd stuff himself with Tunisian pastries until he felt sick and then go to see her, get a blow job and leave. It was probably best that way.

It was a mild night, the night Annick died. It was the end of March, but already it was a spring evening. In the patisserie, Bruno bought an almond turnover, then walked down along the banks of the Seine. The commentary from the loudspeakers of a *bateau-mouche* echoed off the walls of Notre-Dame. He chewed his way through the sticky, honey-covered pastry only to feel more disgusted with himself than ever. He thought perhaps he should try it right here, in the centre of Paris, with the whole world looking on. He closed his eyes, brought his feet together and folded his arms across his chest. Slowly, carefully, with complete concentration, he began to count. When he reached the magic number he opened his eyes, lifted his head. The *bateau-mouche* had disappeared, the riverbank was deserted, the air was as mild as before.

Two policemen were trying to disperse a small crowd gathered outside Annick's building. Bruno went a little closer. The body of a girl lay smashed and strangely twisted on the pavement. Her shattered arms seemed to form two strange limbs around her head. Her face, or what was left of it, lay in a pool of blood. She had obviously brought her hands up to her face in a last, desperate reflex to protect herself from the impact. 'Jumped from the seventh floor,' said a nearby woman, with odd satisfaction, 'killed stone dead.' At that moment an ambulance arrived and two men got out carrying a stretcher. As they lifted her body he saw her shattered skull and turned away. The ambulance drove off in a howl of sirens. So ended Bruno's first love.

The summer of '76 was probably the worst time of his life. He had just turned 20. The heat was stifling, with not a breath of cool air even at night. Girls wore short flimsy dresses which stuck to their bodies with sweat. He walked around all day, his eyes popping out with lust. At night he would get up and go walking through the dark streets of Paris, stopping for coffee on café terraces, hanging around outside nightclubs. He didn't know how to dance. He had a permanent hard-on. He felt as though what was between his legs was a piece of sweaty, putrefying meat devoured by worms. Several times he tried to talk to girls in the street only to be humiliated. At night he would stare at himself in the mirror. He noticed that his hair, which was plastered to his head with sweat, was already beginning to recede. The folds of flesh were obvious even through his shirt. He started visiting sex shops and peepshows which only served to aggravate his suffering. For the first time, he turned to prostitutes.

A subtle but definitive change had occurred in Western society during 1974 and 1975, thought Bruno to himself. He was still lying on the grassy bank by the canal; he had rolled his linen jacket into a ball as a pillow. He tore up a clump of coarse, damp grass. During those years when he was desperately trying to fit in, Western society had tipped towards something dark and dangerous. In the summer of 1976 it was already apparent that everything would end badly. Born of frustrated desire, physical violence, the supreme manifestation of this focus on the individual, was once again about to flare up in the West.

10

Julian and Aldous

*When it is necessary to modify or renew fundamental doctrine,
the generations sacrificed to the era during which the
transformation takes place remain essentially alienated from
that transformation, and often become directly hostile to it.*
(Auguste Comte – *Un Appel au Conservateurs*)

Towards noon, Bruno got back into his car and drove into
Parthenay. He decided he would take the motorway after
all. He stopped at a phone box and called his brother who
answered immediately. He was on his way back to Paris
and wondered if he could see him that evening. He
wouldn't be free the following evening – he was seeing his
son – but this evening. It was important. Michel was
impassive. 'If you want . . .' he said after a long pause. Like
most people, he found he loathed what the sociologists
and commentators liked to call the 'atomised society'.
Like most people, he thought that it was important to stay

in touch with one's family, even if it meant a certain amount of routine. For years he had spent every Christmas with his Aunt Marie-Thérèse at her house in Raincy, where she was living out her declining years with her husband. His uncle was practically deaf – a kind-hearted man, he had voted communist all his life and he refused to go to midnight mass – which always started an argument. Michel listened as the old man talked about emancipating the workforce and sipped *gentiane*; from time to time, he would yell something banal in response. Then the others arrived: his cousin Brigitte. He was fond of Brigitte; he wanted her to be happy, but the fact that her husband was a bastard made that rather unlikely. He was a sales rep with Bayer and cheated on his wife whenever he had the opportunity – as he was a handsome man and travelled a lot, he had rather a lot of opportunities. Every year, Brigitte's face fell a little more.

Michel stopped making his annual visit in 1990, but there was still Bruno. Family relationships last for years, sometimes decades – much longer, in fact, than any other kind of relationship; then, finally, they too gutter out.

When Bruno arrived at about nine o'clock, he had already had a couple of drinks and was eager to talk philosophy. 'I've always been struck by how accurate Huxley was in *Brave New World*,' he began before he had even sat down. 'It's phenomenal when you think he wrote it in 1932. Everything that's happened since simply brings us closer to the social model he described. Control of reproduction is more precise and eventually it will be completely dissociated from sex altogether, and procreation will take place in tightly guarded laboratories where perfect genetic conditions are ensured. Once that's happened any sense of family, of father–son relationship, will disappear. Pharmaceutical companies will break down the distinction between youth and age. In Huxley's world, a sixty-year-old man is as healthy as a man of twenty, he looks as young and has the same desires. When we get to the point that life can't be prolonged any further, we'll be killed off by voluntary euthanasia; quick, discreet, emotionless. The society Huxley describes in *Brave New World* is happy; tragedy and extremes of human emotion have disappeared. Sexual liberation has come to stay – everything favours instant gratification. Oh, there are little moments of depression, of sadness or doubt, but they're easily dealt with using advances in antidepressants. "One cubic centimetre cures ten gloomy sentiments." This is exactly the sort of world we are trying to create, this is the world we want to live in.

'Oh, I know, I know,' Bruno went on, waving his hand as if to dismiss an objection Michel had not voiced. 'Everyone says *Brave New World* is supposed to be a totalitarian nightmare, a vicious indictment of society, but that's hypocritical bullshit. *Brave New World* is our idea of heaven: genetic manipulation, sexual liberation, the war against age, the leisure society. This is precisely the world that we have tried – and so far failed – to create. The only thing in the book that rankles a little with our idea of equal opportunities – or meritocracy- is the idea of dividing society into castes where each performs tasks depending on their genetic make-up. But that's also the only point on which Huxley proved to be a false prophet. Advances in automation and robotics have made the whole idea pointless.

'Oh, Huxley was a terrible writer, I admit. His writing is pretentious and clumsy, his characters are bland ciphers, but he had one vital premonition – he understood that evolution of human society had for centuries been linked to scientific progress and would continue to be. He may have lacked style or finesse or psychological insight, but that's insignificant compared to the brilliance of the original concept. Huxley was the first writer to realise that biology would take over from physics as the driving force of society – long before the SF crowd.'

Bruno stopped and noticed that his brother seemed worried and gaunt. He was clearly tired and had been paying little attention. In fact, he had not bothered to go shopping for days. Poverty was usually less oppressive in the summer months, but there were more beggars than ever outside Monoprix this year. What would it be like when war came? Michel wondered as he watched the slow tread of the beggars from his bay window. When would war break out, and what would that mean to the back-to-school rush? Bruno poured himself another glass of wine; he was getting hungry and was surprised when his brother said in a weary voice:

'Huxley came from a large family of English biologists.

His grandfather was a friend of Darwin's. He wrote a lot in defence of Darwin's theory of natural selection. His father and his brother Julian were also famous biologists. They were pragmatic intellectuals in the English liberal mould – a tradition based more on observation and on experimental models than the French Enlightenment. As a boy, Huxley had the opportunity to meet many economists, judges and, particularly, scientists who were regular visitors to his father's house. He was certainly the only writer of his generation to realise the impact biology would have. It would all have happened much faster if it hadn't been for the war. Nazi ideology completely discredited eugenics and the idea of "improving the race", it was decades before anyone thought about it again.'

Michel went over to the bookshelf and took down *What Dare I Think?* and handed it to Bruno. 'It was written by Julian Huxley, Aldous' brother, and published in 1931, a year before *Brave New World*. All of the ideas his brother used in the novel: genetic manipulation and "improving the species" – including the human species – are here. All of the ideas are presented as something which society should strive for.'

Michel sat down again and wiped his forehead. 'In 1946, just after the war, Julian Huxley was appointed first Director General of UNESCO, which had just been founded. Aldous Huxley had just published *Brave New World Revisited*, in which he tried to portray the novel as a social satire. Years later, Aldous would become a major influence on hippie culture. He had always been in favour of sexual liberation, and he was a pioneer in the use of psychedelic drugs. The founding members of Esalen met him and were very influenced by his ideas. Then the New Age came along and recycled all the ideas of Esalen. Aldous Huxley is probably one of the most influential thinkers of the century.'

They went to a Chinese restaurant on the corner, which offered a set meal for two at 270 francs. Michel had not been out of his apartment for three days. 'I haven't eaten today,' he said, slightly surprised; he was still carrying the book.

'In 1962,' he went on as he stirred his sticky rice, 'Huxley published his last book, *Island*. It's set on a tropical island – probably based on Sri Lanka, from the scenery and the wildlife. On the island a civilisation has developed which has completely bypassed twentieth-century capitalism. The civilisation is technologically advanced, but still at one with nature. The natives are pacifists, and completely immune to family neuroses and Judaeo-Christian inhibitions. Nudism is accepted as normal, sensuality and sexuality are freely practised. The book was second-rate, but it was widely read and it had a big influence on hippies and through them on New Agers. If you look at it closely, the harmonious society in *Island* has a lot in common with *Brave New World*. Huxley was senile by that time; he didn't notice the similarities himself. The society in *Island* is as close to *Brave New World* as hippie liberalism is to bourgeois liberalism –

specifically the Swedish model of social democracy.'

He paused, dipped a prawn into the chilli sauce and then put down his chopsticks. 'Like his brother, Aldous was an optimist . . .' he said with something like disgust. Metaphysical mutation, having given rise to materialism and to modern science, in turn spawned two great trends: rationalism and individualism. Huxley's mistake was in not being able to predict the power struggle between rationalism and individualism – he crucially under-estimated the power of the individual faced with his own death. Individualism gives rise to the idea of freedom, the sense of self, the need to feel that one is superior to others. A rational society like the one he describes in *Brave New World* defuses the struggle. Economic rivalry – a metaphor for animals competing for territory – should not exist in a society of plenty, where the economy is strictly regulated. Sexual rivalry – genes competing over time – is meaning-less in a society where the link between sex and procreation has been broken. But Huxley forgets about individualism. He doesn't seem to understand that, stripped of their link with reproduction, lust and greed still exist – not as pleasure principles, but as forms of egotism. Why has the Swedish model of social democracy never triumphed over liberalism? Why has it never been applied to sexual satisfaction? Because the metaphysical mutation brought about by modern science depends on individuation, narcissism, malice and desire. Any philosopher, not just Buddhist or Christian, but any philosopher worthy of the name knows that, in itself, desire – unlike pleasure – is a source of suffering, pain and hatred. The Utopian solution – from Plato to Huxley by way of Fourier – is to do away with desire and the suffering it causes by satisfying it immediately. The opposite is true of the sex-and-shopping society we live in, where desire is marshalled and organised and blown up out of all proportion. For society to function, for competition to continue, people have to want more and more until it fills their lives and finally devours them.' He wiped his forehead, exhausted. He had not touched his food.

'There are some comforts,' said Bruno gently, 'some humanist touches which help people forget about death. In *Brave New World*, it's tranquillisers and antidepressants, in *Island* it's hallucinogens, meditation and some vague Hindu mysticism. In our own society, people usually use a mixture of both.'

'Julian Huxley gives over the second part of *What Dare I Think?* to discussing religion,' retorted Michel, clearly contemptuous. 'He's well aware that science and materialism have completely undermined traditional spirituality, but he also realises that society cannot function without religion. He spends about a hundred pages trying to set out the principles of a religion which could dovetail with science. The results aren't terribly convincing, and certainly society hasn't followed the route he suggested. In fact, any attempt at fusing science and religion is doomed because of the understanding of mortality, so cruelty and egotism have free reign. It's small comfort,' he concluded, 'but the same goes for love.'

11

After Bruno's visit, Michel took to his bed for two whole weeks. How could society function without religion? he wondered. It is difficult enough for an individual human being. For several days he studied the radiator beside his bed. It was a useful and ingenious device – when it was sufficiently cold to trigger the thermostat, the pipes filled with hot water – but how long could Western civilisation continue without religion? As a child, he liked to water the plants in the kitchen garden. He still had a small black and white photograph of himself at the age of six, holding the watering can, watched over by his grandmother. Later, he liked to go on errands – with the change from the bread money, he was allowed to buy a Carambar. Then he would fetch the milk from the farm, balancing the aluminium churn of still-warm milk at arm's length as he walked back along the track hedged with brambles. Now, the very thought of going to the supermarket was torture, though the stock changed regularly and they were always introducing new frozen ready-meals for one. He'd recently seen ostrich steak in the meat section of Monoprix.

To facilitate reproduction, the two helices which make up the DNA molecule separate before each attracts complementary nucleotides. The point at which they separate is dangerous, as it is then that random mutations – mostly harmful – occur. The impression of intellectual stimulation created by fasting is real, and by the end of the first week, Michel was convinced that perfect reproduction was impossible while DNA was in the form of a double helix. To obtain an exact reproduction across an indefinite succession of cellular generations, it would probably be necessary for the information to be stored in a compact structure – a Mœbius strip or a torus.

As a child, he could hardly bear to observe the deterioration of everything, the breakage, the wear and tear. For years, he continually taped two broken ends of a plastic ruler together again. With all the layers of Sellotape, the ruler was now lopsided. It was impossible to draw a straight line, so it didn't even fulfil the basic function of a ruler. Then it would break again and he would repair it, adding another layer of Sellotape, and put it back in his pencil case.

'One of the marks of Djerzinski's genius,' Frederic Hubczejak would write many years later, 'was his ability to go beyond his first intuition that sexual reproduction necessarily included harmful mutations. For millions of years, human societies had instinctively made the incontrovertible link between sex and death; a scientist who had irrefutably established such a link in molecular biological terms should consider his work done and leave it at that. Djerzinski, however, realised that it was necessary to look beyond sexual reproduction to study the general topological conditions of cell division.'

From his first week at primary school in Charny, Michel had been struck by the cruelty of the boys. It's true that the little beasts were farmers' sons, and therefore closer to animals than most. Nevertheless, it was startling to witness the instinctive, unaffected way they stabbed frogs with a compass point or a dip-pen; violet ink blossoming beneath the skin of the unfortunate animal as it slowly died. They would gather in a circle, their eyes bright, to watch its final agony. Another of their games was to cut the antennae off snails with their round-ended children's scissors. All of the snail's sensory awareness comes from its antennae, crowned by the eyes. Without them, the snail is reduced to a pulpous mass, suffering and bewildered. Michel quickly realised that he had to keep his distance from these young savages; there was less to fear from girls, however, who seemed altogether more delicate creatures. This instinctive notion of the world was confirmed every Thursday night when he watched *The Animal Kingdom*. Amid the carnage and brutality which was the lot of animals, the only glimmer of altruism was the maternal instinct, which had gradually evolved into mother love. The female squid, a pathetic little thing barely eight inches long, unhesitatingly attacks any wading bird which comes near her eggs.

Thirty years later he could not come to any other conclusion: women were indisputably better than men. They were gentler, more affectionate, more loving and more compassionate, they were rarely violent, selfish, cruel or self-centred. Moreover, they were more rational, more intelligent and more hard-working.

What on earth were men for? Michel wondered as he watched sunlight play across the closed curtains. In earlier times, when bears were more common, perhaps masculinity served a particular function, but for centuries now, men clearly served no useful purpose. For the most part, they assuaged their boredom playing squash, which was a lesser evil; but from time to time they felt the need to *change history* – which expressed itself in leading a revolution or starting a war somewhere. Aside from the senseless suffering they caused, revolutions and war destroyed the achievements of the past, forcing societies to build again. Without the notion of continuous progress, human evolution took random, irregular and violent turns for which men (with their predilection for risk and danger, their repulsive egotism, their volatile nature and their violent tendencies) were directly to blame. A society of women would be immeasurably superior, tracing a slow, unwavering progression, with no U-turns and no chaotic insecurity, towards a general happiness.

On the morning of 15 August he went out, hoping that the streets would be deserted, which they were. He took some notes which he would stumble on ten years later while writing his most important paper, *Towards a science of perfect reproduction*.

At precisely that moment Bruno, exhausted and despairing, was taking his son back to his ex-wife. Anne had just come back from a package tour with Nouvelles Frontières to Easter Island or Benin – he couldn't remember which. She had probably made friends with some of the women on the trip. They would have exchanged addresses and she would see them once or twice before growing bored of them. She would certainly not have met any men. She would take him aside for a minute or two and ask how things had been. He would say 'Fine' in the calm, self-assured tone that women seemed to like, before adding, a little facetiously, 'though Victor did watch a lot of television'. He would quickly feel uncomfortable, as since she had given up smoking, Anne wouldn't tolerate it in her tastefully furnished apartment. As he got up to leave, he would be choked with regret and wonder what he could do to make things better between them. He would kiss Victor quickly and then go. His son's holiday would be over.

In truth, the two weeks they had spent together had been a nightmare. Lying on his bed with a bottle of Bourbon in his hand, he would listen to the sounds of his son in the next room – the toilet flushing after he pissed, the buzz of the remote control. Just like his half-brother –

though he did not know it – he stared dumbly at the radiator for hours at a time. Victor slept on the sofa-bed in the living room and spent 15 hours a day watching television. The television was already on by the time Bruno woke up every morning – Victor would be watching cartoons on M6 with the sound down and his headphones on. He was not a bad boy and he clearly did not want to be rude, but he and his father had nothing to say to one another. Twice a day, Bruno would heat something in the microwave and they would eat at the table with hardly a word.

How had it come to this? Victor had just turned thirteen. Some years before, he spent his time drawing pictures he would bring over for his father to see. He copied characters from Marvel Comics: Fatalis, Fantastik, The Pharaoh of the Future – and made up stories for them. Sometimes they would play a game of Mille Bornes and on Sunday mornings they would go to the Louvre. When he was six, Victor had made a card for his father's birthday. On heavy drawing paper, he had written in big, multicoloured letters: 'I LOVE YOU DAD'. Now, that was all over, over and done with. Bruno knew that things would get worse, that they would move from mutual indifference to loathing. In a couple of years his son would want to go out with girls his own age; the same fifteen-year-old girls that Bruno lusted after. They would come to be rivals – which was the natural relationship between men. They would be like animals fighting in a cage; and the cage was time.

★

On the way home Bruno stopped at a local Arab grocers and bought two bottles of pastis. Then, before he drank himself into a stupor, he phoned his brother to arrange to see him the following day. When he arrived at Michel's apartment he found his brother, who had suddenly felt hungry after weeks of fasting, stuffing himself with Italian salami between great gulps of winc. 'Help yourself,' he said vaguely, 'help yourself.' It seemed to Bruno as though he was barely listening. It was like talking to a wall, or a psychiatrist, but he talked nonetheless.

'For years my son turned to me for love and I rejected him. I was depressed, I hated my life, I thought there'd be a time when I felt better. I didn't realise how quickly the years would go by. Between seven and twelve, a child is an astonishing animal – full of joy and convinced that the world is a rational place. He's full of love, and happy to accept what love we're prepared to give. After that it all goes wrong – it all goes horribly wrong.'

Michel bolted the last two slices of salami and poured himself another glass of winc. His hands were trembling violently. Bruno continued: 'There's nothing more stupid, more hateful and more obnoxious than a teenage boy, especially when he's with boys his own age. Boys are monsters, and stupid with it. They're unbelievably conformist – at puberty boys seem to epitomise everything that is evil in mankind and, because they're still children, they're unpredictable. When you think about it, sexuality has to be a corrupting influence. I don't know how people can live under the same roof as kids like that. I think the only reason they can stomach it is because their lives are completely empty, though I suppose my life is completely empty and I didn't manage it. In any case, the world is full of liars; people spend their lives telling appalling lies. "We're divorced now, but we're still good friends. I get to see my son every other weekend . . ." – that's bullshit. Complete bullshit. If people were honest, they don't give a toss about their kids, they don't really love them. In fact, I'd say men aren't capable of love; the emotion is completely alien to them. The only emotions they know are desire – in the form of pure animal lust – and male rivalry. There used to be a time when, late in life, a man would feel a certain affection for his spouse – though not before she'd borne his children, made a home for them, cooked, cleaned and proved herself in the bedroom. The sort of regard that meant they enjoyed sleeping in the same bed. It was probably not what women were looking for, it might even have been a delusion – but it was a powerful feeling. Strong enough that if men still became aroused and wanted to have a bit on the side from time to time, they didn't because they could not imagine life without their wives. If their wives left them, they hit the bottle and died soon afterwards – often in a matter of months. Children existed solely to inherit a man's genes, his moral code and his name. This was taken for granted among the aristocracy, but merchants, craftsmen and peasants also bought into the idea, it became the norm at every level of society. That's all gone now: I work for someone else, I rent my apartment from someone else, there's nothing for my son to inherit. I have no craft to teach him, I haven't a clue what he might do when he's older. By the time he grows up, the rules I lived by will be meaningless – the world will be completely different. If a man accepts the fact that everything must change, then his life is reduced to nothing more than the sum of his own experience – past and future generations mean nothing to him. That's how we live now. For a man to bring a child into the world now is meaningless. Women are different, because they never get past the need to have someone to love – which is certainly not true of men. It's bullshit to pretend that men need to spoil their children, play with them or cuddle them. I know people have been saying it for years, but it's bullshit. After divorce – once the family unit has broken down – a man's relationship with his children is nonsensical. Kids are a trap, they are the enemy – you have to pay for them all your life – and they outlive you.'

Michel got up and went into the kitchen to get a glass of water. He could see coloured wheels spinning in mid-air, he felt like throwing up. First, he had to stop his hands shaking. Bruno was right – paternal love was a lie, a fiction. A lie is useful if it transforms reality, he thought, but if it fails, then all that's left is the lie, the bitterness and the knowledge that it was a lie.

When he came back, Bruno was curled up on the sofa, as still as if he were dead. Night was falling over the towers and the heat of the day was just about bearable. Suddenly,

Michel noticed the empty cage where for years his canary had lived; he would have to throw it out, he had no intention of getting another pet. For a moment, he thought of his neighbour opposite – the girl who worked on *Vingt Ans* – he hadn't seen her for months. She had probably moved out. He forced himself to concentrate on his hands and noticed that they were shaking a little less. Bruno still had not moved; the silence between them continued for some minutes.

12

'I met Anne in 1981,' Bruno went on with a sigh. 'She wasn't really beautiful, but I was tired of jacking off. The good thing, though, was she had big tits. I've always liked big tits . . .' He sighed again. 'A WASP with big tits . . .' To Michel's surprise, his eyes were wet with tears. 'Later, her tits started to go south and our marriage went with them. I fucked up her whole life. That's one thing I can't forget – I fucked up her life. Is there any wine left?'

Michel went into the kitchen to get another bottle. This was all very strange; he knew Bruno had been seeing an analyst and that he'd stopped. Human beings always do what is least painful. For as long as it is less painful to confess, we talk; then we are silent, we give up, we are alone. If Bruno felt the need to talk about how his life was a failure, it was probably because he was hoping for something, some new beginning; it was probably a good sign.

'I'm not saying she was ugly,' Bruno went on, 'but her face was plain, charmless. She never had that luminous beauty that can light up a young girl's face. Her legs were too fat for her to wear mini-skirts, but I convinced her to wear short tops with no bra; looking at big tits from below is a real turn-on. She was a bit embarrassed at first, but she got used to it – she was very inexperienced sexually, she didn't understand the erotic and didn't know the first thing about lingerie. Here I am going on about her as if you didn't know her, but you did meet her, didn't you?'

'I came to your wedding . . .'

'That's true,' said Bruno, suddenly embarrassed and awkward. 'I remember being surprised you turned up. I was sure that you didn't want to see me again.'

'I *didn't* want to see you again.'

Michel thought about the wedding and wondered what on earth had persuaded him to go to that dismal ceremony. He remembered the depressingly austere room in the temple at Neuilly, half-filled with a congregation of the discreetly rich – her father was in finance. 'They were left-wing,' said Bruno, 'but then everyone was left-wing back then. They had no problem with me living in sin with their daughter. We only got married because she was pregnant. The usual story.' Michel could still hear the pastor's voice ringing out in the cold, bare room: something about Christ being true God and true man and about the new covenant between the Almighty and his people. In fact, he hadn't really understood what it was about. After three-quarters of an hour of this, he was nodding off: he woke with a start at the words: 'May the God of Israel bless you, he who had pity on the little children.' He had trouble working out what was going on. Were they Jews? He had to think for a moment before he registered that it was the same God. The pastor went on fawningly, his voice booming with sincerity: 'He that loveth his wife loveth himself: for no man ever yet hated his own flesh but nourisheth and cherisheth it, even as the Lord the Church: for we are members of his body, of his flesh and of his bones. For this cause shall a man leave his father and his mother and shall be joined unto his wife; and they two shall be one flesh. This is a great mystery: but I speak concerning Christ and the church.' It really was a peculiar phrase, '*they two shall be one flesh*'. Michel considered this for a time and glanced over at Anne: she was calm, focused, it seemed as though she was holding her breath; she was almost beautiful. Undoubtedly fired up by Saint Paul, the pastor continued with increasing passion: 'Lord, send thy blessing upon this thy servant who craves thy protection at the hour of her marriage. Grant that she may be in Christ a pure and faithful wife and that she, like Rachel, will be a comfort to her husband and that, like Sara, she will be faithful unto him. Grant that she will remain in the faith and observe thy commandments; cleave to her spouse and renounce all evil. May she be honoured for her modesty and respected for her humility and may she be instructed in the ways of the Lord. Grant, Lord, that she shall be fruitful in childbirth and that these two shall see their children's children to the third and fourth generation. May they grow together to a happy old age, and may they know the rest of the chosen in the Kingdom of Heaven. In the name of Jesus Christ, our Lord, Amen.' Michel pushed his way through the crowd towards the altar, attracting angry glances as he went. At the third row, he stopped and watched the exchange of rings. Head bowed, the priest took the hands of the couple in his own; the intensity of his concentration was overwhelming, the silence in the chapel was total. Then he lifted his head and in a loud voice which sounded both vital and despairing, he exclaimed violently: 'That which God hath joined together, let not man put asunder.'

Later, Michel went up to the priest as he was packing away the tools of his trade. 'I was very interested in what you were saying earlier . . .' The man of God smiled urbanely. He began to talk about the Aspect experiments and the EPR paradox: how two particles, once united, are forever an inseparable whole, 'it seems to be pretty much in keeping with what you were saying about one flesh'. The priest's smile froze slightly. 'What I'm trying to say,' Michel went on enthusiastically, 'is that from an ontological point of view, the pair can be assigned a single vector state in Hilbert space. Do you see what I mean?'

'Of course, of course . . .' murmured the servant of Christ, looking around him. 'Excuse me,' he said abruptly and turned to the father of the bride. They shook hands warmly and slapped each other on the back. 'Beautiful ceremony . . . magnificent . . .' said the banker, his voice choked with emotion.

'You didn't stay for the reception . . .' said Bruno. 'It was really difficult for me – I was at my own wedding and I didn't know anyone there. My father got there very late, but at least he came: he hadn't shaved and his tie was crooked, he looked the very picture of an elderly playboy. I'm sure Anne's parents would have preferred it if she had married someone else, but being liberal middle-class Protestants they had a healthy respect for the teaching profession. Anyway, I had a degree and she only had a diploma. The only problem was that her little sister was really pretty. She looked a bit like Anne – she had big tits too – but she wasn't plain at all, she had a beautiful face. It's amazing how the smallest detail in someone's features can make all the difference. Life's a bitch . . .' He sighed again and poured himself another glass.

'I got my first job as a teacher in September 'eighty-four, at the Lycée Carnot in Dijon. Anne was six months pregnant. We'd made it – we were teachers at last – now all we had to do was live a normal life.

'We rented an apartment on the rue Vannerie not far from the school. "You won't be paying Paris prices here," the estate agent told us, "but it's pretty lively in the summer – we get a lot of tourists here. There's a lot of young people in town now for the Baroque Music Festival." Baroque music?

'I knew from the start that I was doomed. It wasn't that I missed "life in Paris" – I couldn't have cared less about that – I'd always been completely miserable in Paris. It was just that I fancied every woman except my wife. Like most provincial towns, there are lots of pretty girls in Dijon, it was much worse than Paris. Those first couple of years the fashions were a real turn-on. It was unbearable, all those skinny little girls in their little skirts with their little laughs. At school, I saw them in class, at lunchtime I'd see them chatting up boys in the Penalty – the bar next to the school – I always went home to my wife for lunch. On Saturday afternoons, I'd see them in town buying CDs and clothes. I was always with Anne, who only wanted to look at baby clothes. She had an easy pregnancy and she was really happy. She slept a lot and ate all sorts of strange stuff. We stopped having sex, but I don't think she even noticed. At the antenatal classes she'd made friends with some of the other women. Anne was always very sociable, affable and friendly, she was very easy to live with. I was really shocked when I found out she was expecting a boy. That was the worst – I was going to have to endure the worst. I should have been happy – I was only twenty-eight, but I felt dead inside.

'Victor was born in December. I remember taking him to be baptised at the Église Saint Michel – I found it incredibly disturbing: "Those that are baptised shall become the living stones of a spiritual edifice to the glory of the holy mother church" said the priest. Victor was all red and wrinkled in his little white lace gown. There were about a dozen families – it was a collective baptism, like in the early Church. "Baptism binds us to the church," said the priest, "and cleaves us to the body of Christ." Anne was cradling Victor in her arms – he weighed nine pounds. He was very good, he didn't cry at all. "Are we not then of the same body?" The parents looked at each other and seemed rather dubious. Then the priest poured the baptismal water three times on my son's forehead and anointed him with chrism. "This perfumed oil, sanctified by the bishop, symbolises the gift of the Holy Spirit," said the priest. Then he addressed Victor directly: "Victor," said the priest, "you are now a Christian and by the power of Holy Unction you have been incorporated into Christ's body. From henceforth you will participate in his holy, apostolic and catholic mission."

'I was so impressed, I joined a "Living with Faith" group that met every Wednesday. There was a young Korean girl there – she was very pretty, and I wanted to fuck her the first time I saw her. It was a bit delicate because she knew I was married. Anne invited the group to meet at our house. The Korean girl sat on the sofa. She was wearing a short dress. I spent the whole afternoon staring at her legs, but nobody noticed.

'Anne took Victor to see her parents for the mid-term holidays in February and I stayed in Dijon on my own. I tried again to become a Catholic. I'd lie on my Épéda mattress drinking pastis and reading the *Mystery of the Holy Innocents*. It was really beautiful – Péguy is an amazing writer, but in the end it just depressed me. All of that stuff about sin and the forgiveness of sin, and God rejoicing more in the return of the sinner than in the thousands of the just . . . I wanted to be a sinner, but I just couldn't do it. I felt like I'd been robbed of my childhood. All I wanted was for some little bitch to put her full lips round my cock and give me a blow job. I saw a lot of little bitches with pouting lips in the nightclubs and I went to the Slow Rock and l'Enfer a few times while Anne was away; but they were always going out with someone else, always sucking someone else's cock, and I just couldn't stand it.

'It was round this time that cruising on the Minitel took off, everyone was talking about it. I used to stay online for hours – sometimes all night. Victor would be asleep in our room, but he slept through the night, so that wasn't a problem. I was terrified when the first telephone bill arrived – I took it out of the letter box and opened it on the way to school: fourteen thousand francs. Luckily I still had a saving account at the Caisse d'Épargne from my student days, so I transferred everything into our joint account. Anne didn't notice a thing.

'We only begin to live through other people's eyes. As time went by, I noticed that my colleagues at the school looked at me without a trace of bitterness or dislike. I was no longer a threat to them; we were all in the same boat; I was *one of them*. They taught me how the system worked. I got my driving licence and I started to get into CAMIF catalogues. When spring came, we spent the afternoons on the lawn at the Guilmards'. They lived in an ugly old house in Fontaine-les-Dijon, but they had a big garden with a beautiful tree-lined lawn. Guilmard taught maths, and we taught the same classes, pretty much. He was tall and thin with reddish-blond hair and a handlebar moustache – he looked a bit like a German accountant. His wife would help him with the barbecue. There were usually four or five teachers with their partners. In the late afternoons, we'd talk about the holidays – we were usually a bit stoned. Guilmard's wife was a nurse and she had the reputation of being a real slut – in fact when she sat on the grass you could see that she wasn't wearing anything under her dress. They spent their holidays at Cap d'Agde, on the nudist beach. I think they went to a wife-swapping sauna on the place Bossuet – well, that's what I heard, anyway. I never dared to talk to Anne about it, but I really liked them. They were a bit social democrat, not at all like the ageing hippies who used to hang around with Mother in the early Seventies. Guilmard was a good teacher, he thought nothing of staying behind after class to help a kid who was having problems. He gave to some charity for the handicapped as well, I think.'

Abruptly, Bruno fell silent. After a minute or two, Michel got up, opened the French doors and went out onto the balcony for a breath of the night air. Most of the people he knew had lived lives very like Bruno's. Apart from in some high-profile industries like advertising and fashion, it's pretty easy to fit in; the dress code is simple and obvious. After a couple of years of working together, sexual desire wanes and people turn their attentions to gourmet food and wine. Some of his colleagues – many of them much younger – had already started a cellar. Bruno wasn't like that – he hadn't even commented on the wine – Vieux Papes, 11.95 francs a bottle. Half-forgetting that his brother was there, Michel leaned on the railing and looked out at the other buildings. It was dark now and the lights in most of the apartments were out. It was 15 August, a Sunday evening. He came back inside and sat near Bruno, their knees almost touching. Was it possible to think of Bruno as an individual? The decay of his organs was particular to him, and he would suffer his decline and death as an individual. On the other hand, his hedonistic world view and the forces that shaped his consciousness and his desires were common to an entire generation. Just as determining the apparatus for an experiment and choosing a method of observation made it possible to assign a specific behaviour to an atomic system – now particle, now wave – so Bruno could be seen as an individual or as passively caught up in the sweep of history. His motives, values and desires did not distinguish him from his contemporaries in any way.

Generally, the initial reaction of a thwarted animal is to try harder to attain its goal. A starving chicken (*Gallus domesticus*) prevented from reaching its food by a wire fence will make increasingly frantic efforts to get through it. Gradually, however, this behaviour is replaced by another which has no obvious purpose. When unable to find food, for example, pigeons (*Columba livia*) will frequently peck the ground even if there is nothing there which is edible. Not only will they forage indiscriminately, but they start to preen their feathers; such inappropriate behaviour, frequently observed in situations of frustration or conflict, is known as *displacement activity*. Early in 1986, just after he turned 30, Bruno began to write.

13

'No metaphysical mutation takes place,' Djerzinski would write many years later, 'without first being announced – the radical change is preceded by many minor mutations – facilitators whose historic appearance often goes unnoticed. I consider myself to have been one such mutation.'

Drifting through the mass of European humanity, Djerzinski was little understood in his lifetime. In the introduction to Djerzinski's posthumously published *Clifden Notes*, Hubczejak writes: 'An idea which evolves in a single mind, without the counterbalance of debate, can nonetheless avoid the pitfalls of idiosyncrasy and folly. It is significant, however, that Djerzinski presents his idea in the form of a quasi-Socratic dialogue. It should be added that, even at the end, Djerzinski considered himself to be primarily a scientist. He believed that his principal contribution to human evolution was his biophysical work – which he had developed within the classical scientific constraints of consistency and refutability. As far as he was concerned, the philosophical elements of his later works were never more than idle conjectures, which he recorded less for their intrinsic claims to truth than out of personal considerations.'

He felt a little tired; the moon glided over the sleeping city. He knew that he only had to say the word and Bruno would get up, put on his jacket and disappear into the lift. He could easily hail a cab at La Motte Picquet.

When we think about the present, we veer wildly between the belief in chance and the evidence in favour of determinism. When we think about the past, however, it seems obvious that everything happened in the way that it was intended. Djerzinski had long since seen through this perceptual illusion, nor did he subscribe to an ontology which presupposes intrinsic properties and depends on the notion of objectivity. It was this realisation rather than any feeling of compassion or respect which prevented him from uttering the simple, established phrase which would have cut short this broken, tearful creature's confession. This evening, the animal sprawled on the sofa – with whom he shared one quarter of his genetic code – had overstepped the unspoken boundaries of decent human conversation. This evening, Djerzinski had a faint but definite feeling that Bruno's tortuous, pathetic tale was tending towards some conclusion; words would be spoken and – for the first time – these words would have meaning and finality. He stood up and went to the bathroom where, discreetly, without a sound, he vomited. He splashed water on his face and went back to the living room.

'You're not human,' Bruno said quietly, looking up at Michel. 'I knew it from the start, from the way you behaved with Annabelle. But you're the audience life has given me. At the time, I suppose you weren't surprised when you got my article on John Paul II.'

'Every civilisation has had to find some way to justify the sacrifices parents make,' said Michel sadly. 'In the circumstances, you didn't have much choice.'

'But I really did admire John Paul II,' Bruno protested. 'I remember it was in 1986 – Canal Plus and M6 had just started broadcasting, the Globe had just been launched and the Restos du Coeur soup kitchens started up. John Paul II was the only person – the only person – who really understood what was happening in the West. I was stunned when my paper was badly received by my "Living with Faith" group in Dijon; they criticised the Pope's position on abortion and contraception – all that rubbish. I have to admit I didn't make much of an effort to see their point of view either. We used to take turns holding the meeting in our houses; everyone would bring something to eat – a salad or a dessert. I used to spend the evenings smiling like a half-wit, nodding my head and knocking back the wine; I wasn't really listening. Anne was really into it, though. She signed up to help with a literacy programme. The evening when she was out, I'd put a sedative into Victor's bottle, log on to the Minitel and jerk off, but I never actually met anyone in person.

'A couple of months before, I'd bought Anne a silver lamé bodice and suspenders for her birthday. She was a bit wary at first, but I persuaded her to try it on. While she was strapping herself into it, I finished the champagne. Then I heard her small trembling voice saying nervously: "I'm ready . . ." The minute I walked into the bedroom I knew it had been a crazy idea. Her sagging arse was squeezed into the suspenders and her tits had never really recovered from breastfeeding. She needed liposuction, silicone implants, the works . . . though she would never have agreed to it. I closed my eyes and slipped a finger into her G-string; I was completely soft. At that moment Victor started howling from the next room – loud, shrill, unendurable screams. She put on a dressing gown and ran into his room. When she got back I just asked her for a blow job. She wasn't very good at it – you could feel her teeth – but I closed my eyes and imagined it was a Ghanaian girl from my *seconde* class. Thinking about her pink tongue rasping gently on me, I managed to shoot in my wife's mouth. I had no intention of having another child. I wrote the piece about the family the next day – you know, the one that was published.'

'I still have a copy of it . . .' said Michel. He got up and took down the magazine from a bookshelf. Bruno thumbed through it, somewhat surprised, and found the page.

There are families still, more or less,
(Sparks of faith among atheists,
Sparks of love in the pit of nausea),
And we do not know how
These sparks glow.

Slaves working for incomprehensible organisations,
The only way in which we can live our lives is through sex
(Though only, of course, those for whom sex is still permitted,
Those for whom sex is possible)

Now, marriage and fidelity cut us off from any possibility of
  existence,
We will not find – in the office or the classroom – that spirit in
  us which clamours for adventure, for light, for dance;
And so we try to pool our destinies through increasingly difficult
  loves
We try to sell a body which is ever more exhausted, mutinous,
  arrogant
And we disappear
In the shadow of sorrow
To true despair,

We go down the long, solitary road to the place where all is
  dark
Without children, without wives,
We enter the lake
In the middle of night
(and the water on our ancient bodies is so cold)

Just after writing this, Bruno had slipped into an alcoholic coma. He was woken some hours later by the screams of his son. Between the ages of two and four, human children acquire a sense of self, which manifests itself in displays of egotistical histrionics. Their aim in this is to control their environment, making slaves of those around them (specifically, their parents); slaves dedicated to satisfying their every whim. Their egotism knows no bounds – such is the nature of the individual. Bruno picked himself up from the floor; the screaming grew loud and shrill with rage. He crushed two Lexomil, mashed them into a spoonful of jam and headed towards Victor's room. The child had shat itself. Where the fuck was Anne? These wog literacy classes were ending later and later. He took off the soiled nappy and threw it on the floor; it stank. The child swallowed the mixture on the spoon easily and his body stiffened as though he had been struck. Bruno put on his jacket and went to the Madison, an all-night bar on the rue Chaudronnerie. He bought a 3,000 franc bottle of Dom Pérignon on his credit card and shared it with a pretty blonde. In one of the upstairs rooms, the girl jacked him off slowly, pausing every now and then to heighten his pleasure. Her name was Hélène, she came from Dijon and was studying tourism, she was 19. As he slipped inside her, she tightened her vagina and he had three whole minutes of complete contentment. When he left, Bruno kissed her on the lips and insisted on giving her a tip – he only had 300 francs in cash on him.

The following week he decided to show a colleague –

a 50-year-old Marxist who taught literature – what he had written. He was tall and thin; rumour had it he was homosexual. Fajardie was pleasantly surprised. 'You're obviously influenced by Claudel . . . or perhaps Péguy, in his blank verse . . . But it's very original, and that's something you don't come across every day.' He was certain as to what should happen next: '*L'Infini* – it's the only serious literary magazine nowadays. Send it to Sollers.' A little taken aback, Bruno asked him to repeat the name – he later realised he had confused it with a brand of mattress – and sent off his work. Three weeks later he telephoned the publishers, Denoël, and was surprised when Philippe Sollers answered and suggested that they meet. Bruno did not have classes on Wednesday, and it would be possible to get to Paris and back in a day. On the train, he tried to read Sollers' novel, *A Curious Solitude*, but quickly gave up, though he did manage to read some of *Women* – mostly the bits about sex. They had arranged to meet in a café on the rue de l'Université. Sollers arrived ten minutes late, brandishing the cigarette holder which would become his trademark. 'You're in the back end of beyond? Pity. You should move to Paris. You have talent.' He told Bruno that he would publish the piece on John Paul II in the next issue of *l'Infini*. Bruno was stunned; he couldn't have known that Sollers was deep into his 'Counter-reformation' phase, and was publishing a variety of impassioned tracts favourable to the Pope. 'I really admire Péguy!' said Sollers enthusiastically, 'and de Sade, you must read de Sade . . .'

'What about the poem I wrote about families?'

'Excellent, really excellent – you're a real reactionary, that's good. All the great writers were reactionaries: Balzac, Baudelaire, Flaubert, Dostoyevsky. But you have to fuck too, you know? You have to fuck as much as possible – that's important.'

In five minutes Sollers was gone, leaving Bruno in a state of slightly inebriated narcissism. On the way home, he calmed down a little. Philippe Sollers was obviously famous but from reading *Women* it was clear that the only women he managed to pull were cultivated old whores; real chicks preferred pop stars. In which case, what was the point of publishing some shit poem in some shitty magazine?

'Of course, that didn't stop me buying five copies of *l'Infini* when it was published. Thank God they didn't run the piece on John Paul II in the end, it was terrible . . . Is there any wine left?'

'Just one bottle.' Michel went to the kitchen and brought back the sixth and final bottle from the multi-pack of Vieux Papes; he was beginning to feel really tired. 'You're working tomorrow, aren't you?' he asked. Bruno didn't respond. He was staring at a spot on the floor, though there was nothing there, or at least nothing specific, just some blurred stains on the floorboards. He came to life when he heard the cork pop and held out his glass. He drank slowly, in small sips; his gaze had now fallen on some indistinct point on the radiator. Michel hesitated for a moment and then turned on the television:

there was a documentary about rabbits. He turned down the sound. In fact, it might have been a programme about hares, he always confused the two. He was surprised when Bruno began to speak again:

'I was trying to remember how long I was in Dijon. Four years? Five? When you work in something like teaching every year seems the same. The only things that mark out your life are visits to the doctor and watching the kids grow up. Victor was growing up, he was starting to call me "Daddy".'

Suddenly, he started to cry. Curled up on the sofa he sobbed loudly. Michel looked at his watch; it was just after four a.m. On the screen a wild cat had a rabbit in its mouth.

Bruno took out a tissue and wiped the corners of his eyes. Tears continued to stream down his face as he thought about his son. Poor little Victor who drew creatures from the pages of *Strange* and who loved him. He had given the boy few moments of happiness and fewer still of love – now the boy was almost 15 and the time for happiness was over.

'Anne would have liked to have had more children, she actually rather liked the idea of being a mother and a housewife. I was the one who pushed her to apply for a job in Paris so we could move back. She didn't dare to say no, of course. At the time, everyone believed – or pretended to believe – that a woman's career was essential to her self-esteem and, more than anything, Anne had a need to conform with what other people thought. I knew perfectly well that the real reason we were going back to Paris was to make the divorce easier. In the sticks people still meet and gossip, and I didn't want people talking about our divorce, even if they thought it was a good idea. In the summer of 'eighty-nine we went away with Club Med – it was our last holiday together. I remember the stupid fucking games before dinner and spending hours checking out girls on the beach. Anne chatted with the other mothers. When she lay on her stomach you could see her cellulite and when she turned onto her back you could see her stretch marks. It was in Morocco. The Arabs were aggressive and obnoxious and the weather was far too hot. It wasn't really worth getting skin cancer just so I could go back to the chalet at night and wank. Victor really enjoyed himself – he had a great time at the Mini Club . . .' Bruno's voice faltered again.

'I was a bastard; I knew I was being a bastard. Parents usually make sacrifices for their kid – that's how it's supposed to be. I just couldn't cope with the fact that I wasn't young any more; my son was going to grow up and he would get to be young instead and he might make something of his life, unlike me. I wanted to be an individual entity again.'

'A monad . . .' said Michel softly.

Bruno said nothing. He drained his glass. 'The bottle's empty . . .' he remarked absently. He got up, put on his jacket and Michel walked him to the door. 'I do love my son,' Bruno said again. 'If he had an accident, if anything happened to him, I couldn't bear it. I love that kid more than anything in the whole world, but I've never even been able to acknowledge him.' Michel nodded. Bruno walked towards the lift.

Michel went back to his desk and noted on a piece of paper: 'Write something about blood ties'; then he lay down to think, but fell asleep almost immediately. Some days later, when he came across the piece of paper, he discovered the words 'blood is thicker than water' written underneath; for ten minutes he stood there completely mystified.

14

On the morning of the first of September Bruno waited
for Christiane at the Gare du Nord. She had taken a bus
from Noyon to Amiens and a train from there to Paris. It
was a beautiful day. Her train arrived at 11.37. She was
wearing a long print dress with a pattern of scattered
flowers and lace cuffs. He took her in his arms. Their
hearts beat eagerly.

They had lunch in an Indian restaurant and then went
back to his apartment and made love. The floor had been
polished, the curtains had been cleaned and smelled
lovely, and he had put flowers in the vases. He managed
to hold back for a long time, waiting for the right moment
to come; sunlight flickered through the gap in the
curtains, glinting on her black hair, where he could see
one or two grey hairs. She came, and then came again
immediately afterwards. As she did so, her vagina con-
tracted vigorously and he came inside her. He pressed

himself against her and they fell asleep.

When they woke, it was around seven and the sun was sinking between the high-rises. Bruno opened a bottle of white wine. He had never spoken to anyone about the years that followed his return from Dijon; he wanted to now.

'At the beginning of the 1989–1990 academic year, Anne got a job at the Lycée Condorcet. We rented an apartment – small, dark, two-bedroomed – on the rue Rodier. Victor was going to nursery school by now, so I had my days free. It was about then that I started visiting prostitutes. There were lots of massage parlours in the area – the New Bangkok, the Golden Lotus and the Maï Lin; the girls were polite, always smiling, it was a nice atmosphere. At about the same time I started seeing an analyst – I don't remember much about the experience – I think the guy had a beard, but I might be confusing him with someone in a film. I talked to him about my adolescence, and I talked a lot about the massage parlours – I felt he had nothing but contempt for me which made me feel better. In any case, in January I changed shrinks. The new one was good – he had a surgery near the Strasbourg Saint-Denis metro, so I'd tour the peepshows on the way back. His name was Dr Azoulay. There were copies of *Paris Match* in his waiting room. Anyway, I thought he was a good doctor. My case didn't really interest him much, but I didn't hold that against him – after all, it was pretty banal, I was just one more frustrated ageing fucker who didn't fancy his wife any more. At about the same time, he was called as an expert witness in the trial of a gang of teenage Satanists who had cut up some handicapped kid with a chainsaw and eaten him. You have to admit that was a damn sight more exciting. Anyway, at the end of every session, he'd recommend that I take up sport – he was obsessed with sport. Though he was getting a bit of a pot belly himself. Anyway, the sessions were okay, but a bit depressing; the only thing that seemed to bring him to life was my relationship with my parents. At the beginning of February, I had an interesting story for him. It was in the waiting room of the Maï Lin; I'd come in and sat down opposite some guy whose face seemed familiar – I didn't recognise him, there was just something about him. Anyway, he was sent upstairs and I went up straight after. There were only two massage cabins separated by a plastic curtain, so he had to be on the other side. When the girl started stroking my belly with her soapy tits, I realised; the guy in the next cabin getting a quick 'full body' was my father. He had aged terribly – he looked like an OAP, but there was no doubt about it, it was him. Just as I realised this, I heard him come with a little noise like water going down a plughole. After I'd shot off myself, I waited a couple of minutes before getting dressed; I didn't fancy running into him on the way out. But the day I told the story to my analyst, I phoned my father when I got home. He seemed surprised to hear from me – but pleased. I was right – he had retired, he'd sold off his shares in the Cannes clinic; he'd lost a lot of money in the last couple of years, but he was still okay financially – there were people a lot worse off, as he put it. We said we'd meet up some day soon, but we couldn't do it right away.

'At the beginning of March I got a call from the School Inspectorate. One of the teachers had taken maternity leave early, so they had a vacancy until the end of the year at the Lycée de Meaux. Well, I thought about it for three hours and then I realised that I didn't really give a toss. I suppose that's old age for you – you don't care much about anything; you don't feel bitter any more, but you don't feel terribly happy either. You spend most of your time worrying about the state of your insides.

'When I got off the train and walked through the town, I was surprised at how small and ugly it was – there seemed to be nothing of interest in it at all. As a kid, when I got back to Meaux every Sunday night, I felt like I was entering some vast hellish place. Well, I was wrong – it was a pretty small hell, without a single distinguishing feature. The streets and the houses didn't conjure up any memories – even the school had been renovated. I took a tour of the building where the boarders had lived; it had long since been closed and turned into a local history museum. In these rooms, other boys had hit me and humiliated me. They'd spat at me, pissed on me, pushed my head into the toilet and enjoyed it, but I didn't feel anything. Oh, maybe I felt a little sad – but in a very general sort of way. "God himself cannot undo that which has been done," as some Catholic writer said somewhere; when I looked back on my childhood in Meaux, it didn't look too bad to me.

'I walked around town for a bit, I even went back to the Café de la Plage. I thought about Caroline Yessayan and Patricia Hohweiller; but there was nothing there that reminded me of them – I suppose I'd never really forgotten them. I noticed a lot of young immigrants – blacks mostly – a lot more than when I was a teenager; that was the only thing that had really changed. Then I went back to the school and introduced myself. The housemaster was delighted to find out that I was a former pupil; he said he might go and dig out my file but I changed the subject, so at least I didn't have to go through that. I took three classes: *seconde*, *première A* and *première S*. I realised straight away that the *première A* would be the worst: there were three boys and about 30 girls. Thirty 16-year-old girls – blondes, brunettes, redheads, white girls, Arabs, Asians . . . every one of them lovely and every one of them desirable. And they weren't virgins either – you could tell. They slept around, swapped boyfriends – enjoying their youth to the full. I used to walk past the Durex machine every day and they weren't the slightest bit embarrassed to use it right in front of me.

'The problems started when I decided I might be in with a chance. A lot of their parents were probably divorced; I was convinced that I could find one who was looking for a father figure. There was a chance – I was sure there was a chance. But I'd have to be a big, broad-shouldered father figure, so I grew a beard and joined a gym. The beard was a qualified success – there was a lot of grey in it, which made me look like a dirty old man –

a bit like Salman Rushdie; but the gym was a great idea.
Within a couple of months I had well-defined pecs and
deltoids. The problem now – and it was a new one for me
– was my dick. It probably sounds strange now, but in the
Seventies nobody really cared how big their dick was.
When I was a teenager I had every conceivable hang-up
about my body except that. I don't know who started it –
queers probably, though you find it a lot in American cop
shows, but there's no mention of it in Sartre. Whatever,
in the showers at the gym I realised I had a really small
dick. I measured it when I got home – it was five inches
– maybe five and a half or six if you measured right to the
base. I'd found something new to worry about, something
that I couldn't do anything about – it was a permanent
handicap. It was round about then that I started to hate
blacks. There weren't many of them in the school – most
of them went to the Lycée Pierre-de-Coubertin where
the eminent Defrance did his philosophical strip-tease and
propounded his pro-youth filth. I only had one in my A-
stream class, a big, stocky guy who called himself Ben. He
always wore a baseball cap and a pair of Nikes; I was
convinced he had a huge dick. All the girls threw themselves at this big baboon and here I was trying to teach
them about Mallarmé – what the fuck was the point? This
is the way the world ends, I thought bitterly, people
worshipping in front of big dicks, like *hamadryas* baboons.
This black guy was going out with the girl I would have
chosen myself: blonde, very pretty, with a childlike face
and small firm tits. They were always holding hands in

class. I always kept the windows closed while they were working – the girls would get hot and take off their jumpers, their tee shirts stuck to their breasts; hidden behind my desk, I'd jerk off. I still remember the day I gave them a passage from *Le côté de Guermantes* as a pract. crit:

'. . . *the purity of a blood-line into which for many generations there had flowed only what was greatest in the history of France had rid her manner of everything that the lower orders call "airs" and had endowed her with perfect simplicity . . .*'

'I looked at Ben: he scratched his head, he scratched his balls, he chewed his gum. What the hell would it mean to him, the big ape? What would it mean to any of them? I was beginning to wonder whether *I* understood what Proust meant exactly. Here were a dozen pages about the purity of the bloodline, the nobility of genius in the context of the nobility of race, the rarefied atmosphere of great doctors . . . it all seemed bullshit to me. We clearly live in a simpler world. The Duchesse de Guermantes has a lot less dosh than Snoop Doggy Dog; Snoop has less than Bill Gates, but he gets the girls wet. There are two possible criteria, that's it. Of course, you could write a Proustian novel about the jet set, about money and fame – a major star brought face to face with a literary legend. It would go down a storm with the literati, but in the end, who cares? Literary fame is a poor substitute for real stardom, which is a showbiz monopoly – after all, showbiz rakes it in more than any other industry in the world. What's a banker or a minister or a managing director next to an actor or a pop star? Financially, sexually, any way you look at it they're nonentities. Proust's subtle distinctions are completely meaningless nowadays. From the point of view of man as social architect, as a creator of hierarchies, the twentieth century had about as much in common with the eighteenth as the GAN Tower with the Petit Trianon. Proust was fundamentally European – he and Thomas Mann were the last Europeans – but what he wrote no longer bears any relationship to the world as we know it. The passage about the Duchesse de Guermantes is magnificent, of course, but I found it all rather depressing. I found myself increasingly drawn to Baudelaire. Here were real themes – death, pain, shame, dissipation, lost childhood and nostalgia . . . transcendent subjects. It was pretty strange really – it was spring, the weather was beautiful, there were stunning girls everywhere and there I was reading:

> *Be calm, my pain and venture to be still*
> *You clamoured for the Night; it falls; is here:*
> *The city shrouds itself in blackest chill,*
> *Brings peace to some, to others fear.*

> *'Neath pleasure's lash, the grim high executioner,*
> *Mortal souls, that vile and worthless throng,*
> *Reap grim remorse amidst the abject ceremony,*
> *Pain, take my hand and let us now along . . .*

'I stopped for a minute. I could tell the poem had moved them, none of them said anything. It was my last class of the day, in half an hour I would be on the train heading home to my wife. Suddenly I heard Ben's voice from the back of the classroom: 'You've got death on the brain, old man . . .' His voice was loud, but he didn't seem to be trying to insult me – in fact, he sounded rather admiring. I don't really know if he was referring to me or to Baudelaire, but as a response to the text it was pretty appropriate. But I had to deal with it somehow. I just said: "Get out!" He didn't move. I waited thirty seconds; I was so scared I was sweating. I knew that if I waited much longer I wouldn't be able to say anything, but I managed to say again "Get out". He stood up, got his things together very slowly and walked towards me. In any conflict, there is a moment of grace when the opposing forces are equally matched. When he got to me, he stopped – he was a good head taller than I was – for a minute, I thought he was going to hit me, but he didn't, he just walked past me to the door. I had won. It was a Pyrrhic victory, of course, he was in class again the next day. I think he knew what was going on, maybe he caught me looking at her, but he started feeling his girlfriend up right there in class. He'd push her skirt up all the way, put his hand on her thigh, then he'd look right at me and smile, really cool. I wanted the bitch so badly. I spent the weekend writing a racist pamphlet – I had a hard-on all the time I was writing it. This time, Sollers asked me to come to his office. He was sharp and spiteful just like he is on television – better, even. "It's obvious you're a real racist. That's good, it really carries the piece. Well done!"

He pointed to one of the pages with a graceful gesture. He had underlined a section: "*We envy and admire the Negro because we long to regress, like him, to our animal selves; to be animals with big cocks and small reptilian brains which are no more than appendices to their pricks.*" He tapped the page: "It's crude, brutal, very 'red in tooth and claw'. You've got talent. A gift for words. I'm not keen on the subtitle: *We become racist, we are not born that way.* I always think irony is a bit, um . . ." His face darkened, but then he did a little twirl with his cigarette holder and smiled again. He was a real clown, but a nice guy. "It's very original, too, and not too heavy. You're not even anti-Semitic!" He pointed to another passage: "*Only Jews are spared the regret of not being Negroes, because they have long since chosen the path of wisdom, shame and guilt. Nothing in Western civilisation can equal what the Jews have made of guilt and shame; this is why Negroes hate the Jews most of all.*" He sat back in his seat, he seemed really pleased. He folded his arms behind his head; for a second, I thought he was going to put his feet up on the desk, but he didn't. He leaned forward again – he just couldn't stay still.

' "So, what are we going to do?"

' "I don't know. You could publish it."

' "Publish it in *l'Infini*?" He burst out laughing, as though I'd just told a really good joke. "I don't think you realise what you're suggesting, my good man . . . You might have got away with it in Céline's day. These days, there are some subjects about which you can't just write anything you feel like . . . something like this could make life really difficult for me. You think I don't have enough problems? You think that because I'm at Gallimard I can do what I like? People keep an eye on me, you know. They're just waiting for me to make a mistake. No, no – it would be too difficult. Haven't you got anything else?"

'He seemed really surprised that I hadn't brought another piece with me. I was sorry to disappoint him, I really wanted to be his *good man*, I wanted him to take me dancing and buy me whisky at the Pont-Royal. Outside, on the pavement, I had a pang of despair. It was late afternoon, the weather was warm, women walked past me along the Boulevard Saint-Germain; it was then that I realised I'd never be a writer, but I realised that I didn't care. But what was I going to do? I was already spending half my salary on sex; I couldn't believe that Anne hadn't figured out something was wrong by now. I could have joined the *Front National* – but why bother getting into bed with those stupid cunts? In any case, there aren't any women on the far right, or if there are, they only fuck ex-paras. My article was crazy – I threw it into the first bin I came across. I had to stick to my "liberal humanist" position; I knew in my heart that it was my only chance of getting laid. I sat on the terrace at the Escurial. My penis was hot, hard and aching. I had a couple of beers and then walked back to the apartment. As I was crossing the river, I remembered Adjila. She was a pretty little Arab girl in the *seconde*. Good student, serious, a year ahead of her age. She had an intelligent, sensitive face, not at all cynical, she really wanted to make something of herself – you could tell. A lot of girls like that live with thugs and murderers, all you have to do is show them a little kindness. I started to believe it was possible. For the next few weeks, I talked to her more and called her up to the blackboard. She responded, she didn't seem to think anything was up. I didn't have much time, it was June already. When she walked back to her desk, I could see her little arse in her tight jeans. I liked her so much I stopped visiting prostitutes. I'd imagine sliding my cock into her long, soft black hair; I even jerked off over her homework once.

On Wednesday 11 June she turned up in a little black dress. Class would be over at six. She was sitting in the front row. When she crossed her legs under her desk I thought I'd pass out. She was sitting beside a fat blonde who ran off as soon as the bell went. I went over and put a hand on her books. She just sat there, she didn't seem to be in any hurry. All the other kids left and the classroom was quiet again. I was holding her exercise book in my hand, I could make out a word or two: "Remember . . . hell . . ." I sat next to her and put the book down on the desk. We sat there, not saying anything, for more than a minute. I stared into her big black eyes, but I was aware of every little movement of her body, the rise and fall of her breasts. She was half-turned towards me and she parted her legs. I don't remember doing what I did next, I think it was half-involuntary, but the next thing I knew I felt her thigh against the palm of my left hand, then it's all a blur. I remembered Caroline Yessayan and I froze with shame. I had made the same mistake – 20 years on, I had made the same mistake. Just like Caroline Yessayan 20 years earlier, she did nothing for a second; she blushed a little. Then, very gently, she moved my hand away, but she didn't get up, she didn't make any move to leave. Through the bars on the windows, I could see a girl in the playground racing off to the station. With my right hand, I opened my fly. Her eyes widened and she looked at my penis. Her eyes on me felt hot – I nearly came just from her watching me but I knew that she had to actually do something if this were to be mutual. I moved my right hand towards hers, but I couldn't go through with it: imploringly, I took my cock in my hand as if to offer it to her. She burst out laughing; I think I laughed too as I started to wank. I went on laughing and jerking off as she got her things together, as she got up to leave. When she got to the door, she turned round and looked at me one last time; I ejaculated, and everything went black. I heard the door close and her footsteps dying away. I was stunned, as though I'd been struck like a gong. Still, I managed to phone Azoulay from the station. I don't remember the train back to Paris, or the metro; Azoulay saw me at eight. I couldn't stop shaking; he gave me an injection to calm me down.

'I spent three days in Saint Anne's and then they transferred me to an Éducation Nationale psychiatric clinic at Verrières-le-Buisson. Azoulay was clearly worried. There was a lot of stuff about paedophilia in the papers that year, it was like journalists had put the word out: "come down hard on paedophiles". It was starting to become a national obsession, all because they hated old people and loathed the idea of old age. The girl was 15, I was a teacher, I'd abused a position of authority and to make matters worse, she was an Arab. His file on me could have me fired – and probably lynched. After a fortnight or so he began to calm down; term was almost over and it was clear that Adjila hadn't said anything. I was back to being a typical case: depressed teacher, possibly suicidal, needs to rebuild his psyche . . . The odd thing is that the Lycée de Meaux wasn't a particularly *tough* school, but he made a big deal of the traumas I'd suffered there as a child, how going back there had brought them back – he did a pretty good job.

'I was in the clinic for about six months; my father came to see me several times, he seemed more tired and more considerate. I was so out of it on neuroleptics that I didn't have any sex drive at all; but sometimes one of the nurses would take me in her arms. I'd press myself against her and stay there, not moving, for a minute or two, then I'd lie down again. It seemed to do me good, so the chief psychiatrist suggested they continue, if they had no problem with it. He suspected that Azoulay hadn't told him everything, but he had cases a lot more serious than mine – schizophrenics, and dangerous psychotics; he didn't have time to bother with me. As long as I had a doctor treating me, that was enough.

'Of course, there was no way I could go back to teaching, but in 1991 the Éducation Nationale found me a job with the Commission des Programmes de Français.

I couldn't teach any more, and I didn't get the school holidays, but I was on the same salary. I divorced Anne soon after. We worked out a pretty standard formula for maintenance, custody and access; actually, the lawyers don't give you much choice, it's pretty routine stuff. We were first in the queue, the judge read through everything at top speed, the divorce only took about 15 minutes. We walked out together onto the steps of the Palais de Justice just after noon. It was early in March; I knew that the first chapter of my life was over.'

Bruno stopped talking. It was completely dark; neither of them had dressed. He looked up at her. Christiane did something surprising: she leaned close, put her arms around his neck and kissed him on both cheeks.

'The next few years, life went on as normal,' Bruno continued softly. 'I had a hair transplant, which took pretty well – the surgeon was a friend of my father's. I kept going to the gym. I tried going on holidays with Nouvelles Frontières, I tried Club Med again and the UCPA. I had a couple of flings, not many, women my age aren't really into sex any more. Of course, they pretend they are, and some of them are looking for feelings they once had: passion or desire or something like that, but there was no way I could give them that. I never met a woman like you before. I never even dared to hope that a woman like you could exist.'

'People . . .' she said haltingly, 'people have to learn to be considerate. If I'd been in that Arab girl's place, I don't know how I would have reacted. But I believe there was something genuine about you even then. I think . . . well I hope I would have consented to give you pleasure.' She lay down again and put her head on his thigh and licked the tip of his penis once or twice. 'I'd like to get something to eat . . .' she said suddenly. 'It's two in the morning, but there must be somewhere in Paris we can go, no?'

'Of course.'

'Do you want me to make you come first, or do you want a hand job in the taxi?'

'No, now.'

15

The Macmillan Hypothesis

They took a taxi to Les Halles and ate in an all-night brasserie. Bruno had rollmop herrings as a starter. 'Now,' he thought, 'anything is possible.' He had hardly done so when he realised that he was wrong. Though the possibilities were endless in his imagination: he could imagine himself a sewer rat, a salt cellar or a field of pure energy, but in reality his body was in a slow process of decay; Christiane's body was too. Despite the nights when they were as one, each remained trapped in individual consciousness and separate flesh. Rollmops were clearly not the solution, but then again, had he chosen sea bass with fennel it would have been no different. Christiane was mysteriously, obscurely silent. They shared a *choucroute royale* with traditional Montbéliard sausages. In the pleasantly relaxed state of a man who has just been brought lovingly, sensually to orgasm, Bruno had a fleeting idea. It was a professional preoccupation: what role did Paul Valéry play in the formation of the technical French used in scientific disciplines? By the time he had finished his *choucroute* and ordered some cheese, he was tempted to answer 'None'.

'I'm useless,' said Bruno resignedly. 'I couldn't breed pigs, I don't have the faintest idea how to make sausages or forks or mobile phones. I'm surrounded by all this stuff that I eat or use and I couldn't actually make a single thing; I couldn't even begin to understand how they're made. If industrial production ceased tomorrow, if all the engineers and the specialist technicians disappeared off the face of the earth, I couldn't do anything to start things off again. In fact, outside the industrialised world, I couldn't even survive; I wouldn't know how to feed or clothe myself, or protect myself from the weather – my technical competence falls far short of Neanderthal man. I'm completely dependent on my society, but I play no useful role in it. The only thing I know how to do is write dubious articles on outdated cultural issues. I get paid for it, too – well paid for it – much more than the average wage. Most of the people I know are exactly the same. In fact, the only useful person I know is my brother.'

'What has he done that's so extraordinary?'

Bruno thought for a moment, toying with the cheese on his plate, trying to formulate a suitably impressive response.

'He invented a new cow. That's a simplistic way of putting it, but I do know that his research led to the development of genetically modified cows which produce more milk which is of higher nutritional value. He changed the world. I've never done anything, never invented anything – I've contributed nothing to the world.'

'You've done no harm . . .' Christiane's face darkened, she finished her ice cream quickly. In July 1976 she had spent a fortnight at di Meola's estate in Ventoux, where Bruno had been the previous year with Michel and Annabelle. When she mentioned this, they were both struck by the coincidence, but as soon as she had mentioned it, she felt a terrible regret. If they had met there in 1976, when he was 20 and she was 16, how different their lives could have been, she thought. This, she realised, was the first sign that she was falling in love with him.

'Well, I suppose it's a coincidence,' said Christiane, 'but it's not so strange. My idiot parents were part of the same dissolute, vaguely beatnik movement as your mum was in the late Fifties. They probably knew each other, though I'd rather not know one way or the other. I have nothing but contempt for them, in fact I hate them. They're evil – everything they've done is evil, and believe me, I know what I'm talking about. I remember the summer of 'seventy-six very well. Di Meola died about two weeks after I got there; he had cancer and didn't seem to be interested in anything much any more. That didn't stop him trying it on with me – I was quite pretty back then – but he didn't push it, I think by then he was really in pain. For twenty years he'd been playing the wise old sage –

using spiritual initiation to try and bed girls. At least he was consistent right to the end. Two weeks after I got there, he took poison – something mild that took hours to work – and then asked to see everyone on the estate one by one – a private audience – very "death of Socrates". In fact, he was going on about Plato and the Upanishads and Lao-Tzu – the usual suspects. He talked a lot about Aldous Huxley, he said he knew him, and talked about the time they spent together. I think he embroidered it a bit, but I suppose the man was dying. When my turn came, I was very moved, but he just asked me to unbutton my blouse. He looked at my breasts and he tried to say something, but I couldn't make it out – he was having trouble speaking by then. Suddenly he sat up in his chair and reached out to touch my breasts. I didn't stop him. He put his face between my breasts for a minute and then he fell back in the chair. His hands were shaking. He nodded for me to go. I couldn't see any sign of spiritual initiation or wisdom in his face, the only thing I saw in his eyes was fear.

'He died early that evening. He'd asked for a funeral pyre to be built up on the hill. We all collected branches and then the ceremony began. His son David lit the fire, a strange glint in his eyes. I didn't know him really, I just knew that he played in a rock band. The guys he was with looked dangerous – American bikers with tattoos, dressed in leather. I'd gone there with a girlfriend, and that night we were really scared.

'Some tom-tom players sat in front of the fire and began to play a slow, funereal beat. Everyone started to dance. The fire was really hot and everyone started to take off their clothes. Usually at a cremation there's sandalwood and incense; all we had was branches we'd picked up in the forest and probably some local herbs: thyme, rosemary, savory. After about half an hour it smelled just like a barbecue. It was one of David's mates who pointed that out – a big guy in a leather jacket, with long, greasy hair and a couple of front teeth missing. Another guy, who looked a bit like a hippie, explained that the funeral of a chief was a time of great spiritual communion. The guy with the teeth nodded and laughed. David went over to them and said something. He took all his clothes off; the gleam of the firelight on his body was magnificent – I think he probably lifted weights. I thought that things were likely to degenerate so I hurried off to go to bed.

'Shortly afterwards, the storm broke. I don't know why I got up again, but I went back to the fire. There were still thirty or so of them dancing, naked in the rain. Some guy grabbed me roughly by the shoulders, he dragged me to the pyre and forced me to look at what was left of the body. You could see the skull, the eye sockets. The flesh hadn't been completely burned, and there was some of it on the ground mixed with the earth like a puddle of mud. I started screaming and the guy let go of me. I ran off. My girlfriend and I left the next day. I never heard anything about the place again.'

'You didn't see the article in *Paris Match*?'

'No . . .' Christiane looked surprised. Bruno stopped and ordered two coffees before going on. Over the years he had developed a cynical, hard-bitten, typically masculine view of life. The universe was a battle zone, teeming and bestial; the whole thing enclosed within a hard, fixed horizon – clearly perceptible, but inaccessible: the horizon of the moral law. It was written, however, that love embodies and perfects this law. Christiane looked at him tenderly, attentively; her eyes were a little tired.

'It's a really disgusting story,' Bruno went on wearily. 'Actually, I'm surprised the papers didn't make more of it at the time – satanic abuse was a new thing in Europe. Anyway, the trial was in Los Angeles and David di Meola was one of the twelve accused – I recognised the name immediately – he was one of the two who had managed to escape. According to the article, he was probably in hiding in Brazil. The charges were pretty heavy. They'd found hundreds of videos at his house of murder and torture, all neatly labelled and classified. You could see his face in some of them. The video they showed the jury was of an old woman, Mary McNallahan, with her grand-daughter – who wasn't much more than a baby – begging for her life. Di Meola dismembered the baby in front of the grandmother with a pair of secateurs, then ripped out one of the old woman's eyes with his bare hands and masturbated into the bleeding socket. He had a remote control for the camera in his other hand and used it to zoom right in on his own face. She was crouched on the floor, manacled to the wall in a place that looked like a garage. At the end, she was lying in her own excrement. The video was three quarters of an hour long, but the police were the only ones to see it all – the jury asked for it to be turned off after ten minutes.

'The article in *Paris Match* was basically just an interview that the District Attorney, David Macmillan, had given in *Newsweek*. According to him, it was not just a group of young men on trial, but society as a whole; he believed that the case was symptomatic of America's social and moral decay since the late 1950s. On more than one occasion the judge had instructed him to stick to the facts of the case – he thought the parallels Macmillan was drawing with the Manson family were spurious, especially as di Meola was the only one who came from a vaguely hippie or beatnik background.

'The following year Macmillan published a book called *From Lust to Murder: A Generation*, translated into French as *Génération meurtre*. The book shocked me; I was expecting the usual right-wing fundamentalist rant about the return of the Antichrist and how there should be prayers at school. In fact, it was a precise, well-documented book which examined a number of cases. Macmillan was particularly interested in David di Meola and had done a lot of research to put together a full biography.

'Just after the death of his father in September 1976, David had sold the thirty-hectare estate and bought a lot of property in an old building in Paris. He lived in a big studio on the rue Visconti, and he had the rest renovated to be rented out. He divided up the old apartments; the *chambres de bonne* were knocked together and kitchenettes and showers added. When the work was done, he had about twenty studio apartments, which would guarantee him a comfortable income. He hadn't given up on the idea of being a rock star and thought that maybe in Paris he might get the break he'd been looking for. But he was already twenty-six. He took two years off his age when touring the record studios: all he had to do was tell them he was twenty-four – no one ever checked. Brian Jones had the same idea long before. Once, at a party in Cannes – according to Macmillan's witnesses – David had run into Mick Jagger and recoiled as though he'd come face to face with a cobra. Jagger was the biggest rock star in the world: rich, adored, cynical – he was everything David longed to be. To be so seductive, he had to be evil, to be the perfect embodiment of evil – what the masses adored above everything was the image of evil unpunished. Only once had Jagger's power been threatened, a clash of egos within the group – with Brian Jones. But the problem had been resolved in Brian Jones' swimming pool. Though it wasn't the official version, David *knew* that Jagger had pushed Brian into the pool; he could see it happening. It was this original murder which had made him leader of the greatest rock band in the world. David was convinced that man's greatest achievements were founded upon murder, and by the end of 1976 he was ready to push as many people as he had to into as many swimming pools as he could find to succeed. In the years that followed his only achievement was to appear as a session musician on a couple of records – none of which was at all successful. On the other hand, women still found him attractive. Sexually, he became more demanding. He began to sleep with two women at a time – preferably a blonde and a brunette. Most of them agreed because he was exceptionally handsome, he had a strong, virile, almost animal beauty. He was proud of his long, thick phallus and his big, hairy balls. He became less and less interested in penetration, but he still got off on watching a girl get on her knees to suck his cock.

'Early in 1981 he met a Californian guy visiting Paris who was looking for bands to put together a heavy-metal tribute album to Charles Manson. He decided to go for it. He sold the studio apartments – which had quadrupled in price – and moved to Los Angeles. He was thirty-one now; officially he was twenty-nine, but even that was too old. Before meeting the American producers, he decided to lose another three years. Physically, he could easily pass for twenty-six.

'Production was delayed, and from his prison cell, Manson demanded huge sums for the recording rights. David took up jogging and began to hang out with Satanist groups. California had always had more than its fair share of Satanists – the First Church Of Satan was founded by Anton La Vey in 1966 and the Process Church of the Final Judgement was founded in Haight Ashbury in San Francisco in 1967. Branches of these sects still existed and David sought them out. Most of them just indulged in ritualistic orgies with the occasional animal sacrifice thrown in, but through them, he was able to get in touch with more secretive and extreme groups. Notably, he got in touch with John di Giorno, a surgeon who organised "abortion parties". After the procedure, the foetus was ground up and kneaded into bread dough to be shared among the communicants. David quickly realised that real Satanists didn't believe in Satan at all. Like him, they were pure materialists who quickly abandoned all the ritualistic kitsch of pentacles, candles and long black robes, trappings which were simply there to help initiates overcome their moral inhibitions. In 1983 he took part in his first ritual murder – a Puerto Rican baby. While he castrated the baby using a serrated knife, John di Giorno ripped out and ate the eyeballs.

'By now, David had more or less given up on the idea of being a rock star, though he still felt a twinge whenever he saw Mick Jagger on MTV. The *Tribute to Charles Manson* had gone belly up, and though he pretended to be twenty-eight, he was actually five years older and was beginning to feel too old. In his fantasies of domination and power, he began to identify with Napoleon. He admired this man who had rained fire and blood upon Europe and killed hundreds of thousands of people without even a fig-leaf of ideology or political conviction. Unlike Hitler, unlike Stalin, the only thing Napoleon believed in was himself. He had succeeded in establishing a radical separation between himself and the world, and considered others mere tools in the service of his will.

Thinking about his Genoese origins, David imagined that he was related to the dictator who, walking through a battlefield at dawn and surveying the thousands of mutilated and eviscerated corpses said nonchalantly: "Bah . . . one night in Paris will replace these men."

'As the months went by, David and some of the others plunged deeper into cruelty and horror. Sometimes they wore masks and filmed these scenes of carnage – one of them was a producer for a video company and could get the videos duplicated. A good snuff movie was worth a lot – about twenty thousand dollars a copy. One night, at an orgy held by a lawyer friend, he saw one of his films being shown in a bedroom. It had been filmed about a month before and, in it, he had cut off a man's penis with a chainsaw. He was very aroused and dragged a young girl of about twelve – a friend of the lawyer's daughter – and forced her onto her knees in front of him. The girl struggled a bit, but in the end she started to suck him off. On the screen, he watched himself slide the chainsaw gently along the thighs of a forty-year-old man. The guy was tied up, his arms spread-eagled, screaming in terror. David shot his load into the girl's mouth just as the blade cut through the man's penis. He grabbed the girl by the hair and jerked her head round brutally, and forced her to watch the long close-up of the stump as it pissed blood.

'That was the end of the evidence against David. The police came across a master copy of one of the videos, but David had probably been warned in advance – in any case, he managed to get away in time. At this point, David

Macmillan puts forward his theory. What he had proved in his book was that these self-professed Satanists didn't believe in God or Satan or in any supernatural power. In fact blasphemy was simply something they used to spice up their rituals, and most of them quickly lost the taste for it. In fact, like their master, the Marquis de Sade, they were pure materialists – libertines forever in search of new and more violent sensations. According to Macmillan, the destruction of moral values in the Sixties, Seventies, Eighties and Nineties was a logical, almost inevitable process. Having exhausted the possibilities of sexual pleasure, it was reasonable that individuals, liberated from the constraints of ordinary morality, should turn their attentions to the wider pleasures of cruelty. Two hundred years earlier, de Sade had done precisely the same thing. In a sense, the serial killers of the 1990s were the spiritual children of the hippies of the Sixties; their common ancestors would be the Viennese Actionists. In the guise of performance art, Actionists like Nitsch, Muehl and Schwarzkögler had conducted animal sacrifices in public. They would rip out an animal's organs and viscera and spread them in front of an audience of cretins, plunge their arms into the flesh and blood, drawing out the animal's suffering to the limit, while someone photographed and documented the carnage so that they could be exhibited in an art gallery. This Dionysian pleasure in the release of the animal and the evil within, begun by the Viennese Actionists, can be traced through every succeeding decade. According to Macmillan, this decline in

Western civilisation since 1945 was simply a return to the cult of power, a rejection of the secular rules slowly built up in the name of justice and morality. Actionists, beatniks, hippies and serial killers were all pure libertarians who advanced the rights of the individual against social norms and against what they believed to be the hypocrisy of morality, sentiment, justice and pity. From this point of view, Charles Manson was not some monstrous aberration in the hippie movement, but its logical conclusion; and what David di Meola had done was nothing more than to extend and to put into practice the principles of individual freedom advocated by his father. Macmillan was a member of the Republican party and some of his anti-liberal diatribes caused much gnashing of teeth within the party, but his book had a major impact. With his royalties, he went into politics full-time and the following year he was elected to Congress.'

Bruno fell silent. He had long since finished his coffee, it was four a.m. and there wasn't a single Viennese Actionist in the house. In fact, Otto Muehl was currently languishing in an Austrian prison for raping a child. He was in his sixties now, hopefully he would die soon, thereby eliminating one source of evil from the world. There was no reason to get so worked up. Everything was calm, now; a single waiter moved between the tables. They were the only customers left, but the brasserie was open 24 hours a day – it said so above the door and again on the menu – it was practically a contractual obligation.

'They better not try to hassle us, the bastards,' remarked Bruno distractedly. In contemporary society, a human life inevitably goes through a number of crises of self-doubt. It's hardly surprising, therefore, to find at least one establishment in any major European city which is open all night. He ordered a raspberry bavarois and two glasses of kirsch. Christiane had listened closely to his story; her silence was pained. It was time to return to simple pleasures.

16

Towards an Aesthetic of Goodwill

With the dawn, young girls go picking roses. A whisper of wisdom breathes over the valleys and the capitals, stirring the intellect of the most ardent poets, strewing safekeeping to cradles, crowns to youth and to old men an intimation of immortality.

(Lautréamont, *Poésies* II)

Most of the people Bruno had encountered in his life had been motivated solely by the pursuit of pleasure – if one includes in the definition those narcissistic pleasures so central to self-esteem or to the admiration of others. And so different strategies are adopted and these are called human lives.

To this rule, however, he had to make an exception for his half-brother; it seemed impossible to associate the notion of pleasure with him; but what, if anything, did motivate Michel? A uniform rectilinear motion will continue indefinitely in the absence of friction or of another external force. Orderly, rational, sociologically situated at the median of the higher social stratum, Michel's life did not so far seem to have encountered any friction. It was possible that there were dark and terrible struggles among molecular biologists, but Bruno doubted it.

'You have a very pessimistic view of the world . . .' said Christiane, ending the oppressive silence between them. 'Nietzschean,' corrected Bruno. 'Pretty second-rate Nietzsche at that,' he felt he should add. 'I'll read you a poem.' He took a notebook out of his pocket and recited the following verse:

> *It's always the same old shit of course*
> *The eternal return etcetera,*
> *And here I am eating raspberry mousse*
> *In a café called Zarathustra*

'I know what we should do,' she said after a long silence. 'We should go and have an orgy on the nudist beach at the Cap d'Agde. You get a lot of Dutch nurses and German businessmen there, all very correct, very middle-class – very northern European. Why don't we go fuck around with some policemen from Luxembourg.'

'I haven't got any holiday left.'

'Neither have I, school starts again on Tuesday, but I *need* a holiday. I'm tired of teaching, the kids are all little fuckers. You need a holiday too, and you need to get off with a lot of different women. We can do it – I know you don't believe me, but we can. I've got a friend who's a doctor, he can write us a sick note.'

They arrived at the station at Agde on Monday morning and took a taxi to the nudist colony. Christiane hadn't had time to go back to Noyon and had very little luggage with her. 'I have to send my son some cash,' she said. 'He can't stand me, but I still have to support him for another couple of years. I just hope he doesn't turn nasty – he hangs out with a lot of dodgy people – neo-Nazis and Muslims . . . D'you know, if he had an accident on his motorbike and was killed, I'd be heartbroken, but I think I'd probably feel relieved.'

It was September, so they found a spot easily. The nudist colony at Cap d'Agde was divided into five blocks built in the late Seventies and early Eighties with a capacity of 10,000 beds – the largest in the world. Their apartment was 22 square metres: a living room with a sofa-bed, a kitchenette, two bunk beds, a bathroom, separate toilet and a balcony. It had a maximum occupancy of four people – usually a family with two children. They felt at home immediately. The balcony was west-facing, with a view over the port, and so they could drink their apéritifs while watching the sun set.

Though it boasted three shopping centres, a mini-golf course and bicycle rental, the primary attractions for holidaymakers at the Cap d'Agde colony were sex and sunbathing. It was an archetype of a particular sociological concept, which was all the more surprising in that it was not the result of some pre-established plan, but the convergence of individual desires.

That, at least, was how Bruno portrayed it in his article, 'THE DUNES OF MARSEILLAN BEACH: TOWARDS AN AESTHETIC OF GOODWILL', a distillation of his two-week holiday. The article was rightly rejected by *Esprit*.

'What first strikes the visitor to Cap d'Agde,' wrote Bruno, 'is the juxtaposition of the consumer outlets typical of any European seaside resort with shops openly selling erotica and sex. It is surprising to see a bakery or a supermarket cheek by jowl with a shop selling transparent mini-skirts, latex underwear and dresses cut away to reveal breasts and buttocks. It is equally surprising to see women, and couples, some with their children, moving casually from shop to shop, aisle to aisle. At the station, the newsagents offer the usual array of papers and magazines alongside a motley assortment of porn mags, sex toys and wife-swapping personal magazines without raising so much as an eyebrow.

'Holiday clubs usually run the gamut from "family" concerns (Mini Clubs, Kids' Clubs – bottle warmers and sun-loungers) to more trendy establishments (body boarding, night clubs for ravers, "not recommended for under 12s"). The nudist colony at Cap d'Agde – with its high proportion of families and the focus on sexual activity divorced from traditional pick-up rituals –

ignored this standard dichotomy. What is most surprising is how different it is from traditional nudist colonies, which tend to stress the "healthy" aspects of naturism, avoiding any allusion to sexuality. They are big on macro-biotic food and smoking is usually forbidden. Their outlook is very "new age": holidaymakers study yoga, painting on silk and oriental exercise and are satisfied with rough-and-ready accommodation in a wilderness environment. The apartments on the Cap d'Agde, on the other hand, are luxurious even by the standards of other holiday resorts. The only allusion to nature is the manicured lawns and lavish flowerbeds. The food is standard fare, pizzerias jostling with seafood restaurants, French fries and ice-cream parlours. Even nudity seems to take on a different aspect. In traditional nudist colonies, nudity is obligatory whenever the weather permits; this is strictly monitored and all behaviour deemed to be voyeuristic is severely reprimanded. At Cap d'Agde, on the other hand, there is no dress code and, from the supermarkets to the bars, dress ranges from fully dressed to full nudity by way of overtly fetishistic clothing (PVC mini-skirts, lingerie, thigh-length boots). Voyeurism is tacitly condoned: it is commonplace to see men on the beach stop to admire the female genitalia on show; some women shave to make it easier to see the vulva and sometimes the clitoris. Even if one does not take part in the activities of the centre, all this makes for a singular atmosphere, as far removed from the erotic, narcissistic ambience of an Italian disco, as from the sleazy ambience of the red-light districts of major cities. What we have here is a traditional, rather genial, seaside resort with the single distinction that sexual pleasure is recognised as an important commodity. It is tempting to suggest that this is a sexual "social democracy", especially as foreign visitors to the resort are principally German, Dutch and Scandinavian.'

On the second day, Bruno and Christiane met a couple on the beach. Rudi and Hannelore gave them an insight into the sociology of the resort. Rudi was an engineer in a satellite tracking station responsible for the geostationary position of satellite Astra; Hannelore worked in a big bookshop in Hamburg. They had two small children but had decided to leave them with Hannelore's parents this year. The four of them had dinner together that evening in a seafood restaurant famous for its bouillabaisse. After dinner, they went back to the German couple's apartment. Bruno and Rudi took turns penetrating Hannelore while she licked Christiane's vagina, before getting the women to swap over. Then Hannelore fellated Bruno. She had a beautiful body, heavy but firm and toned through regular exercise. She sucked very sensitively; turned on by the whole situation, Bruno came a little too quickly. Rudi, however, managed to delay his orgasm for 20 minutes while Christiane and Hannelore sucked him off together, their tongues sliding over each other around the glans of his penis. Hannelore offered them a glass of kirsch to round off the evening.

The Germans spent little time in the night clubs at the colony. The Cleopatra and the Absolute could not compete with the Extasia, which was outside Marseillan, spectacularly equipped with a backroom, peepshows, heated swimming pool, jacuzzi and recently, the most magnificent mirror room in Languedoc-Roussillon. Far from resting on the laurels it had earned in the early Seventies, the Extasia had managed to preserve its reputation as a night-club legend. Nonetheless, Hannelore and Rudi suggested that they meet up the following evening in the Cleopatra. Though smaller than the Extasia, the Cleopatra, situated in the heart of the complex, had a warm, convivial atmosphere ideally suited to the novice. It was the perfect place to have an after-dinner drink with friends and a good place for women to try out their daring new clothing.

Rudi passed the bottle of kirsch around again. None of them had dressed. Bruno was excited to discover that he was hard again, less than half an hour after coming in Hannelore's mouth; he mentioned this, his voice naively enthusiastic. Touched, Christiane began to masturbate him under the tender gaze of their new friends. As he neared climax, Hannelore knelt between his thighs and started fellating him gently as Christiane continued to stroke him. Somewhat absently, Rudi murmured '*Gut . . . gut . . .*' They left, a little drunk, but in good spirits. Bruno said that together they reminded him of the Famous Five. He told Christiane she was exactly as he had always imagined George; all they needed now was Timmy the dog.

The following afternoon they went to the beach together. The weather was beautiful and very hot for September. Bruno thought how pleasant it was, the four of them walking, naked, along the shoreline. It was nice to know that there would be no problems, that all the sexual issues had been resolved; it was good to know that each of them would do their best to bring pleasure to the others.

The nudist beach at Cap d'Agde is about three kilometres long on a gentle slope, which makes it very safe for swimming even for young children. Most of its length is reserved for family bathing and beach activities (windsurfing, badminton, kite-flying). It is tacitly accepted that couples looking for adventure meet on the eastern part of the beach, just past the bar. The dunes, shored up at the sides, create a slight hill. From the top of the hill, one can see the beach to one side sloping gently to the sea; to the other side the dunes enclose flat expanses of sand dotted with clumps of holly oak. They settled themselves on the beach just below the dunes, looking from side to side.

'During our two-week holiday, we went to the beach every afternoon,' Bruno's article went on. 'Of course, death, or the thought that one might die could make one judgemental about such human pleasures. I intend to show that if we ignore such an extremist notion, the dunes of Marseillan beach are a defining example of the humanist proposition: striving to maximise individual pleasure without causing suffering to another. Sexual pleasure (the most intense feeling of which human beings are capable) is principally dependent on the sense of touch, in particular, the stimulation of areas of the epidermis rich in Krause's corpuscles. These activate neurons capable of triggering an abundant flow of endorphins from the hypothalamus. This simple neo-cortical system has evolved over generations of cultural change to generate a rich *fantasy world* centred (particularly in women) on *love*. My hypothesis is that the dunes of Marseillan beach, far from exacerbating such dangerous fantasies, actually serve to counteract such notions and bring sexual play back to its original form – which is to say, based on the notion of *goodwill*. In this space between the dunes and the shoreline, any couple can take the initiative and begin public fondling; often the woman begins to stroke or lick her partner's sexual organs and the man returns the favour. Neighbouring couples watch with interest, move closer the better to observe their caresses and slowly begin to follow their example. From the original couple, a wave of affection and sexual excite-ment will quickly ripple across the beach. Sexual passion beings to mount, couples come together to indulge in group sex – though it must be stressed that each waits for acknowledgement or explicit consent. If a woman wishes to decline an unwanted caress, she indicates this with a simple shake of the head, and the man makes a formal – almost comic – apology.

'The decorum among the men is even more striking further inland, above the line of the dunes. This is an area dedicated to amateurs of the *gang bang,* usually involving multiple male partners. Here, too, the germ is a couple who begin an intimate caress – commonly fellatio. Rapidly, the couple find themselves surrounded by 10 or 20 single men. Sitting, standing or crouched on their haunches, they masturbate as they watch the scene. Often things go no further, the couple return to their embrace and the crowd slowly disperses. Sometimes the woman will gesture to indicate that she would like to masturbate, fellate or be penetrated by other men. In this case, the men take turns – in no apparent hurry. When she wishes to stop, another simple gesture is sufficient. No words are exchanged; one can hear the wind whistling through the dunes, bowing the great tufts of coarse grass. Now and then, the wind dies away and the silence is almost total, broken only by cries of pleasure.

'It is not my intention to depict the naturist resort at Cap d'Agde as some sort of idyllic phalanstery out of Fourier. In Cap d'Agde, as anywhere, beautiful, firm young women and seductive, virile men will find themselves inundated by flattering propositions. In Cap d'Agde, as anywhere, the obese, the old and the ugly are condemned to solitary masturbation – the sole difference being that whereas masturbation is generally prohibited in public, here it is looked upon with kindly compassion. What is most surprising is that so many diverse sexual practices – many more than one might witness in a porno-graphic film – can take place with such exemplary courtesy and not so much as an undertone of violence. In my opinion, this "sexual social democracy" is an uncommon example of the qualities of discipline and respect for the social contract which allowed Germany to conduct two appallingly murderous wars a generation apart, before building a powerful international economy from the ruins of their country. Indeed, it would be interesting to see what countries which traditionally honour the values of discipline and respect (Japan, Korea) might make of the application of such principles in the Cap d'Agde. This respect, which pleasurably rewards those who respect the contract, is a powerful principle, in that even without a written code, it can be easily enforced on the multifarious minorities at the resort (*Front National* thugs, Arab delinquents, Italians from Rimini).'

At the end of his first week, Bruno stopped writing here. What remained to be said was more tender, more fragile and more uncertain. After spending the afternoon at the beach, they were in the habit of going back to their apartment for an apéritif at about seven o'clock. He usually had a Campari, Christiane a vodka martini. He watched the sunlight play on the brickwork. He enjoyed seeing Christiane wander naked through the apartment, fetching ice or olives. What he was feeling was strange, very strange: his breathing was easier, sometimes he found that he could spend minutes at a time without thinking, he was no longer really afraid. One afternoon, about a week after they arrived, he said to Christiane, 'I think I'm happy.' She stopped dead, her hand on the ice bucket tensed visibly, she breathed out slowly. He went on:

'I want to live with you. I think we've both had enough, that we've both been too miserable for too long. Later we'll have to deal with sickness and infirmity and death, but I think we could be happy together right to the end. I'd like to try, anyway. I think I love you.'

Christiane started to cry. Later, over seafood at the Neptune, they tried to work out what this might mean in practice. She could come and stay at weekends, that would be easy, but it would be difficult for her to get a transfer to Paris. Allowing for alimony, Bruno's salary was not enough for them to live on. In any case, there was Christiane's son to think of; they would have to wait. All the same, it was feasible; for the first time in many years, something seemed feasible.

The following morning Bruno wrote a short, emotional letter to Michel. He declared himself happy, regretted that they had never truly understood one another. He hoped that Michel, too, might find a measure of happiness. He signed the letter: *'Your brother, Bruno.'*

17

When Michel received the letter he was in despair over a theoretical crisis. According to Margenau's theory, human consciousness could be reduced to a field of probabilities in a Fock space, defined as a direct sum of Hilbert spaces. Such a space could be created by elementary electrical activity at a microscopic synaptic level. Normal behaviour could therefore be seen as the elasticity of the field and free will as a rupture within it; but in what topology? There was nothing in the natural topography of Hilbert spaces that might give rise to free will. Michel was not entirely convinced that the problem could even be posed except in the most metaphorical sense. One thing he was certain of was that a new conceptual framework was needed. Every night, before switching off his PC, he sent a request over the Internet for the daily experimental results from the Institute. The following morning, he would digest them. As he did so, he realised that around the world, researchers were trapped in a senseless empiricism. Nothing in their experimental results brought them closer to a conclusion, nor did they provide support for any particular hypothesis. Individual consciousness seemed to emerge among animals for no apparent reason, and seemed largely to predate the capacity for language. Darwinians, with instinctive determinism, put forward hypotheses about how natural selection might have benefited from the emergence of consciousness, but these in no way explained anything; they were Just So stories, no more. Then again, the anthropogenic model was hardly more convincing: life had thrown up something which could contemplate it, a mind capable of understanding it, but so what? That in itself did not make understanding consciousness any easier. Self-consciousness, which is absent in nematodes, was clearly observable in inferior lizards like *Lacerata agilis*, implying the presence of both a central nervous system and something more. What that something was, remained completely mysterious; consciousness did not seem to depend on any single thing, whether anatomical, biochemical or cellular. It was all rather depressing.

What would Heisenberg have done? What would Niels Bohr have done? Step back from the problem, take time to think, take a walk in the country, listen to music. The new was never simply a reworking of the old; detail was added to detail like grains of sand, predefined by the conceptual framework of the experiments; now more than ever a new paradigm was needed.

★

The short, blistering days went by sadly. On the night of 15 September Michel had an unusually happy dream. He was beside a young girl as she gambolled through the forest, surrounded by flowers and butterflies. (An image, he realised later, that had floated to the surface from a 30-year-old memory of *Prince Sapphire*, a television series he used to watch at his grandmother's every Sunday afternoon and which so accurately found an echo in his own heart.) A moment later, he was walking alone through tall grasses across an immense meadow. He could not see the horizon, the grassy hills seemed to stretch out to infinity under the brilliant, clear grey sky. He walked on, however, purposeful and unhurried; he knew that some way beneath his feet ran an underground river; he knew too that, instinctively, his feet would follow its path. All around him the breeze disturbed the long grass.

When he woke he felt joyful and alive, something that he had not felt in the two months since he had left work. He went out and walked under the beech trees down the avenue Émile Zola. He was alone, but he was not lonely. He stopped at the corner of the rue des Entrepreneurs. It was about nine o'clock. Zolacolor was opening up; Asian girls sat behind the cash desks. Between the Beaugrenelle towers, the sky seemed strangely luminous; there seemed no way out here. Perhaps he should have talked to his neighbour opposite – the girl who worked at *Vingt Ans*. Working for a lifestyle magazine, she would surely know how to belong. It must depend on common psychological traits which even he possessed. There was much that she could teach him. He walked back quickly, almost breaking into a run, and bounded up the stairs to the door of his neighbour's apartment. He rang the doorbell three times. No one answered. Flustered, he retreated to his own block; as he waited for the lift he questioned himself. Was he depressed, and did such a question have any meaning? For years he had seen posters appear in the area, asking people to be vigilant and warning them about the *Front National*. The fact that he had no opinion on such a subject one way or the other was already a worrying sign. *Depressive lucidity*, which is usually described as a withdrawal from ordinary human concerns, generally manifests itself by a profound indifference to things which are, genuinely, of minor interest. Thus, it is possible to imagine a depressed lover, while the idea of a depressed patriot seems frankly inconceivable.

Back in his kitchen, he realised that belief in the notions of reason and of free will, which are the natural foundations of democracy, probably resulted from a confusion between the concepts of freedom and unpredictability. The turbulence of a river flowing around the supporting pillar of a bridge is structurally unpredictable, but no one would think to describe it as being *free*. He poured himself a glass of white wine, opened the curtains and lay down to think. The equations of chaos theory made no reference to physical space; their ubiquity meant that they applied as effectively to hydrodynamics as to meteorology, group sociology or the genetics of a population. As a tool for devising models they were excellent, but their predictive capacities were non-existent. On the other hand, the equations of quantum mechanics made it possible to predict the behaviour of microphysical systems with exceptional precision, even perfect precision if one was prepared to accept a purely materialist ontology. It was certainly premature to try and establish a mathematical link between the two. It might even prove impossible. But Michel was convinced that the physical nature and evolution of attractors in neurons and synapses held the key to understanding human actions and opinions.

Looking for a list of recent publications on the subject, he noticed that he had not opened his mail for more than a week. Naturally, most of it was junk mail. With the launch of the *Costa Romantica,* a company called TMR hoped to completely redefine the concept of the luxury cruise. The ship was described as being an 'authentic floating paradise'. The first moments of his cruise – 'the decision is yours!' – might be described thus: 'You step into the great hall. Sunlight streams through the great glass cupola. You take one of the panoramic lifts to the upper deck. Here, from the immense atrium situated on the prow, you can stare out to sea as though you were watching it *on a gigantic screen*.' He put the brochure to one side, telling himself he would study it in detail later. 'Walk along the deck, contemplate the ocean from the comfort of a vast atrium, sail for weeks under a changeless sky . . .' Why not? While they sailed, Western Europe might well be atomised under a hail of bombs. They would disembark, tanned and radiant, onto a new continent.

In the meantime, he had to live, and that was something he could do intelligently, responsibly, joyously. In the most recent issue of *Dernières Nouvelles de Monoprix,* the accent was ever more on 'real' food. Once again, the editor took issue with the notion that convenience and gastronomy were incompatible. Their scrupulous choice of ingredients, their range of produce, their own-brand products, everything, in fact, that Monoprix had stood for since the beginning was based on a premise which directly contradicted this. 'It is possible to have gourmet food, a balanced diet, and to have it now' the editor affirmed. After this first contentious, one might even say combative, article, the rest of the magazine was filled with 'handy hints', educational games and 'useful information'. Michel was therefore able to calculate his average daily calorie intake. He discovered that in the past fortnight, he had not swept or ironed, gone swimming, played tennis or made love; the only three activities he could actually tick off were sitting, lying down and sleeping. All told, he only needed 1,750 kilocalories a day. From Bruno's letter, it was clear that he'd been doing rather more swimming and lovemaking. He recalculated, using these new parameters, and discovered he would need 2,700 kilocalories a day.

There was a second letter, this one from the town council at Crécy-en-Brie. In the light of development plans for a new car park, it was necessary to reorganise the local cemetery, and a number of graves, among them his grandmother's, would have to be moved. According to regulations, a family member had to be present for the removal of the remains. If he would be so good as to arrange a meeting with the funeral directors between the hours of ten thirty and midday . . .

18

Second Meetings

The monorail to Crécy-la-Chapelle had been replaced by a commuter train. The village itself had changed a lot. He stopped for a moment in the square outside the station and looked around him in surprise. There was a Casino hypermarket on the outskirts of Crécy on the avenue Général-Leclerc. All around him, he could see new houses, new office buildings.

It had all happened around the time Eurodisney opened, explained the councillor at the town hall, and the extension of the RER as far as Marne-la-Vallée. A lot of Parisians chose to move here; land prices more than tripled and the last of the farmers sold off their fields. Now there was a complex comprising a gym, a community centre and two swimming pools. There were some problems with delinquency, but no more than anywhere else.

As he passed the old houses and the canals on his way

to the cemetery, he felt the sadness and confusion of anyone returning to their childhood home. As he crossed the
old town wall, he found himself opposite the windmill.
The seat where he and Annabelle liked to sit after school
was still there. In the dark waters huge fish swam against
the current. Sunshine briefly broke through the clouds.

The man was waiting for Michel at the cemetery gates.
'Are you the . . .' 'Yes.' What did they call gravediggers
nowadays? He was carrying a spade and a black plastic bag.
Michel walked beside him. 'You don't have to be there
when I . . .' he muttered as they approached the open
grave.

Death is a difficult thing to understand; only reluctantly
does a person face the reality of it. Michel had seen the
body of his grandmother 20 years before and had kissed her
for the last time. At first, he was surprised by what he saw.
His grandmother had been buried in a coffin, but among
the freshly dug earth there were only fragments of broken
wood, a rotting board and indistinct white fragments.
When he realised what he was looking at he quickly
turned his head and forced himself to look the other way,
but it was too late. He had seen the skull caked with earth,
clumps of white hair falling over empty sockets. He had
seen her vertebrae scattered in the clay. He understood.

The man continued to fill the plastic bag, glancing over
at Michel lying on the ground. 'Always the same . . .' he
muttered. 'Can't help themselves, they have to look.
Coffin's not going to last twenty years, is it?' he said

almost angrily. Michel walked a few paces behind as the gravedigger transported the remains to their new resting place. When he had finished his work, the man stood up and came over to him. 'You alright?' Michel nodded. 'We'll move the headstone tomorrow. Can you sign here for me?'

That was that. After 20 years, that was that. Bones and earth mingled together and the mass of white hair, so much of it, so white. He could see his grandmother darning in front of the television, walking towards the kitchen. That was that. As he passed the Bar des Sports, he realised he was trembling. He went in and ordered a pastis. When he sat down he noticed that the interior was completely different from the way he remembered it. There was a pool table and video games; a television tuned to MTV blared out music. The cover of *Newlook* pinned to the noticeboard promised the Fantasies of Zara Whites and great white sharks in Australia. He gradually slipped into a gentle doze.

It was Annabelle who recognised him first. She had just bought cigarettes and was making for the door when she saw him sitting on the bench. She hesitated for a second or two and then came up to him. He looked up. 'This is a surprise . . .' she said softly; then she sat opposite him on the moleskin seat. She had hardly changed. Her face was still incredibly smooth and pure, her hair was dazzlingly blonde. It seemed impossible that she could be 40: she looked 27 or 28 at most.

She was in Crécy for reasons similar to his own. 'My father died a week ago,' she said. 'Cancer of the bowel. It was long and difficult – and excruciatingly painful. I stayed for a bit to help Mum out. The rest of the time I live in Paris, like you.'

Michel looked down. There was a moment's silence. At the next table two young guys were talking about karate.

'I ran into Bruno about three years ago, at an airport. He told me you were a scientist, you were successful – well known in your field. He told me you never married. I never did do much – I'm a librarian in a local library. I never married either. I've often thought about you. I hated you when you didn't answer my letters. That was twenty-three years ago, but I still think about it sometimes.'

She walked him to the station. It was almost six and getting dark. They stopped on the bridge over the Grand Morin. There were plants in the water, chestnut trees, willows; the water was still and green. Corot had loved this scene and had painted it many times. An old man in his garden looked like a scarecrow. 'We're at the same point now,' said Annabelle, 'the same distance from death.'

She stood on the step of the train and kissed him on both cheeks just before it pulled out. 'I'll see you again,' he said. She answered: 'Yes.'

She invited him to dinner the following Saturday. She was living in a studio apartment on the rue Legendre. It was very small, but the place seemed warm and inviting – the walls and the ceiling were panelled in dark wood like the cabin of a boat. 'I've been living here for eight years,' she said. 'I moved in when I passed my library exams. Before that I worked in the co-production unit at TF1. I'd had enough – I didn't like working in television. I lost two-thirds of my salary when I changed jobs, but I like it much better. I work in the children's section in the local public library.'

She had made a lamb curry with dhal. Michel said little as they ate. He asked Annabelle about her family. Her elder brother had taken over the family business. He was married with three children – a boy and two girls. Unfortunately, the business was in trouble, competition in precision optics was fierce, he had almost filed for bankruptcy on more than one occasion. He drowned his sorrows drinking pastis and voting for Le Pen. Her younger brother had gone into the marketing department at l'Oréal; he had recently been made marketing director for North America; they didn't see much of him. He was divorced, childless. Two completely different fates, but both somehow archetypal.

'I haven't really had a happy life,' said Annabelle. 'I think I was too obsessed with love. I fell for guys too easily; once they got what they wanted, they dumped me and I got hurt. It took me years to come to terms with the cliché that men don't make love because they're in love, they do it because they're turned on. Everyone around me knew that and lived like that – I grew up in a pretty liberal environment – but I never enjoyed the game for its own sake. In the end, even the sex started to disgust me; I couldn't stand their triumphant little smiles when I took off my dress, or their idiot leers when they came and especially their boorishness once the deed was done. They were weak, pathetic and pretentious. In the end, it was too hurtful to know they thought of me as just another piece of meat. I was a prime cut, I suppose, because I was physically perfect, and they were proud to take me out and show me off in a restaurant. Only once did I think I was involved in a serious relationship, I even moved in with him. He was an actor, there was something very imposing about him physically, but he never really made it – in fact I paid most of the bills. We lived together for two years and then I got pregnant. He told me to have an abortion. I did. But even as I was coming back from the hospital I knew it was over. I moved out that night and moved into a hotel for a while. I was thirty, I'd had two abortions and I couldn't take much more. This was in 1988 and everyone was starting to worry about AIDS; for me it was a salvation. I'd slept with dozens of men and there wasn't one of them worth remembering. People think that when you're young you go out and have fun and only later do you start to think about death. But every man I ever met was terrified of getting old. They worried all the time about how old they were. They get obsessed about it when they're quite young – I've seen twenty-five-year-olds worried about getting old – and it just gets worse. I decided to give up, to stop playing the game. I live a quiet life, a joyless life. At nights I read, I make herbal tea and hot drinks. I go to see my parents every weekend, I spend a lot of time looking after my nephew and my nieces. Sometimes I get scared at night; sometimes I feel that I need a man around. I take tranquillisers and sleeping pills, but they're never really enough. I just want life to go by as quickly as possible.'

Michel said nothing; he wasn't surprised. For many women, adolescence is exciting – they're really interested in boys and in sex. Gradually they lose interest; they're not so keen to open their legs, or to get on their knees and wiggle their arse. They're looking for a tender relationship that they never find, for a passion they no longer feel; so they begin the long, difficult years.

Folded out, the sofa-bed took up most of the room. 'I've never actually used it before,' Annabelle said. They lay down side by side and held each other.

'I haven't been on the pill for a long time, and I haven't got any condoms here. Have you got any?'

'No . . .' he smiled at the very idea.

'Would you like me to take you in my mouth?'

He thought for a moment and, at last, said 'Yes.' It was pleasant, though the pleasure was not intense (in fact, it never had been. Sexual pleasure, which is so intense for some, is faint, almost insignificant for others; is this a result of culture, of neural connections or what?). There was a poignancy in the act: it symbolised their second meeting, their interrupted destinies. And, afterwards, it was wonderful to take Annabelle in his arms when she turned away to sleep. Her body was soft and pliant, warm and perfectly smooth; she had a slim waist, big hips and small, firm breasts. He slipped a leg between hers and placed his hands on her stomach, her breasts; in this warmth, this softness, he was at the dawn of the world. He fell asleep almost immediately.

At first he saw a man, a form in space, only his face was visible. The expression in his eyes as they flashed in the darkness was indecipherable. There was a mirror facing him. When he first looked in the mirror, the man felt as though he was falling into an abyss. But he sat down and studied his reflection as though it were a thing apart, a mental image unrelated to him. After a time he began to feel more at ease, but if he turned away, even for an instant, he had to begin again. He had to force himself to shatter the link which bound him to his reflection. The self was an intermittent neurosis, and this man was far from being cured of it.

Then he saw a smooth, white wall, and as though from within, letters began to form upon it. Little by little, the letters rose, creating a moving bas-relief in time to an excruciating throb. At first it resolved into the word 'PEACE', then into 'WAR', then 'PEACE' reappeared. Then, suddenly, the phenomenon ceased and the surface of the wall was as smooth as before. The atmosphere seemed to liquefy, pulsing in waves; the sun was immense, yellow. He could see a distant point, the root of time itself. From one central knot, tendrils snaked out across the universe, their tips cold and sticky. They wound round, encircled and agglomerated part of space.

He saw the brain of the dead man, a part of space, enclosing space.

Last, he saw the mental aggregate of space and its opposite. He saw the mental conflict through which space was structured, and saw it disappear. He saw space as a thin line separating two spheres. In the first sphere there was being, then space, and in the second was non-being and the destruction of the individual. Calmly, without a moment's hesitation, he turned and walked towards the second sphere.

He extricated himself from their embrace and sat up. Beside him, Annabelle's breathing was deep and regular. She had a Sony alarm clock which read 03:37. Could he get back to sleep? He had to get back to sleep. He had some Xanax with him.

In the morning, she made him coffee while she had tea and toast. The weather was beautiful though it was already a little cold. She looked at his naked body; his skinny frame seemed strangely adolescent. They were both 40, and it was difficult to believe. Nonetheless, she could no longer have children without running the risk that they would be genetically malformed; his virility had already largely ebbed. From the point of view of the good of the species, they were a couple of ageing human beings of little genetic value. She had lived a bit: taken cocaine, been involved in orgies, stayed in luxury hotels. Her beauty had put her at the eye of the sexual storm that had been such a major part of her youth, and she had suffered for it – she had almost given her life for it. His indifference had left him on the periphery of that storm, and of life, and he had been barely touched by it; he had been content to be faithful to his local Monoprix and to coordinate research in molecular biology. Their different lives had left few visible marks on their separate bodies, but life itself had long since begun its work of destruction, slowly eliminating the capacity of cells to reproduce and organs to heal. Intelligent mammals capable of loving one another, they looked at each another on this autumn morning. 'I know we've left it a bit late,' she said, 'but I'd still like to try. I still have my train pass from 1974–75, the last year we were at school together. Every time I look at it, I feel like crying. I can't understand how things can have gone so wrong. I just can't accept it.'

19

In the midst of the suicide of the West, it was clear that they had no chance. They continued to see each other, however, once or twice a week. Annabelle visited her gynaecologist and went back on the pill. Michel proved able to penetrate her, but what he liked most was simply sleeping next to her, feeling her living flesh. One night, he dreamed of a fun fair in Rouen, on the right bank of the Seine. There was a Big Wheel, almost empty, turning slowly against a livid sky, dominating a landscape of clapped-out freighters and old rusting cranes. He walked past the sideshows, the lights alternately dim and bright; a glacial wind whipped rain against his face. As he came to the gates of the park, he was attacked by a number of youths in leathers wielding razors. They laid into him for some minutes and then let him go on. Blood was running into his eyes, he knew that he would be blind, his right hand had almost been severed. In spite of the blood and the pain, still he knew that Annabelle would stay by him, she would shield him with her love for ever.

On All Saints' Day they went to Soulac for the week-end and stayed in a holiday home that belonged to Annabelle's brother. The morning they arrived, they walked down to the beach together. He felt suddenly tired and sat on a bench while Annabelle walked on. In the distance, the sea roared and heaved, a constant grey and silver flux. As they broke against the sandbanks on the horizon, the waves threw spray against the sun in a dazzling, beautiful haze. Annabelle's silhouette, barely visible in her pale jacket, walked along the water's edge. Circling around the plastic furniture of the Café de la Plage, an old Alsatian was barely visible, half erased by a mist of water and sunlight.

For dinner, she grilled a sea bass; the society in which they lived accorded them a surplus above and beyond their basic needs, so they could live a little, but the fact was, they no longer wanted to. He had an immense compassion for her, for the boundless reserve of love he could feel simmering inside her, which the world had wasted; he felt compassion and, to be honest, it was perhaps the only emotion which could still touch him. As to the rest, a glacial reticence had taken over his body; he simply could not love.

Back in Paris, they had happy moments together, like stills from a perfume ad (dashing hand in hand down the steps of Montmartre; or suddenly revealed in motionless embrace on the Pont des Arts by the lights of a *bateau-mouche* as it turned). There were arguments, too, the inconsequential Sunday afternoon moments of silence when bodies curl up beneath the sheets, the long shores of silence and apathy where life founders. Annabelle's studio was dark; they had to turn the lights on at four in the afternoon. They were sad sometimes, but mostly they were serious. Both of them knew that this would be their last human relationship and that feeling lent something lacerating to every moment they spent together. They had a great respect and a profound sympathy for one another. But there were days when, caught up in some sudden magic, they knew moments of fresh air and glorious sunshine; for the most part, however, they could feel a grey shadow moving over them and on the earth that supported them, they could make out the end.

20

Bruno and Christiane had also returned to Paris, it was inconceivable not to. On the day they went back to work, he stopped and thought about the unknown doctor who had given him the two weeks of unmerited sick leave, then he set off again towards his office on the rue de Grenelle. As he got to his floor, he realised he looked tanned and healthy – which was ridiculous – but he realised that he didn't care. His colleagues, the thought-provoking seminars, the social development of the adolescent, multiculturalism . . . none of it had the slightest importance for him any more. Christiane sucked his cock, looked after him when he was ill; Christiane was important. At that moment, he knew he would not see his son again.

Christiane's son Patrice had left the apartment a complete tip: pizza trodden into the carpet, empty Coke cans, cigarette butts were strewn about and there were scorch marks on the floor. She hesitated for a moment, thought about checking into a hotel, but then she decided to clean up, to make the place her own again. Noyon was a dirty, dull and dangerous town: she got into the habit of going to Paris every weekend. Most Saturdays, they would go to a club for couples – the 2+2, Chris et Manu, the Chandelles. Their first night at Chris et Manu left a vivid impression on Bruno. Along the dance floor there were a number of booths bathed in a strange purple glow. All around them, couples were fucking, stroking and licking each other. Most of the women were naked, though some wore a blouse or a tee shirt, or had simply hiked up their skirts. In the largest room there were about 20 couples. No one spoke, there was only the steady hum of the air conditioning and the moaning of women as they approached orgasm. He sat on one of the beds next to a tall dark-haired woman with heavy breasts who was being tongued by a man of about 50 who was still wearing a shirt and tie. Christiane opened his trousers and began to jerk him off, glancing around her as she did so. A man came up to them and slipped his hand under her skirt. She unhooked it and it slipped to the floor; she was wearing nothing underneath. The man knelt and began to stroke her as she continued to wank Bruno. Beside him on the bed, the dark-haired woman started to moan louder, he cupped her breasts. He was hard as a rock. Christiane leaned over and began to tease the slit of his penis and the frenum with the tip of her tongue. Another couple came over and sat beside them; the woman, a redhead of about

20, was wearing a black PVC mini-skirt. She watched as Christiane licked his cock; Christiane smiled at her and pulled up her tee shirt to show off her breasts. The other woman hiked up her skirt revealing her cunt, her pubic hair was also red. Christiane took her hand and guided it to Bruno's penis. The woman began to masturbate him while Christiane continued to lick the glans. In a matter of seconds he shuddered with a spasm of pleasure and came all over her face. 'I'm sorry,' he said, 'really sorry.' She kissed him and pulled him close to her, he could smell the spunk on her cheeks. 'It doesn't matter,' she said gently, 'it really doesn't matter.' 'Do you want to go?' she said a little later. He nodded sadly, his excitement had completely dissipated. They dressed quickly and left immediately.

In the weeks that followed he learned to control himself a little better; it was the beginning of a good time for them, a happy time. His life had meaning now, though it was limited to the weekends he spent with Christiane. In the health section of FNAC he found a book by an American sexologist on how to postpone ejaculation using a series of gradual exercises. Essentially, they helped to develop the pubo-coccal muscle, a small arc-shaped muscle at the base of the testicles. Bruno began to work on the exercises; it was something worth working on. Every time they went out he was astonished to see men, often much older than he, penetrate several women one after another, to see them masturbated or sucked for hours on end without

ever losing their erections. He was embarrassed to discover that most had pricks much bigger than his.
Christiane told him time and again it didn't matter, that it
made no difference to her. He believed her – he could see
that she was in love with him – but he could not help but
feel that many of the women they met in clubs were
somewhat disappointed when they saw his penis. No one
ever commented; their courtesy was exemplary, and the
atmosphere was always friendly and polite; but their looks
couldn't lie and slowly he realised that, from a sexual
viewpoint, he just didn't make the grade. But there were
moments of fleeting, unbelievable pleasure in which he
would almost swoon, which made him scream with
genuine pleasure, but they had less to do with his potency
than his genital sensitivity. On the other hand, Christiane
told him he was very tactile, and it was true, he knew that
it was rare for him not to be able to bring a woman to
orgasm. In mid-December, he noticed that Christiane was
losing weight and that there were red marks on her face.
She was still having problems with her back, she told him,
and had increased her medication; the weight loss and the
red spots were just side effects of the drugs. She quickly
changed the subject and he thought she seemed
embarrassed. He felt uneasy about the whole thing. She
was certainly capable of lying to protect him: she was too
gentle, too good-natured. On Saturday nights, she usually
cooked and they had a nice meal together before going
out. She wore skirts slit up the side, and small see-through
tops, suspenders or sometimes a body stocking open at the

crotch. Her pussy was soft, exciting and instantly wet. They were wonderful nights of the sort that he had hardly dreamed of before. Sometimes, when she let herself be fucked by several people, Christiane's heartbeat would become irregular. Her heart would begin to beat a little too fast and she would suddenly start to sweat; at such times Bruno was afraid. They would stop, then; she would press herself against him, kiss him and stroke his neck and his hair.

21

Of course, even here, there was no escape. The men and women who frequented clubs for couples quickly abandoned their search for pleasure (which required time, finesse and sensitivity) in favour of prodigal sexual abandon – an empty experience based directly on the gang bang scenes in the fashionable porn movies shown on Canal Plus. In homage to Marx's 'tendency for the general rate of profit to decline', the cryptic law at the heart of his system, it would be nice to propose a corresponding 'tendency for the general rate of pleasure to decline' for the libertine system in which Bruno and Christiane found themselves, but it would be simplistic and inaccurate. Pleasure and desire, which as cultural, anthropological and secondary phenomena explain little about sexuality itself; far from being a determining factor, they are in fact themselves sociologically determined. In the context of a monogamous system based on romance and love, they can be attained only through the intermediary of the loved one. In the liberal system which Bruno and Christiane had joined, the sexual model proposed by the dominant culture (advertising, magazines, health education groups) was governed by the principle of *adventure*: in such a system, pleasure and desire become part of the process of *seduction*, and favour originality, passion and individual creativity (all qualities also required of employees in their professional capacities). In concentrating on the physical aspects of seduction to the exclusion of intellectual and moral considerations, regulars of such clubs were led to a fantasy version of the dominant culture: the *Sadean* system. In this fantasy world, cocks are invariably enormous and rock hard, breasts are enhanced, cunts wet and shaven. Female regulars, often readers of *Connexion* and *Hot Video*, go out with the sole aim of being impaled on as many pricks as possible. For them, the logical next step would be S&M clubs. Orgasm is a creature of habit, as Pascal would undoubtedly have said if he had been interested in such things.

With his five-inch cock and his inability to maintain an erection between orgasms (he had never really been able to sustain a hard-on for any length of time, except perhaps as a teenager, and the time between ejaculations had grown considerably since then: he wasn't getting any younger), Bruno was not really comfortable in such places. He was happy, however, to have more cunts and mouths open to him than he ever dreamed possible; he felt indebted to Christiane for that. The gentlest moments were those when she caressed another woman; the women were invariably delighted by the deftness of her tongue and the agility of her fingers in finding and stimulating their clitorises; their stimulation of him, however, was usually disappointing. Gaping from multiple penetrations and brutal fingering (often using several fingers, or indeed the whole hand), their cunts had all the sensitivity of blocks of lard. Imitating the frenetic rhythm of porn actresses, they brutally jerked his cock in a ridiculous piston motion as though it was a piece of dead meat (the ubiquity of techno in the clubs, rather than more sensual rhythms, probably contributed to the mechanical nature of their technique). He came quickly, with no real pleasure, and after that, the evening was over as far as he was concerned. They usually stayed for another half hour or an hour; Christiane would let herself be fucked by several men while trying – usually vainly – to get him hard. When they woke, they would make love again and images of the previous night would flood back, softened by sleep; these were moments of extraordinary tenderness.

The ideal scenario would have been to invite a number of couples to spend the evening at their apartment and chat pleasantly while fondling one another. Bruno felt sure that this was the way forward; he knew, too, that he should go back to the exercises recommended by the American sexologist. His relationship with Christiane, which had brought him more joy than anything in his life, was a deep and serious one. That, at least, is what he thought sometimes, as he watched her dress or potter in the kitchen. But during the week, when she was away from him, he more often thought that it was a bad farce, one last sordid joke that life had played on him. Unhappiness is always keenest when faced with a realistic chance of happiness.

The accident happened one night in February at Chris et Manu. Bruno was lying on a mattress, his head raised on several cushions, holding Christiane's hand as she gave him a blow job. She was kneeling over him, legs apart, offering herself to any man who might pass; they slipped on condoms and took her from behind. Five men had already fucked her without Christiane even glancing at them; eyes half-closed, dreamlike, she let her tongue play on Bruno's penis, exploring every inch of its length. Suddenly she gave a single short cry. The man behind her, a well-built guy with curly hair, continued conscientiously to pump her hard and fast; his eyes glazed and distant. 'Stop! Stop!' said Bruno; he thought he had screamed, but his voice did not seem to carry, only a feeble croak escaped his lips. He got up and brutally pushed the guy away. The man stood, stunned, his cock rigid, arms hanging loose at his sides. Christiane had fallen onto her side, her face contorted in a rictus of pain. 'Can you move?' he asked her. She shook her head. He ran to the bar and asked to use the telephone. The ambulance arrived ten minutes later. Everyone in the club had dressed and in complete silence watched the paramedics lift Christiane onto a stretcher. Bruno went with her in the ambulance to the Hôtel Dieu nearby. For hours he waited in the corridor until the duty nurse came to speak to him: she was asleep now; she was out of danger.

On Sunday they took a bone marrow sample. Bruno came back at six. It was dark already, and a chill, fine rain was falling over the Seine. Christiane was sitting up in bed, her back supported on a pile of pillows. She smiled when she saw him. The diagnosis was simple: the necrosis in the vertebrae of her coccyx was so advanced that nothing could be done. She had known for several months that it could happen at any moment; her medication had slowed its progress, but could not stop it. It would get no worse, and there were no complications, but she would be permanently paralysed from the waist down.

She was discharged ten days later; Bruno was with her. Things were different now; in general life is a series of long stretches of dazed monotony, and for the most part, it is miserable. Then, suddenly, things take a decisive turn. Christiane would never have to work again, she was entitled to an invalidity pension; even to a free home help. She wheeled herself towards him, still a little awkward – her forearms were not yet strong enough. He kissed her on both cheeks, then on the lips. 'Now you can come to Paris and move in with me,' he said. She looked up at him, but he could not hold her gaze. 'Are you sure?' she asked softly. 'Are you sure that's what you want?' He didn't answer, or at least he hesitated. There was silence for 30 seconds and then she added: 'You don't have to. You've still got your life ahead of you, you don't have to look after a cripple.' Contemporary consciousness is no longer equipped to deal with our mortality. More than at any time or in any other civilisation, human beings are obsessed with ageing. Each individual has a simple view of the future: a time will come when the sum of pleasures that life has left to offer is outweighed by the sum of pain (one can actually feel the meter ticking, and it ticks inevitably towards the end). This weighing up of pleasure and pain which, sooner or later, everyone is forced to make, leads logically, at a certain age, to suicide. On the subject, it's amusing to note that two highly respected *fin-de-siècle* intellectuals, Gilles Deleuze and Guy Debord, both committed suicide for no reason other than that they could not bear the idea of their own physical decline. Their suicides provoked no surprise and no comment; in general, the suicide of elderly people – by far the most commonplace – seems to us perfectly rational. It is perhaps also useful to cite public reaction to the prospect of a terrorist attack as symptomatic: the overwhelming majority of people would prefer to be killed outright rather than tortured, maimed, or even disfigured. In part, this is probably because they are somewhat tired of life; but the principal reason is that nothing – not even death – seems worse than the prospect of living in a broken body.

★

He turned left at La-Chapelle-en-Serval. The easiest thing would be to plough the car into a tree as he drove through the forest of Compiègne. He had hesitated a couple of seconds too long; poor Christiane. Then he had hesitated a couple of days too long before calling her; he knew she was alone in her council apartment with her son, he could picture her there in her wheelchair by the phone. There was nothing forcing him to look after a cripple, that's what she'd said, and he knew that she had not died hating him. Her broken wheelchair had been found at the bottom of the stairs near the letter box. Her face was swollen and her neck broken. Bruno's name was in the box marked 'in the event of an accident, please contact'; she had died on the way to hospital.

The funeral complex was just outside Noyon on the road to Chauny, you turn off just after Baboeuf. In a white Portakabin, two employees in overalls were waiting for him. It was stuffy and overheated, there were radiators everywhere like a classroom in a technical school. The windows opened onto a series of low-rise modern buildings in a semi-residential zone. The coffin, still open, lay on a trestle table. Bruno approached it, saw Christiane's corpse and felt himself fall backwards; his head hit the ground hard. The men helped him up gently. 'Cry! Go on, let it all out! . . .' the older man urged him. He shook his head; he knew he couldn't bring himself to. Christiane's body would never again breathe, or move or speak. Her body would never again love, nothing now was possible for Christiane, and it was all his fault. This time all the cards had been dealt, all the hands played, the last card was on the table and he had lost. He had no more been capable of love than his parents before him. He floated in a strange state of detachment as though he were lifted off the ground. He watched as they placed the lid on the coffin and screwed it down with an electric screw-driver. He followed them to the 'wall of silence', a grey concrete wall three metres high with funerary trays set into it, half of which were empty. The older of the two men checked his instruction sheet and went to compartment 682; behind him, his colleague rolled the coffin on the trestle. It was cold and damp, it was beginning to rain. Compartment 682 was halfway up the wall. In one quick, efficient motion, the workers lifted the coffin and slid it into the hole. With a pneumatic gun, they sealed up the compartment with quick drying cement, then the elder of the two asked Bruno to sign the register. If he wanted, the man said as he left, he could stay and collect his thoughts.

Bruno drove back along the A1, arriving at the *périphérique* at about eleven. He had taken the day off; it hadn't occurred to him that the ceremony would be so brief. He took the Porte de Châtillon exit and found a place to park on the rue Albert-Sorel just opposite his ex-wife's apartment. He did not have to wait long. Ten minutes later, his son turned the corner of the avenue Ernest-Reyer, his satchel on his back. He seemed worried, and he was talking to himself as he walked. What could he be thinking about? Anne had told him that he was a solitary boy; he would come home at lunchtime and heat up something she had left for him rather than eat with his classmates at school. Had he missed Bruno? Probably, though he had never said anything. Children suffer the world that adults create for them and try their best to fit in with it; in time, they will replicate it. Victor reached the door, keyed in the security code; he was only a couple of yards from the car but he hadn't noticed Bruno. Bruno sat up in his seat and put his hand on the door handle. The door to the building closed behind the boy; Bruno stayed motionless for some minutes, then sat back heavily in his seat. What could he possibly say to his son, what message did he have to give? Nothing. There was nothing. He knew his life was over, but he didn't understand the ending. Everything was dark, indistinct and painful.

He started the car and took the motorway south. Just past the exit for Antony, he turned off towards Vauhallan. The psychiatric clinic run by the Éducation Nationale was just outside Verrières-le-Buisson, near the forest of Verrières; he remembered the park well. He parked on rue Victor-Considérant, walked the short distance to the gates. He recognised the duty nurse. He said: 'I've come back.'

22

Saorge – Terminus

Advertising is so focused on attracting the youth market that it has often blundered into campaigns in which age is treated with condescension, caricature and ridicule. To compensate for the inability of such a society to listen, it is necessary to ensure that every member of every sales force become an 'ambassador' to the elderly.
(Corinne Mégy – *Le Vrai Visage des Seniors*)

Perhaps it was always going to end like this; perhaps there was no other way, no other way out. Perhaps it was necessary to unravel everything that had become tangled, complete everything that had been started. And so Djerzinski had to come to this place: Saorge, latitude 44° north, longitude 7°30 east, at an altitude of just over 500 metres. At Nice, he checked into the Hôtel Windsor, a mid-range hotel with a foul ambience, one of whose rooms had been painted by the mediocre artist Philippe

Perrin. The following morning he took the famously picturesque Nice–Tende train. The train wound its way through the northern suburbs of Nice with council blocks full of Arabs, billboards for Minitel chat-rooms and a 60 per cent *Front National* majority. After Peillon-Saint-Thècle station, the train entered a tunnel, and when it emerged into the brilliant sunshine Djerzinski could see the fantastical silhouette of the town of Peillon perched high in the hills. This was what was called the *arrière-pays niçois*; people came from as far as Chicago and Denver to contemplate the beauty of the hinterland of Nice. Then the train entered the ravines of the Roya, Djerzinski disembarked at Fanton-Saorge; he had no luggage; it was the end of May. He walked for about half an hour. About halfway, he had to go through a tunnel; there was no traffic whatsoever.

According to the *Guide du Routard* he'd bought at Orly airport, the village of Saorge, dominating the whole valley, its tall houses built vertiginously into the hillside, had 'something Tibetan about it'; you could put it that way. In any case, it was here that his mother Janine, who had been rechristened Jane, had chosen to die, after five years in Goa on the west coast of the Indian subcontinent.

'Well, she chose to come here,' Bruno corrected him, 'I'm sure she didn't choose to die. Apparently the old whore converted to Islam, to Sufi mysticism or some such bollocks. She moved into an empty house outside the village with a crowd of hippies. You'd think hippies had disappeared from how little you hear about them in magazines and the papers, but actually, there's more of them than ever, what with high unemployment – the place is swarming with them. I did my own little survey . . .' he lowered his voice, 'the thing is, now they call themselves "neo-rurals", but actually they do sod all. They just sign on and get some rubbish grant supposed to promote hill farming.' He nodded his head with a knowing air, drained his glass and ordered another. He had arranged to meet Michel at Chez Gilou, the only café in the village. With its saucy postcards, framed pictures of trout and a poster for 'Saorge Boules' with its steering committee of at least 14, it evoked an olde-worlde Hunting/Fishing/Nature/Heritage atmosphere completely at odds with the neo-hippie movement vilified by Bruno. He carefully took a pamphlet out of his pocket entitled SOLIDARITY WITH THE BRIGASQUE SHEEP! 'I wrote it last night . . .' he said conspiratorially. 'I was talking to some of the farmers yesterday. They're struggling to make ends meet – they're really angry – their sheep have been decimated. It's all because of the eco-movement and the National Park at Mercantour. They've reintroduced wolves into the wild, hordes of wolves, and they eat the lambs! . . .' His voice became strangulated and suddenly he began to sob violently. In his letter to Michel, Bruno had mentioned that he had moved back to the psychiatric clinic at Verrières-le-Buisson 'probably for good'. They had obviously let him out for the occasion.

'So our mother is dying . . .' Michel interrupted, anxious to get to the point.

'Absolutely! It's the same at Cap d'Agde, apparently they've closed the dunes to the public. The decision was taken by the Society for the Protection of the Littoral, which is completely run by the eco-warriors. People weren't doing any harm, they were just having a quiet orgy, but apparently they were disturbing the terns. Terns are a type of bird. Well fuck the terns!' shouted Bruno. 'They're trying to stop us fucking and now they want to stop us eating sheep's cheese, they're fucking Nazis. The socialists are in on it too. They hate sheep because sheep are conservative, whereas everyone knows wolves are left-wing, which is kind of strange because wolves look like Alsatians and they're clearly pretty much on the extreme right. How do you know who to trust?' He shook his head solemnly.

'What hotel are you staying at in Nice?' he asked suddenly.

'The Windsor.'

'The Windsor? Why?' Bruno became agitated again. 'When did you start staying in high-class hotels? Who do you think you are? Personally,' (he stressed each word, his voice rising) 'I always stay at a Mercure hotel! Did you bother to check it out? Did you know that the Hôtel Mercure at Baie des Anges has attractive seasonal rates? Off-peak, the room only costs three hundred and thirty francs, that's the price of a two-star hotel, with all the comfort of three-star service, a view over the promenade des Anglais and twenty-four-hour room service!'

Bruno was practically screaming now. Despite his customer's somewhat eccentric behaviour, the manager of *Chez Gilou* (was his name really Gilou? That would be ridiculous) was listening carefully. Men are always interested in finance and value for money, it's one of their characteristic traits.

'Oh, here's Twat!' said Bruno jokingly. His tone completely changed and he nodded to a young man who had just come into the café. He was about 22, wearing combat trousers and a *Greenpeace* tee shirt, he was tanned and wore his hair in Rasta dreadlocks. 'Hi, Twat,' said Bruno cheerfully. 'This is my brother. On your way to see the old bitch?' The boy nodded without saying anything; for some reason or another he had decided not to let Bruno get to him.

Outside the village, the road wound along the mountainside towards Italy. Over the first hill, they found themselves in a large valley flanked by forest; the border could not be more than ten kilometres away. To the east, it was possible to make out snow-capped peaks. The deserted landscape seemed serene and abundant. 'The doctor was out,' explained the white Rasta. 'She can't be moved, anyway there's nothing more they can do for her. It's nature's way . . .' he said gravely.

'Did you hear that?' yelled Bruno. 'Did you hear that little fucker? Going on about "nature" – that's all they ever go on about. Now that she's sick they can't wait for her to snuff it, like she's an animal in a trap. That's my mother you're talking about, Twat!' he said haughtily. 'Look at him!' he went on. 'The rest of them are the same – worse probably. They're total wankers.'

'It's pretty around here . . .' said Michel absently.

The house was large and squat, built of rough-hewn stone with a slate roof beside a spring. Before he went in, Michel took out his Canon Prima Mini (retractable zoom lens, 38-105mm, 1,290 francs at FNAC). He turned around completely and focused on a long shot before pressing the button, then he joined the others.

Apart from Twat, the front room had only an indeterminate, clearly Dutch creature with blondish hair knitting a poncho by the fireplace and an old hippie with long grey hair, a grey beard and an intelligent goat-like face. 'She's in here . . .' said Twat, pulling back a piece of fabric nailed to the wall and ushering them into the next room.

Certainly Michel was curious to see the dark-haired creature huddled in the corner of the room, who watched as they came in. After all, this was only the second time he had seen his mother, and everything led him to believe that it would be the last. The first thing that struck him was how thin she was, her prominent cheekbones and twisted arms. Her skin was dark, earth-coloured, and she was breathing with difficulty; she was clearly not long for this world, but over her crooked nose, her huge, pale eyes shone in the half-light. Cautiously, he walked towards her silhouette. 'Don't worry,' said Bruno. 'She can't talk any more.' She might not have been able to talk, but she was certainly still alert. Did she recognise him? Probably not. Maybe she was confusing him with his father; that was possible; Michel knew he looked a lot like his father had at his age. There are people who have a profound effect on one's life, who leave their mark for better or worse; for Janine, now rechristened Jane, there was life *before* and *after* Michel's father. Before she met him, she was just a degenerate little rich girl; afterwards she was to become something else, something much more disastrous. In fact, 'meet' was the wrong word; they hadn't met as such, they had simply run into each other, procreated and gone their separate ways. She had never succeeded in understanding the enigma that was Marc Djerzinski; she had never even come close. Did she think of him now, in the final hours of her calamitous life? It wasn't impossible. Bruno slumped heavily into a chair beside her bed. 'You're just an old whore . . .' he said in a pedantic tone. 'You deserve to die.' Michel sat opposite him at the head of the bed and lit a cigarette. 'Do you want to be cremated?' Bruno went on jovially. 'Well, when the time comes, I'll make sure they incinerate you. I'll put what's left of you in a little pot and every morning when I get up, I'll piss on your ashes.' He nodded contentedly; Jane let out a throaty howl. Just then the Rasta arrived. 'Would you like something to drink?' he offered coldly. 'Of course, my good man!' shouted Bruno. 'What kind of question is that? Go open a bottle, Twat!' The young man went out and came back with a bottle of whisky and two glasses. Bruno poured himself a large glass and knocked it back quickly. 'You'll have to forgive him,' said Michel. 'He's upset . . .' 'That's right,' said his half-brother, 'you just leave us to our misery, Twat.' He emptied the glass, clicked his tongue and poured himself another. 'They better keep out of my way, the fuckers . . .' he said. 'She's left everything to them and they know fucking well that children are absolutely entitled to their inheritance. If we wanted to contest the will, we'd win hands down.' Michel said nothing, he didn't want to discuss the subject. There was a moment of uncomfortable silence. In the next room, no one said a word either; they could hear the weak but raucous breathing of the dying.

'She just wanted to be young, that's all . . .' said Michel, his voice tired now, and forgiving. 'She wanted to be with young people, certainly not her kids who just reminded her that she was part of an older generation. It's not difficult to understand. I want to go now. Do you think she'll die soon?'

Bruno shrugged his shoulders. Michel got up and went into the other room; the grey-haired hippie was on his own now, peeling organic carrots. He tried to talk to him, to find out what the doctor had actually said, but the old beggar could only come up with vague details that were completely off the subject. 'She was a radiant woman . . .' he said emphatically, carrot in hand. 'We think she's ready for death, she's reached an intense level of spiritual

awareness.' What the fuck did that mean? There was no
point in getting into it. It was obvious the old guy wasn't
actually saying anything, he was just making noises with
his mouth. Michel turned on his heel and went back to
Bruno. 'Fucking hippies . . .' he said as he sat down again,
'they're still convinced that religion is some sort of
individual experience based on meditation, spiritual
exploration and all that. They don't understand that it's
just a purely social thing about rites and rituals,
ceremonies and rules. According to Auguste Comte, the
sole purpose of religion is to bring humanity to a state of
perfect unity.'

'Auguste Comte yourself!' interrupted Bruno angrily.
'As soon as people stop believing in life after death,
religion is impossible. If society is impossible without
religion, which is what you're saying, then society isn't
possible either. You're just like those sociologists who go
on about how youth culture is just some passing fad born
in the Fifties which had its finest hour in the Eighties and
so on. Actually, man has always been terrified by death,
he's never been able to face the idea of his own
destruction, or even physical decline, without horror. Of
all worldly goods, youth is clearly the most precious and
we don't believe in worldly goods any more. "If Christ
did not rise from the dead," says Saint Paul bluntly, "then
our faith is vain." Christ didn't rise from the dead, he lost
his fight with death. I wrote a film script on the theme of
the New Jerusalem. The film takes place on an island
populated by naked women and small dogs. Men have

been wiped out by some biological disaster along with nearly every species of animal. Time has stood still, the weather is constant and mild, trees bear fruit all year long. The women are eternally young and nubile and the little dogs forever lively and happy. The women swim and stroke each other, the little dogs gambol and play around them. The dogs come in all shapes and sizes: poodles, fox-terriers, Shi-tzus, King Charles spaniels, Yorkshire terriers, beagles. The only big dog is a clever, gentle Labrador who acts as a counsellor to the others. The only sign that men have ever existed is a video of speeches by Edouard Balladur, which has a soothing effect on some of the women and on the dogs. There's also a video of *The Animal Kingdom* presented by Claude Darget; no one ever watches it, but it is there as a testimony to the barbarism of previous eras.'

'So they let you write . . .' said Michel quietly. He was not surprised. Most psychiatrists were particularly interested in their patients' scribblings. Not that they ascribe a particular therapeutic value to them, but it gives them something to do and anything is better than having them slash their wrists with a razor.

'There is drama on this little island,' went on Bruno, his voice filled with emotion. 'For example, one of the little dogs swims too far out to sea. Luckily his mistress notices that he's in difficulty, jumps in a boat and quickly rows out just in time to save him. The poor dog has swallowed too much water and passed out; it looks like he's dead, but his mistress gives him the kiss of life and revives him and everything ends happily.' Suddenly he was silent. He seemed serene now, almost rapt. Michel looked at his watch and glanced around. His mother was quiet. It was almost noon; everything seemed too calm. He got up and went back into the other room. The grey-haired hippie had disappeared, leaving his carrots on the table. Michel poured himself a beer and walked over to the window. He could see for miles across hills covered with pines. Between the snow-capped peaks it was just possible to see the shimmering blue of a lake. The air was warm and full of fragrance; it was a beautiful spring morning.

It was difficult to tell how long he had been standing there; his mind had left his body and was floating peacefully among the peaks when he was brought back to reality by what he at first thought was a scream. It took him several seconds to focus on what he was hearing; then he walked quickly into the other room. Still seated at the end of the bed, Bruno was singing at the top of his voice:

> *They've all come*
> *the boy and his brother*
> *the screams have brought them running*
> *To see their dying mother . . .*

Inconsequential; inconsequential, shallow and ridiculous – such is Man. Bruno stood up and belted out the next verse:

> *They've all come*
> *The wop and the bum*
> *to pay their respects*
> *to their dear old mum*

Only the buzzing of a fly as it crossed the room broke the silence which followed this performance, before it landed on Jane's face. *Diptera* can be recognised by the fact that they have a single pair of membranous wings at the second thoracic ring, a pair of balancing antennae (to stabilise flight) on the third thoracic ring and a proboscis which pierces or sucks. When the fly began to move across Jane's eye, Michel knew something was wrong. He leaned over his mother, careful not to touch her. 'I think she's dead,' he said after a brief examination.

The doctor had no trouble confirming this diagnosis. He was accompanied by a county clerk and that was when the problems started. Where was the body to be transferred? A family mausoleum, perhaps? Michel did not have the faintest idea, he felt confused and exhausted. If he had known how to form warm, affectionate relationships with his family, they wouldn't be in this position – making themselves ridiculous in front of some functionary who remained icily polite. Bruno was clearly uninterested in the proceedings; he sat off to one side playing Tetris on his Gameboy. 'Well . . .' said the clerk, 'we could offer you a plot at Saorge cemetery. It would be a little far for you to come if you don't live in the area, but from the point of view of immediate transport it's obviously the most practical solution. The burial could take place as early as this afternoon, we're not too busy at the moment. I don't suppose there'll be any problems with the death certificate . . .' 'No problem at all,' said the doctor, 'I've brought the paperwork . . .' He brandished a sheaf of forms with a little smile. 'Fuck,' said Bruno to himself, 'Game Over . . .' and as he said this the Gameboy played a cheerful little tune. 'Are you happy with the idea of burial, M. Clément?' said the clerk, his voice sounding a little strained. 'Absolutely not!' Bruno jumped up. 'My mother wanted to be cremated, it was very important to her!' The clerk frowned. The cemetery at Saorge was not equipped to deal with cremations; it required specialised equipment and there simply wasn't the demand to justify it. Cremation would make things very difficult. 'It was my mother's dying wish . . .' said Bruno importantly. There was silence. The county clerk thought quickly. 'There is, of course, a crematorium in Nice . . .' he said nervously. 'We could arrange transport there and back if you'd still like to have her buried here. Of course, you would be responsible for the expense . . .' No one spoke. 'I'll give them a call . . .' he went on. 'I'll have to find out when they might have a window.' He checked his address book, took out a mobile phone and began to dial, when Bruno interrupted again. 'Oh, don't worry about it . . .' he made a large gesture. 'Let's just bury her here. Who gives a shit about her last wishes? You're paying for it!' he said authoritatively, turning to Michel. Michel said nothing, but took out his cheque book and enquired as to the price of a plot on a 30-year lease. 'A very good choice,' said the clerk. 'With a thirty-year lease, you've got time to make plans.'

The cemetery was about a hundred metres above the village. Two men in overalls carried the coffin. They'd gone for the basic, stripped pine model stocked at the local undertakers; the funeral business seemed to be remarkably well organised in Saorge. It was late in the afternoon, but the sun was still warm. Bruno and Michel walked side by side two paces behind the men; the grey-haired hippie walked beside them, he had insisted on going with Jane to her final resting-place. The path was stony and arid; all this had to make some kind of sense. A bird of prey – probably a buzzard – glided slowly, low in the sky. 'The place is probably full of snakes . . .' Bruno inferred. He picked up a sharp white stone. Just as they turned into the cemetery, an adder appeared between two bushes against the cemetery wall; Bruno aimed and threw the stone with all his strength. It shattered on the wall, just missing the reptile's head.

'Snakes have their place in nature too . . .' said the grey-haired hippie sharply.

'Nature? I wouldn't piss on it if it was on fire,' Bruno was beside himself with anger again, 'I'd shit on its face.'

'Fucking nature . . . nature my arse!' he muttered angrily to himself for several minutes. However, he behaved himself as the coffin was lowered, content to nod his head, making quiet burbling sounds, as though the ceremony had evoked thoughts which were as yet too vague to be put into words. After the ceremony, Michel tipped the two men – he assumed it was customary. He had 15 minutes to catch his train; Bruno decided to go with him.

They parted on the platform at Nice. Though they did not know it yet, they would not see one another again.

'How are things at the clinic?' asked Michel.

'Yeah, not bad, pretty okay really, they've got me on lithium.' Bruno smiled mischievously. 'I'm not going to go back to the clinic just yet. I've got another night left. I'm going to go to a whorehouse, there are loads of them in Nice.' He frowned and his face darkened. 'Since they put me on lithium I can't get it up at all, but it doesn't matter, I'd still like to go.'

Michel nodded distractedly and climbed into the carriage: he had reserved a sleeping car.

Part Three

Infinite Emotional

1

When he got back to Paris he found a letter from Desplechin. According to article 66 of the CNRS code, Michel had to apply to be reinstated or ask that his leave be prolonged, no later than 60 days before the end of the original term of leave. The letter was polite and witty, Desplechin made caustic comments about the bureaucracy; Michel realised the deadline had passed three weeks earlier. He put the letter on his desk, feeling deeply unsettled. For a year, he had been completely free to determine the direction of his research, and what had he come up with? Nothing, absolutely nothing. He turned on his computer and felt queasy when he discovered he had received another 80 e-mails, though he had only been away for two days. One of them was from the Institute of Molecular Biology at Palaiseau. The colleague who had taken his position had initiated a research programme on mitochondrial DNA; unlike cellular DNA it seemed to have no mechanisms for repairing code damaged by radical attacks – this was hardly a surprise. The most interesting message was from the University of Ohio: in the course of a study on *Saccharomyces*, they had demonstrated that those that reproduced sexually evolved more slowly than those that reproduced by cloning; random mutation seemed to be more efficient than natural selection. The experimental model was engaging and completely contradicted the standard hypothesis that natural selection was the driving force behind evolution, but it was really only of anecdotal interest. As soon as the genome had been completely decoded (which would be in a matter of months), humanity would have complete control of its evolution; when that happened sexuality would be seen for what it really was: a useless, dangerous and regressive function. But even if one could detect the incidence of mutations and eliminate all deleterious effects, there was nothing yet which shed any light on what they determined; nothing which provided a definite meaning or practical application for them. It was clear that this should be the focus of research.

Cleared of all the books and files which had cluttered the shelves, Desplechin's office seemed vast. 'Yep . . .' he smiled discreetly, 'I'm retiring at the end of the month.' Djerzinski stood open-mouthed. It is possible to know someone for years, decades even, learning little by little how to avoid personal questions and anything of real importance, but the hope remains that some day, in different circumstances, one could talk about such things, pose such questions. Though it may be indefinitely postponed, the idea of a more personal, more human relationship never fades, quite simply because human relationships do not fit easily into narrow, fixed compartments. Human beings therefore think of relationships as potentially 'deep and meaningful'; an idea that can persist for years until a single, brutal act (usually something like death) makes it clear that it is too late, the hoped for 'deep and meaningful' relationship will never happen. In his 15 years of professional experience, Desplechin was the one person with whom Michel would have liked to have a relationship beyond the utilitarian, infinitely irritating, chance juxtapositions of office life. Well, now it was too late. Devastated, he glanced at the boxes of books piled on the floor of the office. 'I think it might be better if we went for a drink somewhere . . .' suggested Desplechin, picking up the thread of the conversation.

They walked past the Musée d'Orsay and settled themselves at a table on a nineteenth-century terrace. At the next table, half a dozen Italian tourists were babbling excitedly like innocent birds; Djerzinski ordered a beer and Desplechin a neat whisky.

'What are you going to do, then?'

'I don't know.' Desplechin looked as if he genuinely did not know. 'Travel . . . probably a bit of sexual tourism.' He smiled; when he smiled, his face still had great charm; disillusioned certainly, there could be no doubt that he was a broken man, but charming none-theless. 'I'm joking . . . Truth is, I'm just not interested in sex any more. Knowledge, on the other hand . . . There's still a desire for knowledge. It's a curious thing, the thirst for knowledge . . . very few scientists have it, you know. Most of them are happy to make a career for themselves, move into management, but it's incredibly important in the history of the species. It's easy to imagine a fable in which a small group of men – a couple of hundred in the whole world, at most – work intensively on something difficult, abstract, completely incomprehensible to the uninitiated. These men remain completely unknown; they have no apparent power, no money, no honours; nobody can understand the pleasure they get from their work. In fact, they are the most powerful men in the world, for one simple reason: they hold the keys to rational certainty. Everything they declare to be true will be accepted sooner or later by the whole population. There is no power in the world – economic, political, religious or social – that can compete with rational certainty. Western society is primarily interested in philosophy and politics; the most vicious, the most ridiculous conflicts have been about philosophical and political ideas; it has also had a passionate love affair with literature and the arts, but nothing in its history has been as important as the need for rational certainty. The West has sacrificed everything to this need: religion, happiness, hope – life itself. You have to remember that when passing judgement on Western civilisation.' He fell silent, deep in thought. He let his gaze wander across the table for a moment, then put down his glass.

'I remember a boy I knew in the *première* when I was sixteen. He was very confused, very tortured. His family were rich, very traditional; and actually he completely accepted their values. One day when we were talking he said to me, "The value of any religion depends on the quality of the moral system founded upon it." I stood there, speechless with surprise and admiration. I didn't know if he had come to this conclusion by himself, or whether he'd read it in a book somewhere, all I know is that it impressed me deeply. I've been thinking about it for forty years, and now I think he was wrong. It seems impossible to me to think of religion from a purely moral standpoint; but Kant was right when he said that the Saviour of mankind should be judged by the same universal ethics as the rest of us. But I've come to believe that religions are basically an attempt to explain the world; and no attempt to explain the world can survive if it clashes with our need for rational certainty. Mathematical proofs and experimental methods are the highest expressions of human consciousness. I realise that the facts seem to contradict me, I know that Islam – by far the most stupid, false and obscure of all religions – seems to be gaining ground; but it's a transitory phenomenon: in the long term, Islam is doomed just as surely as Christianity.'

Djerzinski looked up; he had been listening closely. He would never have imagined that Desplechin was interested in such things; Desplechin hesitated, then went on:

'I lost touch with Philippe after the *baccalauréat*, but a couple of years later I found out that he'd committed suicide. Anyway, I don't think the two things are connected: being homosexual, Catholic and a monarchist can't exactly have been easy.'

At that moment, Djerzinski realised that he had never really thought seriously about religion. This, despite the fact that he knew that materialism, having destroyed the religious faith of previous centuries, had itself been destroyed by recent advances in physics. It was curious that neither he nor any of the physicists he had met had had the slightest spiritual doubts.

'Personally,' said Michel, the idea coming to him only as he spoke, 'I think that I needed that basic, pragmatic positivism that most researchers have. Facts exist and are linked together by laws; the notion of cause simply isn't scientific. The world is precisely the sum of information we have about it.'

'I'm no longer an active researcher . . .' said Desplechin with disarming simplicity. 'Maybe that's why I'm starting to think about metaphysical questions late in the day. But you're right, of course. We have to go on investigating, experimenting, finding new laws – nothing else is important. Remember Pascal: "We must say summarily: 'This is made by figure and motion,' for it is true. But to say what these are, and to compose the machine, is ridiculous. For it is useless, uncertain, and painful." Once again, he's right and Descartes is wrong. So tell me . . . have you decided what you're going to do? I'm sorry about . . .' he made an apologetic gesture '. . . all this trouble with deadlines.'

'Yes. I need to get a position at the Galway Centre for Genetic Research in Ireland. I need to set up hundreds of simple experiments, in very specific conditions of temperature and pressure with a good range of radioactive markers. What I need more than anything is a lot of processing power, but if I remember right they have two Crays running in parallel.'

'Are you thinking of taking your research in a new direction?' Desplechin's voice betrayed his excitement. He realised this and smiled again, almost in self-mockery. 'The thirst for knowledge . . .' he said quietly.

'I think that it's a mistake to work only from natural DNA. DNA is a complex molecule which has evolved more or less by chance; there are redundancies, long sequences of junk DNA, a little bit of everything. If you really want to test the general conditions for mutation, you have to start with smaller self-replicating molecules with a maximum of a hundred bases.'

Desplechin nodded, his eyes shining, he was no longer trying to hide his excitement. The Italian tourists had left, they were the only people left in the café.

'It would be a long haul,' Michel went on. 'There's nothing in principle to distinguish configurations prone to mutation, but there has to be some structural stability at a sub-atomic level. If we can work out a stable configuration with even a couple of hundred atoms it's just a matter of the speed and power of replication. But I'm getting a bit ahead of myself.'

'Maybe not . . .' Desplechin's voice had the dreamy quality of a man who has just glimpsed fantastical new ideas from a great distance.

'My work would have to be completely independent of the centre's bureaucracy. Some of this is no more than pure speculation: too long and too complicated to explain.'

'Of course. I'll write to Walcott, the director there. He's a good man, he'll leave you in peace. You've already done some work with them, haven't you? Something about cows . . .'

'Something small, yes.'

'Don't worry. I'm retiring anyway . . .' (this time there was a trace of bitterness in his smile), 'but I still have some influence. From an administrative point of view, you'll have a completely independent facility which can be extended year on year for as long as you like. Regardless of who gets my job, I'll make sure there's no way the decision can be reversed.'

They parted just past the Pont Royal. Desplechin extended his hand. He had never had a son; his sexual preference precluded it and he had always found the idea of a marriage of convenience ridiculous. For several seconds as they shook hands, he thought that this kind of relationship was infinitely more satisfying; then he realised that he was very tired; he turned and walked back along the quay, past the *bouquinistes*. For a minute or two, Djerzinski watched as the man walked away in the fading light.

2

He had dinner at Annabelle's the following evening and explained clearly and precisely why he had to move to Ireland. His research programme had been all mapped out, everything was coming together. The important thing was not to become fixated on DNA but to look at the phenotype as a whole as a self-replicating system.

At first Annabelle didn't say anything, but she could not stop the corners of her mouth turning down. Then she poured him another glass of wine; she had cooked fish that evening and more than ever her little studio seemed like a ship's cabin.

'You weren't planning to take me with you . . .' Her words broke the silence; the silence continued. 'It didn't even occur to you . . .' she said, her voice a mixture of surprise and childish petulance; then she burst into tears. He didn't move; if he had raised a hand at that moment she would certainly have pushed him away; you have to

let people cry, it's the only way. 'It's strange. We understood each other completely when we were twelve . . .'
she said through her sobs.

She looked up at him. Her face was pure and extraordinarily beautiful. She was talking without thinking: 'I
want to have your child. I need someone to be close to
me. You don't have to help raise him or look after him,
you don't even have to acknowledge him. I'm not asking
you to love him or even to love me; I just want you to
give me a baby. I know I'm forty, but so what? I'm prepared to take the risk. This is my last chance. Sometimes
I regret having the abortions, even though the first guy
who got me pregnant was a shit and the second was an
irresponsible fool. When I was seventeen, I never
imagined that life would be so constrained, that there
would be so few opportunities.'

Michel lit a cigarette to give himself time to think. 'It's
a strange idea . . .' he said between his teeth. 'It's a curious
idea to reproduce when you don't even like life.'
Annabelle stood up and began to take off her clothes.
'Let's make love anyway,' she said. 'It must be more than
a month since we made love. I stopped taking the pill a
couple of weeks ago; I'll be fertile about now.' She put her
hands on her stomach and moved them up to her breasts,
parted her thighs slightly. She was beautiful, desirable,
loving: why then did he feel nothing? It was bizarre. He
lit another cigarette, then suddenly realised that thinking
about it would get him nowhere. Whether or not one has
a child is not a decision one can make rationally. He

stubbed the cigarette out in the ashtray and murmured: 'Alright.'

Annabelle helped him off with his clothes and masturbated him until he could penetrate her. He felt nothing except the softness and the warmth of her vagina. He quickly stopped moving, fascinated by the geometry of copulation, entranced by the suppleness and richness of her juices. Annabelle pressed her mouth to his and wrapped her arms around him. He closed his eyes and felt the presence of his penis more acutely; he started to move inside her once again. Just before he ejaculated he had a vision – crystal clear – of gametes fusing followed immediately by the cell dividing. It felt like a headlong rush, a little suicide. A wave of sensation flowed back along his penis and he felt his sperm pump out of him. Annabelle felt it too, she exhaled slowly; they lay there, motionless.

'You were supposed to come in for a smear about a month ago . . .' said the gynaecologist in a weary voice, 'instead of which, you stop taking the pill without consulting me and then you go and try to get yourself pregnant. You're not a girl any more!' The surgery seemed cold and humid; when she left Annabelle was surprised by the June sunshine.

She telephoned the following morning. The smear had thrown up 'pretty serious' anomalies; they would have to do a biopsy and a D&C. 'As for getting pregnant, now would not be a good time. Let's take one thing at a time, okay?' He didn't sound worried, just a little annoyed.

And so Annabelle had her third abortion – the foetus was only two weeks old, so a little suction was enough. The technology had advanced since her last termination and it was all over in less than ten minutes. The results arrived three days later. 'Well . . .', the doctor seemed terribly old, sad and wise, 'I'm afraid there's no doubt about it. I'm afraid you have stage one uterine cancer.' He resettled his glasses on his nose and looked at the papers again; the impression of general competence was greatly enhanced. He was not surprised: cancer of the uterus often attacks women in the years before menopause, and not having had children simply increased the risk. There was no question as to the treatment. 'We have to do a hysterectomy and a bilateral salpingo-oophorectomy. They're standard surgical procedures nowadays, complications are almost unheard of.' He glanced at Annabelle; it was irritating that she hadn't reacted, she simply sat there open-mouthed; she would probably have a breakdown. It was standard procedure for practitioners to refer patients to a therapist for counselling – he'd prepared a list of addresses. Above all it was important to remain positive: emphasise that the end of fertility did not mean that one's sex life was over; on the contrary, many patients found their desire increased.

'You mean, they're going to remove my uterus . . .' she said incredulously.

'The uterus, the ovaries and the fallopian tubes; it's best

to avoid any risk of the cancer spreading. I'll prescribe hormone replacement therapy for you – in fact it's commonplace to prescribe it for the menopause nowadays.'

She went back to her parents at Crécy-en-Brie. The operation was scheduled for 17 July. Michel and her mother went with her to the hospital in Meaux. She wasn't scared. The operation lasted a little more than two hours. Annabelle woke up the following morning. Through her window she could see blue sky and the wind in the trees. She barely felt anything. She wanted to see the scar on her abdomen, but didn't dare to ask the nurse. It was strange to think that she was still the same woman, but her reproductive organs had been removed. The word 'ablation' hung in her mind for a moment before giving way to a more visceral image. 'They've gutted me,' she thought, 'gutted me like a chicken.'

She left hospital a week later. Michel had written to Walcott to tell him that his departure had been postponed; after some vacillation, he agreed to stay with her parents in her brother's old room. Annabelle noticed that he and her mother had become closer while she had been in hospital. Her older brother also dropped by more often, now that Michel was there. In fact they had nothing much to say to each other; Michel knew nothing about small businesses and Jean-Pierre was completely ignorant as to the issues raised by research in molecular biology; nevertheless, over a nightly apéritif they'd managed to establish a semi-illusory male bond. She needed to rest and to avoid lifting heavy objects, but at least she could now wash herself and eat normally. In the afternoons she would sit in the garden; Michel and her mother would pick strawberries or plums. It was strange, as though she were on holiday or as if she were a child again. She felt the sun caress her face and her arms. More often than not, she did nothing, though sometimes she did a little embroidery or made stuffed toys for her nephews and nieces. A psychiatrist in Meaux had given her a prescription for sleeping pills and some strong tranquillisers. For whatever reason, she slept a lot and her dreams were happy and peaceful; the mind is a very powerful thing, as long as it remains in its sphere. Michel lay beside her in the bed, his hand on her waist, feeling her abdomen rise and fall regularly. The psychiatrist came to see her frequently, muttered, worried, talked about 'dissociation'. She had become very gentle and her behaviour a little strange; sometimes she would laugh for no reason and sometimes her eyes would suddenly fill with tears. Then she would take another Tercian.

After the third week she was allowed out, and she would take short walks along the river or in the surrounding woods. It was August, and the weather was beautiful; day followed day, each one identically radiant, without so much as the murmur of a storm or anything that might signal an ending. Michel held her hand; often they would sit together on the bench beside the Grand Morin. The grass on the riverbank was scorched, almost white; in the shadow of the trees, the river wound on forever in dark green ripples. The world outside had its own rules and those rules were not human.

3

On 25 August a routine examination revealed metastases in the abdomen; under normal circumstances, she could expect it to spread and the cancer would become generalised. Radiotherapy was a possibility, in fact it was the only possibility, but it was important to realise that it was an arduous treatment and the chances of success were only 50 per cent.

The meal was a silent affair. 'You'll get better, darling . . .' said Annabelle's mother, her voice trembling a little. Annabelle put her arm around her mother's neck and pressed her forehead to hers; they sat like that for almost a minute. After her mother had gone to bed, she stayed in the living room, leafing through some books. Michel watched her every move from the armchair. 'We could get a second opinion . . .' he said after a long silence. 'Yes, we could,' she said softly.

She could not make love, the scar was too fresh, too

painful, but she held him in her arms for a long time. In the silence, she could hear him grind his teeth. Once, as she stroked his face, she found it wet with tears. She stroked his penis gently, it was exciting and calming all at once. He took two Mepronizine and at last he fell asleep.

At about three a.m. she got up, put on a dressing gown and went down to the kitchen. She rummaged in the dresser and found the bowl inscribed with her name that her godmother had given her for her tenth birthday. She emptied the contents of a tube of Rohypnol into the bowl and added a little sugar and water. She did not feel anything, unless perhaps a very general, almost metaphysical sadness. That was life, she thought; her body had taken a turning which was unfair and unexpected and now it could no longer be a source of joy or pleasure. On the contrary, it would gradually, but quite quickly, become another source of pain and embarrassment. And so she would have to destroy her body. A big wooden clock loudly counted off the seconds; her mother had been given it by her grandmother, she had had it the day she married. It was the oldest piece of furniture in the house. She added some more sugar to the bowl. She was far from accepting; life seemed to her like a bad joke, an unacceptable joke, but acceptable or not, that was what it was. In a few short weeks her illness had brought her to the feeling so common in the elderly: she did not want to be a burden to others. Towards the end of her adolescence, her life had speeded up, then there had been a long dull stretch; now, at the end, everything was speeding up again.

Just before daybreak, as he turned over in bed, Michel noticed that Annabelle was gone. He dressed and went downstairs: her body was lying on the sofa in the living room. Near the body, on the table, she had left a note. The first line read: 'I have decided to die, surrounded by those I love.'

The head of emergency services at the hospital in Meaux was a man of about 30, with dark curly hair and an honest face; he immediately made a good impression on them. There was little chance that she would regain consciousness, he explained, but they could stay with her if they wished, he had no problem with that. Coma was a strange condition and one which was poorly understood. It was probable that Annabelle was unaware of their presence. There was, however, some weak electrical activity in the brain, which had to correspond to some mental process, but as to what that mental process might be, nature was defiantly enigmatic. The medical prognosis was far from certain; there were cases where a patient remained in a coma for weeks, even months and then suddenly regained consciousness; more often, unfortunately, coma slipped just as suddenly towards death. She was only 40, at least they knew that her heart was strong; that was the only thing they could say for sure.

Day was breaking over the town. Sitting beside Michel, Annabelle's brother shook his head and muttered. 'It's not possible . . . It's not possible . . .' he repeated endlessly, as though the words themselves had power. But it was, it was possible. Anything was possible. A nurse walked past them pushing a trolley full of rattling bottles of serum.

Later, the sun ripped through the clouds and the sky turned blue. It would be a beautiful day, as beautiful as the others. Annabelle's mother stood up with difficulty. 'We should get some rest . . .' she said, struggling to control her voice. Her son rose too, his arms hanging limply by his sides, and followed her like a robot. Michel shook his head to indicate that he wasn't coming. He didn't feel in the least tired. In the moments that followed, he was strangely aware of the presence of the visible world. He was sitting on a plastic chair in a sunlit corridor. This wing of the hospital was very quiet. From time to time, a door opened and a nurse came out and hurried towards another corridor. The noise of the town some floors below was greatly muted. In a state of complete mental detachment, he went over the events, the circumstances and the stages of the destruction of their lives. Everything seemed clear, conclusive, unexceptional, seen in the frozen light of a restrictive past. Now it seemed unthinkable that a girl of seventeen should be so naïve; it was particularly unbelievable that a girl of seventeen should set so much store by love. If the surveys in magazines were to be believed, things had changed completely in the 25 years since Annabelle had been a teenager. Young girls today were more sensible, more sophisticated. Nowadays they worried more about their exam results and did their best to ensure they would have a decent career. For them, going out with boys was simply a game, a distraction based as much on narcissism as on sexual pleasure. Later, they would try to make a good marriage, basing their decision on a range of social and professional criteria as well as shared interests and tastes. Of course, in doing this, they cut themselves off from any possibility of happiness – a condition indissociable from traditional and transient emotions which are incompatible with the practice of reason – but in doing so they hoped to escape the moral and emotional suffering which had so tortured their forebears. This hope was, unfortunately, rapidly disappointed; the passing of the pains of love simply left the field clear for boredom, emptiness and an anguished wait for old age and death. The second part of Annabelle's life had been, therefore, much more dismal than the first of which, in the end, she had no memory at all.

Towards noon, Michel pushed open the door to her room. Her breathing was very shallow, the sheet which covered her chest was almost still – though, according to the doctor, it was sufficient for oxygenation. If her respiratory rate dropped further, they intended to put her on a respirator. For the time being, a drip was hooked up to her arm just above the elbow and an electrode fixed to her temple, that was all. A ray of sunlight crossed the immaculate sheet and lit a lock of her magnificent blonde hair. A little paler than usual, her face, eyes closed, seemed completely at peace. All worries seemed to have disappeared, to Michel she had never seemed so happy. It is true that he had always had a tendency to confuse happiness with coma; nonetheless she seemed to him completely happy. He stroked her hair, kissed her forehead and her warm lips. It was too late, of course, but it was nice. He stayed in the room with her until nightfall. Back in the corridor, he opened a book of Buddhist meditations compiled by Dr Evans-Wentz (the book had been in his pocket for some weeks; a small book with a dark red cover).

> *May all creatures in the east,*
> *May all creatures in the west*
> *May all creatures in the north*
> *May all creatures in the south*
> *Be happy, and remain happy*
> *And may they live in friendship*

It wasn't entirely their fault, he thought; they had lived in a painful world, a world of struggle and rivalry, vanity and violence; they had not lived in a peaceful world. On the other hand, they had done nothing to change it, had contributed nothing that might make it a better place. He should have given Annabelle a child, he thought, and then he remembered that he had done, or that he had tried to, that at least he had accepted the idea; and that thought filled him with joy. Now he began to understand the peace and gentleness he had felt in these last weeks. There was nothing more he could do now, no one could battle against the empire of sickness and death; but at least for some weeks she had felt loved.

If a man practises the thoughts of love
And does not abandon himself to wantonness;
If he severs the bonds of passion
And turns his gaze towards Faith

Because he was able to practise love
He will be born again in the sky as a Brahma
And will soon merit deliverance
And will forever inherit Nirvana,

If he does not kill, nor think of harm
If he does not seek glory in the humiliation of others
If he practises universal Love
At his death, he will have no thoughts of hatred.

Annabelle's mother came by to see if there was any change. No, there were no developments; deep coma could be a very stable condition, the nurse reminded her patiently, it could be two weeks before a prognosis could be made. She went in to see her daughter and came out after a minute sobbing. 'I don't understand . . .' she said, shaking her head. 'I don't understand how life can be like this. She was a lovely girl, you know, always very affectionate, she never gave me any trouble. She never complained, but I knew she wasn't happy. She deserved better from life.'

She left shortly afterwards, visibly shattered. Strangely, Michel was neither hungry nor tired. He paced up and down the corridor, then went down to the lobby. The West Indian at the information desk was doing a crossword; he nodded to him. He got a hot chocolate from the vending machine and walked to the windows. The moon hung between the buildings; a few cars drove along the avenue de Châlons. He knew enough about medicine to know that Annabelle was but a whisper away from death. Her mother was right to refuse to understand; man is not made to grasp death, neither his own, nor that of others. He walked up to the security guard and asked him for a piece of paper; a little surprised, the man handed him a sheaf of headed notepaper. (Later, it was this letterhead which would help Hubczejak to identify the text among all the papers at the Clifden house.) Some people cling fiercely to life, they leave it, as Rousseau said, with bad grace; he knew already that that would not be the case with Annabelle.

> *She was a child meant for happiness,*
> *And gave to everyone her heart's treasure*
> *She could have given her life for others,*
> *Among the newborn of her bed*
>
> *By the cry of children*
> *By the blood of the race*
> *Her ever-present dream*
> *Will leave a trace*
> *Written in time*
> *Written in space*
>
> *Written on the flesh*
> *Forever sanctified*

In the mountains, the air
And in river waters clear
In the changing sky

Now you are here,
On your deathbed
So still in your coma
And here you love still.

Our bodies will become cold, barely present
In the grass, my Annabelle,
Which will be the death too
Of every individual.

We will have loved little
In our human form
Perhaps the sun, the rain on our graves, the
    wind and the frost
Will end all our pain.

4

Annabelle died two days later, and from the family's point of view it was probably for the best. When death occurs it's usual to come out with some shit like that, but it's true that her mother and brother would have found it difficult to cope with prolonged uncertainty.

In the steel and white concrete building, the same place where his grandmother had been interred, Djerzinski realised for the second time the power of emptiness. He crossed the room to where Annabelle lay. The body was the same one he had known, only its warmth was slowly ebbing away. Now her skin was almost cold.

Some people live to be 70, sometimes 80 years old believing that there is always something new just around the corner, as they say; in the end they practically have to be killed or at least reduced to a state of serious incapacity to get them to see reason. This was not how it was for Michel Djerzinski. He had lived alone all his adult life, in a vacuum. He had contributed to the sum of human knowledge; that was his vocation, it was the way he had found to express his talents; but love was something he had never known. And Annabelle, despite her beauty, had not known love either; and now she was dead. Her body now lay, useless, like pure weight in the light. They sealed the coffin.

In her last letter she had asked to be cremated. Before the ceremony they had coffee at the Relais H in the hospital waiting room; at the next table a gypsy on a drip talked about cars with two friends who had come to visit him. The lighting was poor — just a couple of lights in the ceiling, set into an ugly plaster relief representing huge corks.

They walked out into the sunshine. The crematorium was not far from the hospital building, in the same complex. The crematorium itself was a large white concrete cube set in the middle of an equally white plaza; the reflected light was blinding. Currents of warm air wove around them like a myriad of small snakes.

The coffin was placed on a moving platform leading to the furnace. They had thirty seconds of silent thought and then one of the staff started the motor. The cogs that moved the platform creaked a little; the door closed. It was possible to watch the blaze through a Pyrex porthole. At the moment when the flames leapt from the huge burners, Michel turned his head away. For about 20 seconds, a red smudge persisted in his field of vision, then it was gone. One of the staff collected the ashes in a small rectangular box of white pine, and gave it to Annabelle's elder brother.

They drove slowly back to Crécy. The sun shone through the leaves of the chestnut trees along the allée de l'Hôtel de Ville. He and Annabelle had walked along that same road after school 25 years before. A dozen people were gathered in the garden of her mother's house. Her younger brother had come from the States for the occasion; he was thin, nervous, visibly stressed and dressed a little too elegantly.

Annabelle had asked that her ashes be scattered in the garden of her parents' house; that too was done. The sun was beginning to sink. It was like powder – a whitish powder. She settled gently like a veil on the ground between the roses. At that moment they heard the bells of the level crossing ringing in the distance. Michel remembered the afternoons when he was 15 and Annabelle used to come to the station to meet him and take him in her arms. He looked at the earth, the sun, the roses; the suppleness of the grass. It was incomprehensible. Everyone was silent; Annabelle's mother had poured wine for a toast. She offered him a glass and looked into his eyes. 'You can stay for a couple of days if you like, Michel,' she said in a low voice. No, he would go; he would go back to work. He did not know how to do anything else. The sky seemed to be streaked with sunlight; he realised that he was crying.

5

As the aeroplane dipped towards the clouds that seemed to stretch out endlessly beneath the sky, he had the feeling that his whole life had been leading up to this moment. For several seconds more, there was simply a brilliant blue vault and a vast plain where matt white and radiant white alternated, and then they dropped into a middle zone, grey and fluid, where his senses were confused. Below, in the world of men there were fields and trees and animals; everything was green, damp and infinitely detailed.

Walcott was waiting for him at Shannon airport. He was a big man with rapid gestures; his baldness was surrounded by a crown of reddish-blond hair. He drove the Toyota Starlet quickly past hills and meadows. The Centre was situated just north of Galway on land adjoining the village of Rosscahill. Walcott took him on a tour of the facilities and introduced him to the technicians who would work with him on programming the calculations for his experiments on molecular configurations. The equipment was all ultramodern, the rooms immaculately clean – it had all been financed with money from the EU. In a refrigeration room, Djerzinski glanced at the two huge Crays, built like towers, whose control panels glowed in the darkness. Their millions of parallel processors were simply waiting to integrate Lagrangian models, wave functions, spectra analyses, Hermite operators; this was the universe he would now inhabit. He folded his arms across his chest but he could not dispel the feeling of sadness, of cold inside. Walcott offered him a coffee from the vending machine. Through the windows it was possible to make out the lush slopes plunging towards the dark waters of Lough Corrib.

On the road down to Rosscahill they passed a long sloping field with a herd of fine-looking dun cows. They seemed rather small. 'Recognise them?' asked Walcott with a smile. 'Yep . . . those are the descendants of the first cattle you worked on, ten years ago now. The Centre was very small at the time and none too well equipped, we were really grateful for your help. The cattle are strong, they've had no trouble breeding and they have a fine milk yield. Do you want a look?' He parked in a lane. Djerzinski stood at the dry-stone wall that enclosed the field. The cows were ruminating calmly, rubbing their heads against each other's flanks; two or three of them were lying down. It was he who had created the genetic code which governed their cell reproduction, or, more accurately, he had improved on it. To them, he should be like God, but they seemed completely indifferent to his presence. A bank of fog rolled slowly down the mountain, gradually shrouding them as it went. He went back to the car.

At the steering wheel, Walcott was smoking a Craven A; the windscreen was blurred with rain. In his soft, discreet voice (its discretion in no way seemed indifferent), he asked: 'I believe you had a death in the family?' So Michel told him about Annabelle, and about her death. Walcott listened, nodding from time to time, or letting out a soft sigh. When Michel had finished, he was silent for a while; he lit and stubbed out another cigarette and said: 'I'm not Irish myself. I was born in Cambridge. I'm still very English, they tell me. People often say that the English are very cold fish, very reserved, that they have a way of looking at things – even tragedy – with a sense of irony. There's some truth in it; it's pretty stupid, though. Irony won't save you from anything; humour doesn't do anything at all. You can look at life ironically for years, maybe decades; there are people who seem to go through most of their lives seeing the funny side, but in the end, life always breaks your heart. Doesn't matter how brave you are, or how reserved, or how much you've developed a sense of humour, you still end up with your heart broken. That's when you stop laughing. After that, there's just the cold, the silence and the loneliness. You might say, after that, there's only death.'

He turned on the windscreen wipers and started the engine. 'Most of them around here are Catholics,' he said.

'Well, that's all changing now. Ireland is just coming into the modern world. Quite a few hi-tech companies have set up here to take advantage of the tax breaks and the low social security payments. Round here, there's Roche and Lilly. And Microsoft, of course; every kid in the country dreams of working for Microsoft. People don't go to mass as much as they used to, there's more sexual freedom than there was a couple of years ago, there are more nightclubs, more anti-depressants. The classic story . . .'

They drove back along the lake. The sun emerged from behind the bank of mist, scattering iridescent glints on the water. 'All the same . . .' Walcott went on, 'Catholicism is still a powerful force here. Most of the technicians at the Centre are Catholic. It doesn't make my working relationship with them any easier. They're nice enough, very polite, but they think of me as someone apart, someone you can't really talk to.'

The sun emerged from the fog, forming a perfect white disc; the whole lake was bathed in light. On the horizon, the Twelve Bens Mountains formed a palette of greys like images from a dream. They said nothing. As they came into Galway, Walcott spoke: 'I'm an atheist myself, always have been, but I can understand why they're Catholic here. There's something very special about this country. Everything seems constantly trembling: the grass in the fields or the water on the lake, everything signals its presence. The light is soft, mutable. You'll see. The sky itself is alive.'

6

He rented an apartment on Sky Road in Clifden, in an old coastguard's house which had been converted into tourist apartments. The rooms were decorated with wheels and storm lamps, anything they thought might please the tourists; they didn't bother him. In this apartment, as in his whole life now, he knew he would always feel as though he were staying in a hotel.

He had no intention of returning to France, but in the first weeks he had to go to Paris a number of times to arrange the sale of his apartment and the transfer of his bank accounts. He would take the 11.50 a.m. from Shannon. The plane flew over the sea, the sun was blistering white on the water, the waves snaking and twisting like worms far below. Beneath this twisting mass, he knew, molluscs were breeding; fish with sharp, fine teeth fed on the molluscs only to be devoured by bigger fish. Often, he slept; he had nightmares. When he woke, the plane was flying over the countryside. Half-awake, he would stare in astonishment at the uniform colour of the fields. The fields were brown, sometimes green, but the colours always muted. The suburbs of Paris were grey. The plane fell slowly, gently nosed its way into the city, irresistibly drawn to life, to the beating of a million lives.

By mid-October the Clifden peninsula was completely covered by a thick blanket of fog rolling in from the Atlantic. The last of the tourists had gone. It was not cold, but everything was bathed in a deep, soft grey. Djerzinski did not go out much. He had imported three DVDs, representing more than 40 gigabytes of data. From time to time he would turn on his computer and study a molecular configuration, then he would lie down on his huge bed, his cigarettes always within reach. He had not gone back to the Centre yet. Outside the window the mass of fog shifted slowly.

Around 20 November the sky cleared and the weather became cold but dry. He began to take long walks along the coast road. He would walk past Gortrumnagh and Knockavally, usually on to Claddaghduff and sometimes as far as Aughrus Point. This was the westernmost point of Europe, the very edge of the Western world. Before him, the Atlantic Ocean stretched out four thousand kilometres to America.

According to Hubczejak, these two or three months of solitary reflection, during which Djerzinski did no work, set up no experiments and made no calculations, should be considered as a key period during which the principal elements of his later work fell into place. The last months of 1999 were, in any case, a strange period for Western civilisation as a whole, marked as they were by a sense of waiting, a sort of dull preoccupation.

December 31st 1999 fell on a Friday. In the clinic at Verrières-le-Buisson, where Bruno would spend the rest of his life, there was a small party for the patients and the care staff. They drank champagne and ate paprika-flavoured crisps. Later that evening Bruno danced with one of the nurses. He wasn't unhappy; the medication was working, he no longer had any feelings of desire. He enjoyed the afternoon snack, and watching game shows on television with the others before the evening meal. He expected nothing, now, of the progression of days, and the last night of the second millennium was a pleasant one for him.

In cemeteries all across the world, the recently deceased continued to rot in their graves, slowly becoming skeletons.

Michel spent the evening at home. He was too isolated to hear the noise of the party in the village. Many times, warm, peaceful images of Annabelle flitted across his memory, and images too of his grandmother.

He remembered that when he was 13 or 14 he used to buy flashlights, and small mechanical objects which he liked to take apart and put together again endlessly. And he remembered an aeroplane with a motor which his grandmother had given him, which he had never succeeded in flying. It was a beautiful plane, painted in camouflage; in the end, it stayed in its box. Through the slow drift of his consciousness, certain things seemed to characterise his life. There were people and thoughts. Thoughts occupy no space; people occupy a portion of space; they can be seen. Their images form on the lens, pass through the choroid and strike the retina. Alone in the empty house, Michel watched his modest parade of memories. Throughout the evening, a single conviction slowly filled his mind: soon he would be able to get back to work.

All across the surface of the globe, a weary, exhausted humanity, filled with self-doubt and uncertain of its history, prepared itself as best it could to enter a new millennium.

7

Some say:
'The civilisation we have built is still fragile,
We are only just emerging from the darkness.
We carry with us still the terrible image of centuries of misery;
Would it not be better to leave such things buried?'

The narrator stands, gathers himself together and recalls;
Patiently but firmly he rises and recalls
That a metaphysical revolution has taken place.

   Just as the Christians could summon up images of ancient
civilisations, just as they could form an image of these civilisations
as a whole, unassailed by questions or by doubt,
Because they had crossed a threshold
A threshold
They had stepped over the fracture;
   Just as the men of the age of materialism could take part,
unknowing, unseeing, in the ceremonial rituals of Christianity.

Just as they could read and reread the ancient literature of a Christian age, without ever leaving their quasi-anthropological perspective

Unable to comprehend the arguments which had enflamed their ancestors, the vacillations between grace and sin;

So, now, we can listen to this story of materialism and its time
As an antique story of men.
It is a sad story, but we will not be saddened by it
Because we are not like these men.
Born of their flesh and their desires, we have cast aside their
    categories and their appurtenances
We do not feel their joys, neither do we feel their suffering
We have set aside,
Disinterestedly,
Without the least effort,
Their universe of death.

These centuries of pain which are our inheritance
We can now bring from the half-light.
Something has happened, like a second coming
And we have the right to live our lives.

Between 1905 and 1915, working almost entirely alone, Albert Einstein succeeded in elaborating a general theory of gravity, space and time, from a first intuition which was the specific theory of relativity. In doing so, he had a profound influence on the evolution of astrophysics. This chance, solitary labour, accomplished, according to Hilbert, 'to the glory of the human spirit', had no obvious practical application and remained inaccessible to the scientists of his time. It can be compared to Georg Cantor's work to establish a typology of the infinite, which created set theory, or the work of Gottlob Frege, which redefined the basis of logic. According to Hubczejak, it can also be compared to the work of Djerzinski at Clifden between 2000 and 2009 – especially as, like Einstein, Djerzinski did not have the mathematical resources necessary to test his idea rigorously.

His first work, *The Topology of Meiosis*, published in 2002, had a considerable impact. It established, for the first time, on the basis of irrefutable thermodynamic arguments, that the chromosomal separation at the moment of meiosis can create haploid gametes, in themselves a source of structural instability. In other words, all species dependent on sexual reproduction are by definition mortal.

Three Conjectures on Topology in Hilbert Spaces, published in 2004, was a shock. Some interpreted it as a reaction against a continuous dynamic, as an attempt – with strangely Platonic resonances – to re-establish an algebra of forms. While they accepted the significance of his conjectures, many serious mathematicians underlined the absence of rigour in his propositions and the somewhat anachronistic character of his approach. In fact, as Hubczejak confirms, Djerzinski did not have access to recent mathematical publications at the time, and it would seem that he was not very interested in them. There is little information on his work between 2004 and 2007.

He was a regular visitor to the Galway centre, but his relationships with the staff there were purely utilitarian. He had developed a working knowledge of Cray assembly code and could therefore dispense with the services of programmers. Only Walcott seems to have had any personal dealings with him. He, too, lived in Clifden and would often spend the afternoon with Djerzinski. According to him, Djerzinski talked often about Auguste Comte, in particular, the letters to Clotilde de Vaux, and to the *Subjective Synthesis*, the philosopher's last, unfinished work. Comte could be considered to be the founder of positivism, even in the scientific sense. No metaphysical or ontological system of the time appealed to him. It is probable, as Djerzinski points out, that had Comte been in the intellectual circle of Niels Bohr between 1924 and 1927, he would have maintained his intransigent position on positivism and allied himself to the Copenhagen interpretation. In any case, the philosopher's insistence on the reality of social structures as opposed to the fiction of individual existence, and his continued interest in the historical process, streams of consciousness and his deep sentimentality, lead one to think that he might have been at home with more recent developments – particularly the replacement of an ontology of objects with an ontology of states – established by the work of Zurek, Zeh and Hardcastle. Only an ontology of states was capable of restoring the practical possibility of human relationships. In the ontology of states, the particles are indiscernible, and can be limited to an observable number. The only entities which can be identified and named in such an ontology are wave functions, and, using them, state vectors – from which arose the analogous concept of redefining fraternity, sympathy and love.

They walked along the Ballyconnelly road; the ocean glittered at their feet. Far off, on the horizon, the sun sank over the Atlantic. More and more often, Walcott got the impression that Djerzinski's thinking was straying into uncertain, even mystical territory. He himself remained steadfast to a radical instrumentalism in the staunch Anglo-Saxon tradition, clearly delineated by the Vienna school. He was slightly suspicious of Comte's work, which he thought too romantic. Contrary to the materialism it sought to replace, positivism could provide the foundation for a new humanism; in fact, it would be a first attempt at a true humanism (since materialism was antithetical to humanism and would eventually destroy it). Nonetheless, materialism had a historic importance: which was to break down the first barrier, represented by God; Man had done this and found himself plunged into doubt and uncertainty. But now a second barrier had been broken down – this time in Copenhagen. Man no longer needed God, nor even the idea of an underlying reality. 'There are human perceptions,' said Walcott, 'human testimonies, human experiences; reason links these and emotion brings them alive. All of this happens without any metaphysical intervention, without any ontology. We don't need ideas of God or Nature or Reality. In experiments, it is possible to get a group of observers to agree on reasonable intersubjectivity; these experiments are linked by theories, which should, as far as possible, be succinct and which must, by definition, be refutable. There is a perceived world, a world of feelings, a human world.'

Djerzinski knew that this position was irrefutable: was the need to find meaning simply a childish defect of the human mind? On a trip to Dublin at the end of 2005, he first saw the Book of Kells. Hubczejak is convinced that this first encounter with the illuminated manuscript, of great formal complexity, which was probably the work of seventh-century Irish monks, was a decisive moment in the evolution of Djerzinski's ideas. It was probably, according to Hubczejak, his long study of the book which allowed him – in a series of intuitions which in retrospect seem miraculous – to overcome the complexities of the calculation of energy stability in the macromolecules he encountered in biology. Without necessarily subscribing to Hubczejak's statement, it is certainly true that the Book of Kells has, down the ages, elicited from its admirers a response akin to ecstasy. In 1185, Giraldus Cambriensis made the following description of the book:

The book is a concordance of the four Gospels in the Vulgate text with as many drawings as there are pages, each decorated in wondrous colours. Here, one can contemplate the visage of divine majesty miraculously rendered; there, the mystical representations

of the evangelists, some having six wings, some four, some two.
Here, we see the eagle, there the bull, here the face of a man, there
the face of a lion and numberless other drawings. In looking at
them casually, it might appear that they are no more than idle
drawing rather than formal compositions. One might not see the
subtleties, whereas all is subtlety. But if one takes the pains to
study the book attentively, you will penetrate the innermost
secrets of art; you will find embellishments of such intricacy, such
compactness and density, such a wealth of knots and interlacing
links, in such fresh and lustrous hues, you might believe it was
not the work of man but of angels.

Hubczejak may be right when he affirms that any new
philosophy, even one which takes an axiomatic form,
founded on pure logic, is in fact a new visual conception of
the universe. In giving mankind the gift of physical
immortality, Djerzinski has clearly given us a deeper understanding of time; but his greatest contribution, according to
Hubczejak, is to have laid the foundations for a new
philosophy of space. Just as the world of Tibetan Buddhism
is inseparable from the contemplation of the infinite circular
forms of mandalas, just as one can create an image faithful
to Democritus' thoughts as he watched sunlight burst upon
white stones on a Greek island on an August afternoon, so
one comes closer to the thinking of Djerzinski in studying
the infinite architecture of cross and spiral which are the
basic ornamental forms used in the Book of Kells, or in
reading *Meditations on Interweaving*, inspired by it and
published separately from the *Clifden Notes*.

'Natural forms,' wrote Djerzinski, 'are human forms. Triangles, interweavings, branchings, appear in our minds. We recognise them and admire them; we live among them. We grow among our creations, human creations, which we can communicate to men, and among them we die. In the midst of space, human space, we make our measurements and with these measurements we create space, the space between our instruments.

'Uneducated man,' Djerzinski goes on, 'is terrified of the idea of space; he imagines it to be vast, dark and yawning. He imagines beings in the elementary form of spheres, isolated in space, curled up in space, crushed by the eternal weight of three dimensions. Terrified of the idea of space, human beings turn in upon themselves; they feel cold, they feel afraid. At best, they move in space and greet one another sadly when they meet. But this space is within them, it is nothing but their mental creation.

'In this space of which they are so afraid, human beings learn how to live and to die; in their mental space, separation, distance and suffering are born. There is little to add to this: the lover hears his lover's voice over mountains and oceans; over mountains and oceans a mother hears the cry of her child. Love binds, and it binds for ever. Good binds, while evil unravels. Separation is another word for evil; it is also another word for deceit. All that exists is a magnificent interweaving, vast and reciprocal.'

Hubczejak rightly notes that Djerzinski's great leap was

not his rejection of the idea of personal freedom (a concept which had already been much devalued in his time, and which everyone agreed, at least tacitly, could not form the basis for any kind of human progress), but in the fact that he was able, through somewhat risky interpretations of the postulates of quantum mechanics, to restore the possibility of love. It is important here to evoke once more the image of Annabelle: though he had not known love himself, through Annabelle, Djerzinski had succeeded in forming an image of it. He was capable of realising that love, in some way, through some obscure process, was possible. This was probably his guiding thought in the last months of his theoretical work, about which we know so little.

According to the testimony of those few people who visited Djerzinski in Ireland, during those final weeks, he seemed to have come to have made his peace. His anxious, faltering expression seemed to have been stilled. He often took long, dreamy walks along Sky Road with only the sky itself as witness. The road west snaked across the hills, some gentle, others steep. The ocean glittered, refracting a shifting light onto the rocky islands beyond the headland. Dropping over the horizon, the mass of cloud seemed luminous and confused, its presence strangely physical. He walked effortlessly for a long time, his face bathed by the delicate mist. His work, he knew, was done. In the room he had converted into a study, its window open onto Errislannan Point, he had put his notes in order. There were hundreds of pages on an extraordinary diversity of subjects. The results of what might properly be called his scientific work were contained in 80 pages of typed manuscript. He had not thought it necessary to include his calculations.

On 27 March 2009, in the late afternoon, he went to the central post office in Galway. He sent a copy of his work to the *Académie des Sciences* in Paris, and another to the British magazine *Nature*. No one can be certain of what happened next. The fact that his car was found near Aughrus Point led many to think of suicide – and indeed neither Walcott nor his colleagues at the Centre seemed surprised at this. 'There was something about him,' said Walcott, 'something monstrously sad. I think he was probably the saddest man I have ever met, even the word "sadness" seems inadequate; there was something broken in him, something completely devastated. I always got the impression that life was a burden to him, that he no longer knew how to make contact with any living thing. I think he held out for exactly as long as was necessary to finish his work, and I don't think any of us will ever know how much effort he had to make to do so.'

Djerzinski's disappearance was a mystery, and when a body could not be found, rumours sprang up that he had gone to live in Asia, probably in Tibet to compare his work with Buddhist teaching. This hypothesis is now discredited. In part, because there is no trace of him leaving Ireland and in part because the drawings on the last pages of his notebook, which some had interpreted as mandalas, were later found to be combinations of symbols much like those in the Book of Kells.

We now believe that Michel Djerzinski died in Ireland, where he had chosen to live out his last years. We also believe that, having completed his work, and with no human ties to bind him, he chose to die. Many witnesses attest to his fascination with this distant edge of the Western world, constantly bathed in a soft shifting light, where he had come so often, where, as he wrote in one of his last notes 'the sky, the sea, the light converge'. We now believe that Michel Djerzinski went into the sea.

Epilogue

Though we know much about the lives, the physical appearances and the personalities of the characters in this book, it must nonetheless be considered a fiction. A plausible recreation based on recollections, rather than a definite, attestable truth. Though the publication of the *Clifden Notes*, a complex blend of memories, personal impressions and theoretical ideas jotted down by Djerzinski while he was working on his theory between 2000 and 2009, tells us much about the details of events in his life, and the choices, conflicts and dramas which were to shape his thought, there are many areas in his biography and in his personality which remain obscure. What follows, however, belongs to History, and the events which followed the publication of Djerzinski's work have been pored over, commented on and analysed so often that a brief résumé seems sufficient.

In 2009, the magazine *Nature* published a separate

section entitled 'Towards perfect reproduction'. These eight pages of highly condensed synthesising, Djerzinski's last work, were to send shock waves throughout the scientific community. Throughout the world, molecular biologists tried to reproduce his experiments and pored over the details of his calculations. After several months, the first results came in and, week after week, more and more experiments confirmed his original hypotheses with exact precision. At the end of 2009 there could no longer be any doubt: Djerzinski's results were flawless and could be considered to have been proven. The practical consequences of this were dizzying: any genetic code, however complex, could be noted in a standard, structurally stable form, isolated from any mutations. This meant that every cell contained within it the possibility of being perfectly copied. Every animal species, however highly evolved, could be transformed into a similar species, reproduced by cloning and therefore immortal.

Hubczejak was 27 when he, like thousands of researchers across the world, first discovered Djerzinski's work. He was completing his doctorate at Cambridge. He was nervous, distracted, always on the move – he had been roaming Europe for a number of years, where he had studied at the universities of Prague, Göttingen, Montpellier and Vienna – searching, as he put it 'for a new paradigm, but for something more: not just a way of seeing the world but a way of situating myself within it'. He was certainly the first, and for many years the only, defender of the most radical of Djerzinski's proposals: that humanity must disappear, that humanity would give way to a new species which was asexual and immortal, a species which had outgrown individuality, individuation and progress. It is superfluous to note the hostility with which such a project was greeted by the defenders of revealed religion; Judaism, Christianity and Islam were for once agreed, and heaped derision and opprobrium on work which 'gravely undermines human dignity in its uniqueness and its relationship with the Creator'. Only Buddhists demurred, noting that the Buddha, in his teachings, had battled with the impediments represented by old age, sickness and death and that the Enlightened One would not necessarily have rejected a technical solution. Hubczejak could therefore count on little support from organised religion. It is perhaps more surprising to note that traditional humanists also rejected the idea out of hand. Though it may be difficult for us to understand this now, it is important to remember how central the notions of 'personal freedom', 'human dignity' and 'progress' were to people in the Age of Materialism (defined as the centuries between the decline of medieval Christianity and the publication of Djerzinski's work). The confused and arbitrary nature of these ideas meant, of course, that they had little practical or social function – which might explain why human history from the fifteenth to the twentieth centuries was characterised by decline and destruction. Nonetheless, the educated or semi-educated classes, having succeeded in inculcating these ideas, clung desperately to them. It is hardly surprising that Frédéric Hubczejak had such difficulty in making himself heard in those early years.

The story of the years in which Hubczejak finally managed to have his project, initially greeted with unanimous disgust and condemnation, accepted by a growing proportion of global opinion until it was eventually granted funding by UNESCO, reveals an extraordinarily brilliant and pugnacious individual, a pragmatic and agile mind, the archetype of an intellectual propagandist. Certainly, he was not of the stuff of great scientists, but he was capable of turning to his advantage the enormous respect the scientific community had for Djerzinski and his work. He was not an original nor a profound thinker, but in annotating and prefacing *Meditations on Interweaving* and the *Clifden Notes*, he presented Djerzinski's work in a precise and intelligent light, making them accessible to a wider public. Hubczejak's first article, 'Michel Djerzinski and the Copenhagen Interpretation,' is, despite its title, a long meditation on a quotation from Parmenides: 'That which is there to be spoken and thought of must be'. In his next paper, 'A Treatise on Concrete Limitations', and the more soberly titled 'On Reality', he attempts a curious synthesis of the logical positivism of the Vienna circle and the religious positivism of Comte, nor is he averse to his own flights of lyricism, as evinced by the oft-quoted passage, 'There is no *endless silence of infinite space*, for in reality there is no space, no silence and no void. The world we know, the world we create, the human world, is as round, smooth, simple and warm as a woman's breast.' Whatever his failings, he understood how to communicate to the public the idea that humanity could and should control the evolution of species – and in particular its own evolution. In his struggle, he had the support of a number of neo-Kantians who had made use of the sudden popularity of Nietzschean ideas to seek control of the wellsprings of power in among the intelligentsia, the universities and the press.

The general consensus is that Hubczejak's genius lay in his clever, playful ability to marshal the confused, bastard, late-twentieth-century ideology known as 'New Age Thinking' to his advantage. He was the first of his generation to see beyond the ridiculous, contradictory and obsolete superstitions it adopted to the fact that New Age thought appealed to a sense of suffering symptomatic of a very real psychological, ontological and social breakdown. Beyond the repellent mix of fundamentalist eco-babble, respect for tradition and the 'sacred' which it shared with its spiritual forebear, the Esalen commune, New Age thought had a genuine desire to break with the twentieth century, its immorality, its individualism and its libertarian and antisocial aspects. It was based on the notion that a society cannot function without the guiding hand of religion; it was, in effect, a call to arms, a search for a new paradigm.

Hubczejak was keenly aware that compromise is essential. And when he founded the Movement for

Human Potential in 2011, he did not hesitate to recycle some of the ideas of the New Age, ranging from what he refers to as 'The structure of the cortex of Gaïa', to his celebrated comparison 'ten billion people on the face of the planet, ten billion neurons in the human brain', from his appeal for a world government based on a 'new alliance', to the sloganeering 'THE FUTURE IS FEMININE'. This was done with an agility which drew admiration even from his critics; he was careful to avoid both the non-rational and the sectarian and to use the leverage that this afforded him with the scientific community to its full advantage.

A certain cynicism in the study of human history tends to identify 'artfulness' as a key component in success although, in the absence of a strongly held conviction, it is incapable of producing any significant change. All those who had the opportunity to meet Hubczejak, or to debate with him, are agreed that his persuasiveness, his magnetism and his extraordinary charisma were all rooted in simple personal conviction. He said exactly what he believed regardless of the circumstances – and to his critics, weighed down by the limitations of outdated ideologies, such simplicity was disarming and devastating. One of the principal objections to his project concerned the suppression of sexual difference which is so central to human identity. To this, Hubczejak would respond that his intent was not to recreate the human species to the smallest detail, but to create a new, rational species, and that the end of sexuality as a means of reproduction in no way heralded the end of sexual pleasure – quite the contrary. The coding sequences responsible for the formation of Krause corpuscles in the embryo had recently been identified. At the time, such corpuscles were sparsely spread on the surface of the glans penis and the clitoris. There was nothing, however, to prevent these being multiplied in future to cover the entirety of the epidermis offering new, and undreamed of, erotic possibilities.

Probably the most profound criticisms focused on the fact that every member of the species created by making use of Djerzinski's work would carry the same genetic code, meaning that one of the fundamental elements of human individuality would disappear. To this, Hubczejak would respond that this unique genetic code of which, by some tragic perversity, we were so ridiculously proud, was precisely the source of so much human unhappiness. To the notion that human personality might disappear, he proposed the concrete example of identical human twins who, through their individual experiences and despite their shared genetic code, developed different personalities while maintaining a mysterious fraternity – which, as Hubczejak pointed out, was precisely the element necessary if humanity were to be reconciled.

There can be no doubt that Hubczejak was sincere when he presented himself as a logical successor to Djerzinski, like an executor whose sole purpose was to put into practice the ideas of his master. Evidence for this might be found in his staunch loyalty to the bizarre idea proposed on page 342 of the *Clifden Notes*: the number of individuals in any new species must always be a prime number; it was necessary therefore to create one person, then three, then five . . . and to follow the sequence of prime numbers. The purpose of having a population divisible only by itself and one was symbolically to draw attention to the dangers which sub-groups constitute in any society; but it would appear that Hubczejak accepted this without ever wondering what it might mean. More generally, his unrelentingly positivist reading of Djerzinski led him constantly to underestimate the extent of meta-physical change which would necessarily accompany such a biological evolution – an evolution which had, in effect, no analogue in the history of humanity.

This gross misinterpretation of the philosophical subtleties of the project, and even his inability to recognise philosophical subtleties in general, in no way hampered or even delayed its implementation. This reveals the extent to which, in all Western societies and particularly in the most advanced sections, represented by the New Age movement, there had been an acceptance of the idea that a fundamental shift was indispensable if society was to survive – a shift which would credibly restore a sense of community, of permanence and of the sacred. It is also a measure of how little the public understood or cared about questions of philosophy. The global ridicule inspired by the works of Foucault, Lacan, Derrida and Deleuze, after decades of reverence, far from leaving the field clear for new ideas, simply heaped contempt on all those who were active in 'human sciences'. The rise to dominance of the scientific community in many fields of thought became inevitable. Even the occasional, sporadic interest which New Age devotees took in this or that belief or 'ancient spiritual tradition' was no more than proof of a profound, almost schizophrenic despair. Like others in society, and perhaps more so, they only truly believed in science; science was to them the arbiter of unique, irrefutable truth. Like others in society, they believed in their hearts that the solution to every problem – whether psychological, sociological or more broadly human – could only be a technical solution. Thus it was without any great risk that Hubczejak launched his 2013 campaign – the first to take on public opinion on a planetary level – with the slogan 'THE REVOLUTION WILL NOT BE MENTAL, BUT GENETIC'.

The first fund of credits was voted through by UNESCO in 2021 and a group of scientists immediately set to work under Hubczejak's direction. In practice, from a scientific standpoint, he had very little to do with the project, but he was to prove himself in his lightning reflexes in the domain of public relations. The extra-ordinary speed with which the results came in was a shock; it was only later that it became apparent that many of the scientists were members of the Movement for Human Potential and had not waited for the green light from UNESCO, but had been working covertly on the project for some time in laboratories in Australia, Brazil, Canada and Japan.

The creation of the first being, the first member of this

new intelligent species made by man 'in his own likeness', took place on 27 March 2029, 20 years to the day after Michel Djerzinski's disappearance. In homage to Djerzinski, and though there was only one French national on the team, the synthesis took place at the Institut de Biologie de Palaiseau. The worldwide broadcast of the event reached a huge audience – dwarfing that, almost 60 years earlier in July 1969, of the first steps of man on the moon. Before the broadcast, Hubczejak made a short speech where, with a typical directness, he declared that humanity should be honoured to be 'the first species in the universe which had developed the conditions for its successor'.

Today, some 50 years later, reality has largely confirmed the prophetic tone of Hubczejak's speech – more so than perhaps even he envisaged. There remain some humans of the old species, particularly in areas long dominated by religious doctrine. Their reproductive levels fall year on year, however, and at present their extinction seems inevitable. Contrary to the doomsayers, this extinction is taking place peaceably, despite occasional acts of violence which will continue to decline. It has been surprising to note the meekness, the resignation, perhaps even the relief of humans at their own passing away.

Having broken the filial chain that linked us to humanity, we live on. Men consider us to be happy; it is certainly true that we have succeeded in overcoming the monstrous egotism, cruelty and anger which they could not; we live very different lives. Science and art are still a part of our society, but without the stimulus of personal vanity, the pursuit of Truth and Beauty has taken on a less urgent aspect. To humans of the old species, our world seems a paradise. It has even been known for us to refer to ourselves – with a certain humour – by the name which they dreamed of, 'gods'.

History exists, it is elemental, it dominates, its rule is inexorable. But outside the strict confines of history, the ultimate ambition of this book is to salute the brave and unfortunate species which created us. This vile, unhappy race, barely different from the apes, had such noble aspirations. Tortured, contradictory, individualistic, quarrelsome, it was capable of extraordinary violence, but nonetheless never quite abandoned a belief in love. This species which, for the first time in history, was able to envisage the possibility of its passing and which, some years later, proved capable of bringing it about. As the last members of this species are extinguished, we think it just to render this last tribute to humanity, a homage which itself will one day disappear, buried beneath the sands of time. It is necessary that this tribute be made, if only once. This book is dedicated to mankind.